VENUS on MARS

a novel by

Jan Millsapps

High Praise for
VENUS on MARS

"A profound story – full of heart, wonder, wisdom – and brilliantly told."

–Harriet Ellenberger, co-founder of *Sinister Wisdom*

"The writing is eloquent. The characters, and the scenes through which they move, are vividly realized."

–William Sheehan, Historical Fellow at Lowell Observatory and author of *The Planet Mars*

"Three women – three generations – all linked by a mysterious journal, one man, and the enigmatic planet Mars. With great imagination and a lyrical flair, Jan Millsapps has fashioned an engaging tale about finding your place in the cosmos."

–Marcia Bartusiak, author of *The Day We Found the Universe*

"Millsapps writes across the unbounded interplanetary gulf that separates Earth from the brooding red planet Mars. Every word is carefully crafted and delicately placed, every page magical to read. Even if the reader knows nothing about astronomy, *Venus on Mars* is a feast."

–Dana Berry, producer of *Hubble's Amazing Universe, Finding the Next Earth,* and Emmy-nominated *Alien Earths*; author of *Race to Mars* and *Smithsonian Intimate Guide to the Cosmos*

VENUS on MARS

a novel by

Jan Millsapps

Jaded Ibis Press
sustainable literature by digital means™
an imprint of Jaded Ibis Productions

$\mathcal{D}$edication

In honor of
Margaret "Bunny" Bundschuh

Ms. Bundschuh is depicted on the cover of the May-June 1973 Jet Propulsion Laboratory (JPL) employee newsletter, *Lab/Oratory* (pictured below).

She worked in JPL's inventory management and acquisitions departments from 1967 until her retirement in 2010, and represents more than four decades of progress women have made toward achieving gender equality in the workplace.

At left, Ms. Bundschuh stands in front of JPL's Space Simulator and holds a scale model of Mariner 10, which flew by both Venus and Mercury in 1974.

VENUS ON MARS

To augment your reading experience, use your smart phone or tablet to scan the QR Codes inside this book. Each code links to additional online content. You can download a free QR Code reader wherever apps are available for your mobile device.

CONTENTS

AUTHOR'S PREFACE
Becoming a Martian

Mars looms larger in our lives than when I began researching and writing *Venus on Mars* several years ago. Curiosity had not yet touched down on Mars while we watched on live television. The popular rover had not yet become a "twitterverse" sensation, endearing herself to millions, 140 characters at a time. She had not yet made astounding discoveries, like the presence of liquid water underneath the rocky Martian surface – that may just be pure enough to drink outright.

A few years ago, Mars was still impossibly remote. NASA's thirty-year space shuttle program was winding down and no new spaceships were being built to ferry us back and forth to the ISS, much less to transport us further into space. We had not yet heard about private ventures preparing to send humans to Mars, nor the crowd-sourced funding campaigns and reality TV shows that would be used to finance them.

Certainly I had never thought of myself as someone who might be among the first to colonize Mars, not until I received this email on December 30, 2013, from the Mars One Selection Committee:

> You and only 1057 other aspiring astronauts around the globe have been pre-selected as potential candidates to launch the dawn of a new era – human life on Mars. Congratulations. You have made it to the next round. Now. Catch your breath.

And, while catching my breath, I realized that I'm already a Martian – without having to endure the arduous physical journey or face the profound uncertainties that will come with our eventual human habitation of Mars.

Mars is no longer just for rocket scientists and astronauts. We've entered a new era of "Mars Madness" that encourages us all to think of ourselves as Martians, to participate in the broader Mars story that has emerged during the past few years, and to share this "Marsness" across the social networks we occupy on a daily basis.

Mars is for everyone, from a kindergartner in Kenya using one finger to push herself across the rugged red landscape on *Google Mars*, to an Aeronautical Engineer at M.I.T.

building a better spacesuit to wear when she gets there, to dedicated high school science teachers preparing the next generation of Martians worldwide for careers yet to be invented and adventures not yet envisioned.

"Mars is there, waiting to be reached," says Apollo 11 astronaut Buzz Aldrin.

As you read and reflect on the story in this book, I encourage you to reach out, to establish your own connection with Mars and worlds beyond, and to think - perhaps even to act - more expansively with regard to your own place in the universe.

Jan Millsapps
January 1, 2014
San Francisco

EDITOR'S NOTE

At first, I did not appreciate the untidy journal forming the heart of this narrative. Its jumbled entries were in no perceptible order – the dense and disorderly sentences extending in all directions and sometimes written one on top of another – and the meaning of its words more often than not stubbornly elusive. Any binding had long since fallen apart and the pages once held in place by it had begun to wander freely through the unsettled air that often signals an approaching storm. Some entries had been lost forever, while others had not yet arrived to beg inclusion. Even today, nearly three quarters of a century after the chronicler's demise, it remains a work in progress.

The irresolute words within were penned by Miss Wrexie Louise "Lulu" Leonard, an amateur astronomer who worked as a secretary at Lowell Observatory in Flagstaff, Arizona, from 1895 to 1916. Miss Leonard was a frequent and dedicated observer of the heavens, and, as evidenced in her journal, an unrestrained thinker about celestial matters as well.

She kept her ideas secret, however; the journal was not discovered until after her death in 1937. The book then passed quietly through several generations, landing in my hands in the summer of 1971, an exhilarating time when gleeful Earthlings were taking baby steps into space. There was no room in that bold era of "one small step for man, one giant leap for mankind" for the quaintly worded notions of a Victorian lady, albeit a woman ahead of her time.

But many years have passed and spectacular events have taken place on Earth and elsewhere in the universe that finally have persuaded me the revelations within must be made public – not only the unusual journal, but also the stories of other lives touched by it, mine included.

An editor's task, I know, is to neaten a work like this, to organize its ideas and present them as palatable concepts easily ingested by readers, but I have decided to let disorder reign ("disorder is the absolute way of our unwieldy universe," Miss Leonard wrote), adding only a brief note or important date here and there for clarification and illumination. The current arrangement of pages I believe to be the most accurate reflection of the unruly spirit of the journal's creator, the living chronicle of an extraordinary life struck by the stars.

Departures

- 1 -

*G*oodbye.

I'm off, in dramatic fashion, on a long and potentially perilous journey to a destination that does not yet exist. I shall travel on faith alone, believing with all my soul that the place where I will terminate my journey will be built in time for my arrival.

I shall miss you. I may never see you again, certainly not here, not now. The thunderous explosion has flung us far apart already, and with our collective velocity increasing more as each moment passes, it is nearly assured we will never find each other again.

Still we remain connected, generated by the same spark, incubated in the same womb. As identical as we were at birth, we will each evolve with distinctly unique qualities, becoming even more differentiated over time, so much so that even if we were to achieve a future encounter, it's doubtful we would recognize each other as once familiar companions.

Instead, we will find others, and we will connect with them, because no entity in the universe should be alone forever, and there is so much more we can achieve in concert: stars, planets, entire solar systems and far-flung island universes. Each of us has a distinct place in the cosmos, which we must find and inhabit, but in the same moment, we must expand beyond where we are, to where we will be.

As I lift my skirt and step cautiously across the rock-strewn desert, I am inventing my future: views never seen in a territory not yet charted, an ever-expanding route through a complex universe that future beings will calculate all the way to infinity.

THE BIG BANG

-$\mathcal{2}$-

Yeah, well, I'm headed straight home.

Three days funeralizing in The Big Easy, with wet bear hugs by weepy folks I never heard of, all saying, "You look so much like her." A big fat lie. I'm thin. My eyes are blue, my vision 20-20. I take after my dad, I've been told.

Long before she died my mom made it clear she wanted to be buried in her home parish, so I had to arrange to have her hefty remains shipped from Boston to New Orleans, driving non-stop from Pasadena to meet her here, along with the rest of her family I've never known.

As soon as she's lowered into her final resting place, I pay the preacher and the mortuary with cash, just like they wanted (no faith in checks from the Bank of Pasadena, a place they've never heard of – might as well be in outer space), and I high-tail it toward my little Karmann Ghia parked by the cemetery curb.

"Wait!"

I turn and see a tall, frail man with graveyard mud on his boots limping toward me, each determined step supported by a diamond-encrusted cane. He stops to catch his breath and then thrusts a package at me.

"You're supposed to have this," he explains. "I promised your mother. She said, 'Make sure it passes to the next generation.'"

The package is wrapped in cloth and tied with strings. I grab hold of it, but he clearly isn't ready to let go.

"I'm Ollie Broussard," he says. He waits for my recognition to kick in. When it doesn't, he adds, "Your mother's oldest brother." He looks at me with solemn brown eyes and a sad frown. I can tell he is not pleased with me as representative of the next generation.

"What is it?" I ask, trying to ease the package from his grip. I don't want to stop and open it mid-getaway, though my curiosity has been piqued.

He raises thick eyebrows over widened eyes and gives me a *you'll-find-out-soon-enough* nod. Finally, he releases the package into my custody.

At that moment a chorus of distant church bells peals, as they always do in New Orleans, on the hour. Time to get out of here.

What's the speed limit in a cemetery?

- 3 -

Boston (a few days earlier)

Despite her poor vision, Letha Broussard Dawson had always enjoyed good health. She was strong in body and in spirit, so the sudden realization that she was about to die came as quite a shock.

Her body jerked to one side and then turned leaden. There was no way she could lift her arm to reach the telephone and call for help. Her head ached, and she heard a faint ringing in her ears. The small sitting room whirled crookedly before her, skewing the color television with the seashell lamp perched on top, toppling the tall open windows graced with fluttering sheer curtains, and upsetting the knickknacks she kept on the round table beside her chair: two plump, ragged Hummel children hugging each other, individually wrapped peppermints in a green leaf-shaped candy dish, a spindly snake plant emerging from a plain clay flowerpot, and a worn stenographer's pad.

She struggled to catch her breath, but there was no breath to catch.

Just before she died, she thought of Venus, the spirited and sometimes reckless daughter she'd leave behind.

Venus had left Letha years ago, hitchhiking across the country in boots and miniskirt to pursue an independent life in which her mother would play only a small and remote part: a Sunday afternoon phone call during which Letha did most of the talking; a week-long visit each summer if Venus could get away—so busy with her prized job involving complicated duties Letha could not begin to fathom, working with all the rocket scientists out at the Jet Propulsion Laboratory in California.

Letha thought next of her long lost husband Vernon, who'd struggled mightily to restore her failing vision, before he himself had become invisible, disappearing from her life with no warning. She thought of the poor but proud family she'd left behind in New Orleans when, as a young woman of eighteen, she'd eagerly climbed aboard a smelly, rumbling Trailways bus and handed the driver a ticket she'd paid for with money earned cleaning rich people's houses and taking care of snotty nosed children and drooling old folks over in the Garden District.

Her big brother Ollie had walked her downtown to the bus station at Tulane and Loyola to see her off. It was not yet dawn and he'd been concerned for her safety.

"Now, don't you forget where you come from," he'd warned her.

She'd laughed it off, but as the bus pulled away she couldn't stop looking out the back window at Ollie, barefoot, in denim overalls, planted under a streetlight on the sidewalk in front of the bus depot, one arm raised to offer a stiff and solemn goodbye. Ollie didn't move, but he kept shrinking and then disappeared completely as the bus turned a corner and roared toward Highway 90. Just as the sun rose over the delta waters, the bus – and Letha – headed east and then north out of town.

Before she died, Letha silently thanked Ollie for the promise he'd made her, one she knew he'd keep. Her tensed muscles let go of the fountain pen she'd been holding and it clattered to the floor.

Letha wouldn't be able to complete the enormous task she'd kept putting off—the letter she'd planned to write to Venus, explaining the significance of the book and why it must be read—but she knew her daughter would figure it out on her own.

Once Ollie gave her the book, the girl would take her time for sure. But eventually well-honed curiosity would overcome her stubborn streak. She'd sneak a peek, and then she'd be fascinated. No way would she stop reading, close the book, and ignore its lessons. Difficult lessons that must be learned, one way or the other.

Roadside Diversions

-1-

Nothing visible through my windshield except pouring rain, the thwack-thwack of the wipers barely keeping up. It's unbearably hot and stuffy inside the close confines of this little car, and the air conditioner won't work with the wipers on high.

I'd turned off the radio so I could concentrate on driving, slowing to a second-gear crawl, trusting without knowing for sure that other drivers would do the same. Just as I see the Fort Worth exit ahead and prepare to pull off the road, a neon beacon zaps its message through the thick grayness: Roadside Café, a glowing white structure surrounded by a rain-glossed parking lot spotted with modest sedans and rugged pickup trucks. I park as close to the door as possible and hold my purse over my head as I rush inside.

I've taken refuge in a red leatherette booth and have ordered a tossed salad and iced tea (instead of a "Texas-style" steak). Now I'm trying to make sense of the jumbled thoughts I've been reading in the little leather-bound book the man – Uncle Ollie – gave me. The words inside were penned by my Great Aunt Lulu around the turn of the century. She'd printed her full name on the fly leaf, large and proudly:

Wrexie Louise Leonard

I'd heard of her – my mom talked about her Aunt Lulu a lot – but I'd never met her. She died before I was born.

Leafing through the delicate pages, brown and brittle with age, I watch her big writing prance across the paper, in a hurry to produce the next word, yet restrained for the sake of neatness. Bold letters slanted forward as if all were being pushed by the same brisk wind. Rows evenly spaced like soldiers in formation, though written without ruled lines to guide her.

Lulu had allowed herself luxurious flourishes in her y's and g's that dipped and spread below the neatly formed lines. Sometimes when she'd reached the bottom of the page she would turn it and write all around the margins, filling in every scrap of space.

There are also "times two" pages scattered throughout the book: The first one is written normally; the second is written perpendicularly on top of the first to form a dense crosshatch pattern that initially seems impossible to read. But when I really concentrate, focusing on one angle and then on the other, I find it easily legible:

Some part of what took off so long ago now resides in me, in you, and beneath this domed roof where we gather each night. When we look through the telescope at distant celestial objects, we are seeing into the past: minutes, centuries, universes ago. Here we sit in the dark, seeing ourselves before we got here, while we were still on the way, even prior to our departure. Seeing and being seen simultaneously, here and there, then and now, an unfinished portrait captured over billions of miles. Who can say what we looked like at any given point along the way? How we felt, what we thought, with whom we wanted to travel, from whom we wanted to distance ourselves (as if we had any say in the matter)? It's the cumulative effect that counts, not the tiny, insignificant instances. Moments achieve meaning only through duration, and sometimes repetition. An instant is nothing.

Her words are more than seventy years old, but the concepts boldly modern. College-level astronomy voiced more like poetry than scientific fact. A Victorian lady's voice slipping easily from earthbound ideas to cosmological perspectives I barely understand, sprinkled with hints of a love affair. This part I get, even though it's written perpendicularly on top of the part I've just read, and I have to turn the book sideways to continue:

But here's an instant to recall, and perhaps to cherish. I am here now, as are you. It's cold and we have only our own body heat for comfort. Lighting a lantern is forbidden; we cannot afford to stir up the air. Air currents cannot be trusted – they throw all the heavens into disarray. You told me that and, shivering, I repeated it back to you, our mutual vow to maintain calm air and undisturbed darkness.

Hold me. We are long-ago cousins, timeless soul mates who have found each other again, despite inconceivable odds.

Great Aunt Lulu, I'd been told, was exotic for our pedestrian family. She traveled the world with her boss, a famous astronomer (the "you" in her journal, I wonder?), spending intimate time with him along the way.

Though well connected to the turn-of-the-century scientific community, she herself was not a learned woman. How could she have known so much about the far-flung universe? How could she have expressed herself so eloquently?

"You want some more iced tea?"

The waitress – Linda, her nametag announces – stands by my table holding a frosted glass pitcher. She purses her unevenly painted lips and smiles like an old friend, revealing bad teeth.

"Okay."

Outside the rain is still pouring. I'm tired of driving and welcome this chance to linger over the strange hand-written book. The book that now belongs to me.

"You look tired, honey." Looks like Linda wants to linger, too. "You on a long trip?"

"Yeah."

She still doesn't go away, just stands there holding the pitcher. I feel compelled to expand my one-word answers.

"Just buried my mother in New Orleans," I tell her, "and now I gotta get back to Pasadena before I lose my job."

She stares at me for a moment, and I imagine she's about to take off her apron and sit down across from me in the booth for a long chat. She'll tell me about her miseries. How that no-good husband of hers can t keep a job so she has to work two shifts. How her hair is turning gray and her last dye job was a disaster. That she's gained six pounds in the last two weeks and hopes to hell she isn't pregnant. Again.

But instead she tops off my iced tea, tilts her head like a songbird and chirps, "Well, then, you have a nice trip, hon." Then she glides behind the counter to fill other cups and glasses and sling steaming plates of food in front of other customers.

Suddenly I'm sobbing in my booth, no way to stop myself.

I pull a twenty from my billfold and toss it on the counter as I flee the diner, hoping no one will notice how generously I've over-tipped the flippant waitress for the mediocre lunch she served me.

Outside my tears merge with the downpour that's power-washing my face and hair.

Rain soaks my clothes all the way down to my two-day-old undies. I stumble across the parking lot and plunge breathlessly into the cozy, dry sanctuary of my car, quickly pulling the door shut behind me.

As I search blindly with one hand in my shoulder bag for my keys, a sudden sharp tap on the window startles me. It's Linda.

I roll my window halfway down, and she thrusts her bundled apron through. It's folded around the book I'd foolishly left behind. Then she reaches in with her other hand and drops bills and coins into my damp lap: my change.

"You be careful out there," Linda warns me. "It's God-awful sometimes."

I start the car and creep away in low gear, shivering in my wet clothes.

Why do I think Linda wasn't talking just about the rain, the wind, the low visibility, the miserable road conditions? Even as the rain tapers off, the dark storm clouds disperse and I can finally roll down the window to breathe the rain-freshened air, I'm haunted by her warning.

Out there is not a fixed location so much as an ongoing condition in my so-far-casually lived life. I've been *out there*. I'm *out there* now, and I'll be *out there* for the foreseeable future, my own meandering journey just as endless as the one Great Aunt Lulu describes in her journal:

Across distances so vast there is no human way to measure them, and through time extending forward and backward beyond both memory and prescience, I struggle to maintain my equilibrium, my identity, my daily existence in which I sleep and wake, work and rest, think and move. The train I've boarded picks up speed, hurling me past barren fields, abandoned towns, dry river beds and deserts scattered with leathery carcasses of long-dead creatures, until I can no longer locate myself with any degree of precision.

Onboard, there is no fixed location to call home, no way to say where I am, because my position changes before the words "I am here" leave my mouth. Out the window I gaze at a blurred, muted vision of past merging with a gauzy, indistinct future gradually revealing itself.

The first time I made this crossing I was young and untested, wearing a pretty new outfit and far too excited about my present situation to consider any thought beyond the immediate needs of my own naively adventurous spirit in this time – this place. I recall how pleased I was to be wearing crimson stockings underneath my skirt!

Eventually the color in my stockings faded; the journey became common, and its repetitiveness fatiguing. I entered a time of sharp impatience over the imposing delay a three-day trip would cause in my life. Arriving could not come soon enough, nor departing again. I felt myself racing over hurdles of train schedules to finish a sprint with no known prize beyond beginning the next sprint. If the train dared to run late, I was beside myself with irritation primed to erupt into anger. The ladies' waiting room at the train station became my own private, tortuous purgatory.

I have come full circle, able at last to understand the value of the crossing itself, endlessly repeated over unfolding time, revealing its meaning though duration, repetition, and occasional variation. Finally I am able to grasp and appreciate the uniqueness of a blended version made up of all journeys, a clarified view not offered to the young and fidgety, but presented only to those prepared over time to accept and understand its profundity. One crossing becomes many, and all can be reduced to one: the indisputable one I am currently experiencing.

I'm going nearly eighty, barreling down a deserted westbound highway, pleased for now by the visceral thrill of forward momentum alone. All I know for certain is that most of Texas still lies ahead and that I need to keep driving. Not because I want to get back home, but because the enigmatic pages I've just read from Great Aunt Lulu's journal suggest that my future depends more on the journey I'm making than on my eventual destination.

My name is Venus Dawson, I announce to the wind blowing across my face. I'm twenty-seven years old; I don't have a clue, nor do I know how to get one. My mother is dead, my father long disappeared, and all I have left is this naively pretentious book written by some nutty great aunt who looked at the stars and thought she understood the universe.

Talk about somebody who was "out there."

-2-

Except for the simple prayer she'd offered up nightly for her daughter's continued well-being – *please take care of her* – Letha had not been inclined toward any religion. Even so, she'd always imagined there would be an afterlife – but never one like this!

The smell came first, something rotting. The window light flickered and then dimmed; hidden in the encroaching shadows of her sitting room, Letha was able to make out a narrow channel filled with water rushing away from her toward a sparkling oasis she'd known was there her entire life, but had never been able to locate – as if the paint-by-number landscape in the poorly realized painting hanging on the opposite wall had become a garish portal to her afterlife, and the turquoise river depicted in it the route she'd take to get there.

She traveled supine along the surface of the water, soft on her body as the satin lining her casket, now a sturdy boat ferrying her to her next destination. She turned her head to see a network of similar containers in the distance; each must be carrying its own passenger. Overhead, the bleak rose-colored sky gave way to lush foliage growing wildly over the watery channels to create a thick and tangled canopy of green. The growth was so vigorous she could see its progress.

She heard the wind howling, its shrill sound growing in intensity, and knew the storm they'd predicted on last evening's weather report was building strength. She felt safe beneath the trees, whose leaves barely moved in response to the turmoil above, and buoyed by the polished water, moving confidently forward within the perfectly engineered banks. She was alone, but she did not feel that way. Others were watching reverently, invisible pallbearers waiting until she completed her journey before clearing their throats and stepping forward to reveal themselves.

Death was not a problem, Letha realized, letting go of all earthly concerns: the unpaid bills, her worn-out bedroom slippers, her distant daughter, the devoted-up-to-a-point husband who'd abandoned her, and her own lifelong struggle to see the world clearly. The complexities of her earthbound existence: that's where the unpleasant odor had been coming from. Now that she'd left the cemetery behind, the air around her smelled like fresh laundry. She saw gigantic white sheets undulating on clotheslines strung high above her, someone's wash hung out to dry before being brought in, ironed, folded and put away. Or perhaps they were loose white sheets of paper grown enormous, filled with that oddly jaunty handwriting going one way and then the other? Papers from the book released from their binding like souls from their earthly remains, flowing, like the words adorning them, in all directions at once, speaking in tongues, spilling secrets to past and future beings who'd dare to read and dare even more to grasp at understanding their significance.

Letha reached up and tried to snare one of the errant pages as it sped over her head, but the page picked up a stronger breeze and raced beyond her grasp. In that exact moment, however, she recalled every word she'd read from the book she'd first opened so long ago, the same potent but elusive words now hurrying to install themselves in her daughter's soul while there was still time:

The race is well underway by the time I am invited to join it. The clockwork universe is slow, steady and unstoppable, while the round, red guest of honor whose exact arrival time has been known for centuries edges closer each day. It's we humans who must hurry now.

On your "good seeing" scale of ten, a favorable venue is chosen. The measurement is not so much about longitude and latitude, but more about the air circulating high above, which must be clear and calm. Not a ten, not all the time, but the best we can achieve in the days remaining. At least it is on this hemisphere, on this continent, and the railroad that will bring us to the base of the mesa already has been built.

I get fitted for a new travel ensemble while distant workers wrestle frantically with lumber, mules, mud, and rough, inclined terrain in their efforts to prepare the necessary route toward the heavenly event, which cannot be postponed like a festive dinner or dance. I am spared not only the hard labor, but also the difficult negotiations over land, access to it, and placement of telegraph poles and lines to connect it to the rest of the world. Rather, I lunch with friends near the State Street offices in Boston, bidding them farewell with hugs, tears and promises to write daily with news, gossip and sincerely voiced concerns for each other's well-being. My trunks have been packed and delivered to the station. I linger anxiously in the ladies' waiting room, my nerves unsettled as always before a journey.

I will travel with the two men standing just outside: one smoking a cigar, outfitted in a finely tailored three-piece suit – the blue-eyed one whose inspiration, energy and bank accounts have made everything possible; the other a glassmaker who shepherds his creation – an enormous, finely crafted, Parisian looking glass, 24 inches across, ground and polished, that will enable us to see far beyond the horizon ahead, past mountains, clouds and settlements in remote territories, onto the surface of another world, the red one fast approaching our own.

"You must remember," the glassmaker says to me of the mysterious, rose-colored planet soon to make its proximate appearance, "to look *on* it, not *at* it, and never at the glass itself, which is merely a route from seer to seen."

Though exquisite in its design and construction, the glass is only the mediating device. What can be observed when using it depends on the acuity, dedication and sometimes the imagination of the observer in relation to the actual thing being seen. The glass alone is not an end in itself but rather part of a larger effort to bring far-away worlds and the beings who populate them closer to our own. Though it cost many thousands of dollars, the glass offers nothing until the intelligent eye encounters it; only then will the distant object of scrutiny reveal itself honestly.

It will be dark, and the sky will be crowded with stars three days from now when the bone-tired mules make one more trip to drag us all up the hill in a rugged wagon that will rattle our worn-out bodies even more determinedly than the speeding train we've just abandoned. I shall inwardly rejoice that my long journey has come to an end. Soon I can pull out my hatpin, remove my hat, pull off my shoes, roll my stockings down, and loosen my corset. Tonight I shall sleep peacefully, without being jostled about, without the incessant noise of wheels on rails. When next I write in this little book of mine, my pen will not shake so, my uneven lines will smooth themselves, and my words will be considerably more legible.

But the most challenging part of my journey is only now beginning. Did you hear what the glassmaker told me? *I have just been given the secret to clear and undisturbed vision!*

There is no resting on this knowledge; rather, the burden of good seeing necessitates that I employ my vision with dedication, with each opportunity I am awarded, in the interests of observing the distant stars and planets, of understanding the entirety of the universe as it unveils itself over time. There is always more waiting to be seen, always more begging my understanding.

When she was a younger woman, Letha would cradle the worn book in both hands, positioning its fragile pages close to her imperfect eyes. She'd adjust her thick eyeglasses and read – piecemeal at first, as if sampling holiday candies whose exquisite tastes must be savored. Soon, however, she would succumb to the book's allure and allow herself to devour its contents cover to cover. Often, after reading from the book, she'd repeat its cautionary words out loud:

We are bound for a place where good seeing has been promised, and yet, despite the cloudless skies and calm air, I can already see that the clarity of everyone's vision will be challenged.

The younger Letha had listened to her own voice reciting these words with intense concentration and yet without full understanding. Now each sentence played itself over in her head, revealing its meaning anew, as if dying had refreshed her memory, her comprehension – and more.

"I see," she whispered to herself as she stepped unsteadily from her satin-lined box onto what seemed to be a vast desert plateau.

And see she did – her troublesome vision had been restored! Not only could she detect the smallest details in her immediate presence – like the tortoise-shell buttons trimming her soft blue crepe dress, and the tiny green-brown leaves on the scrub brush growing low around her feet – but she also could see great distances clearly, past nude hills spread in all directions, and beyond the deep-hued storm clouds boiling in the sky. When she turned her head one way and then the other, she could see backward and forward, beyond the limited span of her own life, into the lives of generations past and beings not yet conceived.

"I see."

She repeated the words reverently to herself, reveling in the all-encompassing, perfect clarity she now possessed: Her earthly vision had been nothing like this!

In the reflective surface of her shiny, black, patent-leather pumps, she studied the massive disturbance now directly overhead that would soon unleash itself: She could already see the storm tearing the desert to shreds.

She should start walking, try to find shelter. But which direction should she choose? All routes seemed the same – east, west, forward, backward. But Letha, who did not believe in dilly-dallying, chose one and began walking briskly.

She stopped abruptly when she saw her husband, Vernon Dawson, standing in the exact location from where he'd vanished so many years ago, just outside his optical shop in Kenmore Square, underneath the giant eyeglasses that hung above the entryway. It was as if no time had passed at all. Either he'd remove a keychain from his pocket, unlock the front door and go inside, pull up the shades and flip the "Closed" sign to "Open," thereby maintaining their lives together. Or else he'd shrug, smile sadly, pocket his keychain and walk away, never to be seen again. She did not know whether she'd traveled backward in time or he'd traveled forward; she only knew that they were once again in the same place at the same time.

Letha pinched color into her cold cheeks, moistened her slack lips with her tongue and ran one hand through her matted hair. The dust-laden wind whipped her determined face as she took one careful step toward him, steadied herself, then took another, mentally preparing the long-unasked question she needed him to answer: *What he was about to do, and why.*

Perhaps then she could find some way to explain it all to Venus – not that her daughter would care. Venus was a practiced expert when it came to not caring.

-3-

An endless expanse of unblemished blue sky, long straight stretches of blacktop highway, and sweetly insipid John Denver crooning just beneath the relentless static on the radio: *Take me home, country roads.* Out here, decent radio stations are few and far between. Unless you like country-western. And I don't.

I'm making gradual progress across the enormous State of Texas. Its breadth, unfortunately, gives me plenty of time to think.

When she was alive, my mom was my only connection to my past, yet she kept the facts mostly to herself for reasons she never revealed. When I was very young I'd pepper her with constant questions, my need to know growing more insistent with each unanswered query.

What happened to him? Why'd he run away? Will he ever come home again? What color were his eyes? When was his birthday? Did he like ice cream sodas? Did he pull for the Red Sox? Do I really have a daddy or did you just make him up?

That last question never failed to annoy her.

"He was real," she'd reply crisply, and no more questions were allowed.

Gradually, I discontinued my inquiries, discouraged by her limited answers. Instead, I pretended not to care about my father's absence from our lives. What bits of family history I'd managed to worm out of my mom over the years were, at best, complicated and incomplete.

Vernon Dawson, a dispensing optician – her husband, my dad – disappeared when I was a baby. One day he went to work as usual but never came home. My mom scoured the office near Kenmore Square where he'd last been seen for clues, but found none. Eventually she'd sold the office and all its contents to an up-and-coming, full-service ophthalmologist, providing her money to raise me comfortably enough, although she ordered the blandly practical dresses I wore to school from the Montgomery Ward catalogue instead of taking me shopping for a more stylish outfit at Filene's, and we could not afford for me to take tap-dancing lessons like the other girls in my grade, making me forever clumsy and lethargic in my movements.

I'd excelled in scholarship, though – smart as a whip, my mom would always say when

I'd bring home another all-A's report card. Outstanding grades during high school earned me a partial scholarship to Boston University, but I'd gone for several years without ever declaring a major, then, uninspired, had dropped out early in my junior year, hitchhiking across the country and settling eventually in Los Angeles, working one temporary job after another to stay afloat before I'd landed at JPL just as the space program was taking off and NASA was into a big-time hiring spree.

Sunday afternoons, when long-distance rates were lowest, I'd phone my mom back in Boston, always a querulous experience.

"Are you going out with anyone?" she'd ask at least once during our conversation, less concerned about whatever career I was pursuing that week, and more that I'd failed, so far, to find a suitable husband. She'd gotten married at nineteen, she never tired of reminding me.

"I'm working on it," I'd always reply.

Sometimes I'd make up an imaginary boyfriend and describe him to her, just to shut her up, fishing for details in nearby Hollywood. I knew she never went to the movies or read the fan magazines because she couldn't see well enough to enjoy them.

"Troy. He's tall and blond, works as a loan officer at the Bank of Pasadena. On weekends we go hiking in the San Bernadino Mountains. He's Methodist."

This particular load of crap would get me through the next few phone calls, but I can't think she ever believed Troy was real, so a few weeks later when we were both tired of hearing about him, I'd tell her he'd been promoted and transferred to a bank in Riverside, so we weren't seeing each other any more.

"But I'm just fine," I'd assure her, and this part was true. I'd feel relieved of the burden of lies I'd been busy concocting, but then the whole cycle would start all over with the very next phone call.

"I don't want you to be all alone after I'm gone," she'd say solemnly. "There's nobody to turn to when things get bad."

Like now. I startle myself with this thought.

Midway through the lonely Lone Star State, and I have no parents, no siblings, no relatives I actually know, no boyfriend, and I've never been the type to nurture the occasional friendship I've encountered. I'm not just alone; I'm absolutely, undeniably, indisputably alone. When I bought a shiny red billfold last month, I tossed the blank "emergency contact" card into the trash; if anything happened to me, I didn't want anyone bothering my nearly blind mom about it, and I couldn't think of any other name to write down. I had considered my boss, briefly, but decided it would be too embarrassing for someone to call the very important Arthur Dickson, Ph.D., to my bedside in the emergency room. He wouldn't know what to say; he'd just stare at my unconscious form and wonder what he was doing there, why they hadn't called someone else, someone who knew me better. They'd tell him it was *his* name I'd put on the card, and he'd think – oh shit – that I actually *liked* him. I don't like him at all, I remind myself; I'd rather die alone than have him summoned to watch.

It was an uncomfortable feeling, tossing the card. It meant that I'd made an irreversible decision to go it alone. Now, even if I meet someone new – an actual Cary or Bobby or Frankie – and decide that is a name I can write on the card, there'll be no card to write it on.

I shake my head to clear it, suck in my breath, and ram my foot on the accelerator. I'm determined to get through the rest of Texas without crying again.

-4-

"Vernon." a confounded but clear-eyed Letha spoke softly to her husband, taking care not to let him know what an incongruous yet wildly momentous event this was. Her dead heart had come to life again, beating rapidly as she approached, pushing air into her failed lungs in quick short bursts. He stood in the same position, but was no longer in Kenmore Square – now he stood on the boarding platform outside a squat rustic train depot she'd never seen before, wearing an old-fashioned three-piece suit, smoking a cigar instead of the pipe she'd thought he favored.

He turned toward Letha when she spoke, a brief flash of recognition in his deep-set blue eyes, but looked away quickly when he heard the train approaching. He put his keychain away, pulled a round watch from his vest pocket and checked to see if the train was on schedule, then snapped the watch shut and replaced it in his pocket, shifting his weight impatiently from one foot to the other. Above him the orange sky was churning, its impending fury barely held in check, and Letha realized that, although the resemblance was uncanny, this elegant man was not her husband.

Letha watched as the man climbed on board the train and disappeared inside it. Porters struggled to load a cart piled high with his baggage onto the train quickly and without scraping the polished-to-perfection leather trunks and cases. As the train crept away, he watched her from his window, and a slight smile crossed his lips.

He must be mistaken as well, confusing her with someone else – perhaps the woman outfitted head-to-toe in an old-fashioned Victorian ensemble. The one who'd come to see him off, who'd turned away, as the train left the station, to dab at her eyes with a fine linen handkerchief.

Aunt Lulu.

'm not calling him, not yet.

"You take some time for yourself now," Dr. Dick told me before I left for the funeral, but I knew he didn't mean it. His actual name is Arthur Dickson, Ph.D., but I prefer the more amusing – and descriptive – nickname I've heard others use in the break room. Dr. Dick is the director of the Image Processing Lab at JPL, where I work.

Soon the voluminous data coming in from the Mariner space probe now enroute to Mars would arrive, page after page of teletyped numbers and mountain-high stacks of couriered machine tapes that weren't going to transform themselves into the well-defined Martian peaks and valleys the scientists wanted to see, wanted to show the world. There would be new stacks of job folders, labeled, prioritized, and lined up on my desk, awaiting my attention. Among these would be requests, special requests and "special requests – urgent" from the science team, all demanding Martian close-ups that must be nursed from a nondescript gray wash into detailed visibility. They all wanted Venus to do the job for them, because they could make all manner of sick jokes about it. Venus does Mars. Mars needs the Venus touch. Only Venus can get a rise out of Mars. And much worse.

When I was first hired at JPL and introduced to the all-male image processing team as Venus Dawson, their new darkroom assistant, they cheered and whistled. One grinned and said, "You showed up in the nick of time."

Later in the cafeteria I saw the sign announcing next week's event:

LADIES! SHOW US YOUR SOLAR SYSTEM STYLE

Dress as your favorite planet for a chance to be crowned JPL's

"MISS SOLAR SYSTEM"

The winner will get the rest of the day off and will ride on the JPL

float in next January's Rose Parade.

GOOD LUCK! MAY THE BEST GAL WIN!

When I told another man on the team that I had no intention of dressing up for a beauty contest, he said, "You gotta be kidding me. You're *Venus*. Tame that hair, put on some makeup and hike up your mini-skirt. You'll win for sure."

"I don't think so," I said. "I'm just not beauty queen material."

I thought I'd managed to gracefully excuse myself from the competition, but I had not yet learned how far my co-workers would go to have their way at my expense.

When I found out they'd entered my name without my permission, I called in sick the day of the contest. In my absence Miss Saturn was crowned winner – a blonde bombshell all dolled up in a gold lamé mini-dress and twirling three yellow hula hoops all at once to represent the planet's rings. She was photographed for the cover of *Lab-Oratory*, the JPL newsletter, wearing her costume, now augmented by the shiny night-sky blue diagonal sash with sparkling silver letters proclaiming her "Miss Solar System." Then she left the premises to enjoy her partial day off, which she spent getting her roots done and phoning her girlfriends to tell them the news.

The next morning when I showed up for work, Dr. Dick was waiting for me, puffing furiously on his cigarette and blocking the doorway to Building 168, where we worked.

"You'd have won and made us proud," he scowled. "Miss Saturn," he said, and pointed across the campus to the administration building, "she's from over in Procurement."

"I don't even know what Venus looks like," was the only excuse I could offer. But it was the honest truth. Even though two Mariners had flown past the planet already, very little was known about its surface. The only thing anyone could say for certain about the brightest "star" in the sky – the planet circling just inside Earth's orbit – was that it was unbearably hot and entirely shrouded by clouds.

"Cotton," Dr. Dick replied. "Lots of cotton rolls wrapped around your hot little body. How hard would that have been?" Then he stamped out his cigarette and stalked off.

I'd promised to call him from the road when I was on my way back to Pasadena

I'm still on my way, I reason, as mile after mile of Texas rolls under my tires. As the new Mariner hurls itself toward Mars. As Miss Saturn and her lovely rings dance circles around hot, sluggish Venus.

I haven't broken my promise – yet.

I pull into a rest stop with rustic picnic tables strategically placed underneath real shade trees whose leaves shimmer in the subtle but resolute breeze I can almost feel, and I get out the book that just keeps getting stranger, about a journey that's even stranger. I'm paused here to cool off and rest, but Great Aunt Lulu – she just keeps on tripping:

This is a journey unlike any I've experienced, one wildly out of control. Once we leave the train shed, we are cut loose from our itinerary, the train careening wildly away from carefully laid tracks.

I bump into my fellow passengers, endlessly repeating, "Pardon me," as I try to separate myself from the coalescing mass, but this becomes more difficult as others climb aboard and are thrown against us, and still others against them. The train does not slow for new passengers; there are no seats remaining in the coach where I am riding, and yet the speeding crowd grows denser as we rush ahead, accelerating into a never-ending spiral, now racing forward without caution, now circling back to invite others to join this mad scramble toward a destination that remains unknowable even as we arrive there, again and again.

I see enormous ones in the distance and smaller ones closer by, plus those nuanced fragments not yet a part of something larger, stubbornly resisting what seems inevitable. Over time we will settle into predictable and routine lives, traveling the same staid route year after year, circling a yellow star that lavishly fuels our existence. There is a balance here that might easily be disturbed, and yet we have been thus, and will be the same, for so long I have lost count and become complacent in my comfortably repetitive journey.

Then a curious thing happens: New identities emerge from the one we hold in common, identities within identities, beings never duplicated, always evolving as unique creatures who spawn yet more unique creatures. One such creature has constructed this train. Another calls, "All aboard!" And the young one in a fancy dress and hat climbs the makeshift wooden stairs and settles into a thickly upholstered seat in a private coach, beside the older, blue-eyed one who makes her feel, always, just a bit lightheaded.

She closes her eyes to steady her nerves as the train rolls forward. She feels his warm hand resting on her arm, offering silent reassurance and undeniable evidence of his presence in her life. She leans her cheek against his shoulder, the pleasure of their shared momentum growing stronger as the train picks up speed. She listens to the repetitive sound of heavy wheels on iron rails, and strains to hear a whisper of his unvoiced promise: the reasoned guidance he will provide along the unknown route they seem destined to travel together.

In Pursuit of Clarity

– *1* –

Summer 1936

merica was just beginning to emerge from the Great Depression when eighteen-year-old Letha Broussard board-ed the Trailways bus in New Orleans, but most of the South lagged behind, and she didn't have time to wait: Her eyesight was failing.

Her store-bought eyeglasses provided some benefit but not enough for reading the magazine she'd brought along. The tiny letters on its slick pages were stubbornly soft. The more she strained to see them, the less crisp they became and the more annoying her headache. So she put the magazine away and spent her time peering out the window of the bus, its forward movement blurring even more the soft green forests and rust-hued farmland stretching between gray-washed cities: Birmingham, Atlanta, Greensboro, Richmond, Washington, D.C., the bus often stopping at little more than a rural crossroads for new or departing passengers.

She watched patiently as the taller buildings and busier streets of Philadelphia, New York, and finally Boston came into view. She adjusted her fancy straw hat with the yellow ribbons as they arrived at the grand South Station, its clock tower and the carved eagle on it soaring into the sky. Letha emerged, squinting in the sunlight.

This is far enough, she decided. She'd heard that Boston was the cultural and intellectual center of the universe – so it must be good enough for Miss Letha Broussard. There were great universities here, a symphony orchestra and an art museum. Surely she could find someone who could treat her failing vision.

Letha rented a room at the YWCA for seven dollars and fifty cents per week, and hauled her carryall up six flights of stairs because she was afraid to take the loud mechanical elevator. Now, as she set it onto the bed neatly made with crisp white sheets and a soft chenille bedspread, she realized she'd entered a grown-up, far-away world in which she could pay for a bed made in clean sheets, in a cheerful private room that also held a comfortable chair by a window offering a splendid view of the emerald-green Boston Common. In the cafeteria downstairs there were meals someone else would prepare for her: breakfast for twenty cents, lunch for thirty-five and dinner for half a dollar. There was even a swimming pool in the basement of the building where she could take swimming lessons for a dollar – with a towel, swimsuit and the required medical examination all provided!

There were, however, more pressing needs: She must find work immediately. She could clean houses and take care of children or the elderly; she'd done these things before. But when she saw the notice posted in the lobby – a free class demonstrating how all kinds of office machines were operated – she decided she'd learn to operate these machines, then get a job in one of the tall buildings soaring all around her. Yes, she'd become a business girl who'd earn enough money to get herself new eyeglasses, a new outfit and a good haircut. Soon enough she'd need a new winter coat as winters in Boston, she'd been told, could be fierce.

Letha hummed to herself as she unpacked her one good dress; change of underwear; her nightgown, robe and slippers; and her one pair of silk stockings. She removed her brush, comb and hand mirror. She glanced at herself and saw only a blur of skin, hair, and lips – nothing she could identify as the person she knew herself to be. She set mirror down. She found her eyeglasses, wrapped in tissue, inside her purse. She put them on, lifted the mirror and looked again. Better, but still not crisp. Still not the Letha Broussard she wanted to see. She told herself that she would add defining details along the way. After all, she was here, in elegant and enlightened Boston, ready to begin her transformation.

Unrestrained girlish laughter in the hallway reminded her that she was not alone. As she made her way downstairs for dinner she wondered how many other girls had traveled here, or elsewhere, on the same determined quest, making their uncertain ways on buses and trains, toward some future version of themselves they imagined but were not yet able to see.

26 August 1896 (my first look!)

Traveling exhausts the soul, yet sometimes transforms it as well.

We have arrived at dusk on top of the mesa via winding, uphill terrain they dare call a road, a low rock wall the only sign of human progress visible along the way. Still noisy from my trip, I chatter as I follow you inside where you shush me with your warm arms, until at last I am able to hear my own welcomed silence. Without a word, you take my hand and lead me through the spreading darkness to the instrument already prepared for our arrival. You gaze into it first, murmuring your approval, then step aside.

Look now, you tell me.

I put one eye to the eyepiece and see hovering right in front of me an enormous red disk, its polar caps splendidly trimmed in ermine. I had anticipated seeing our planetary neighbor as if it were visiting our own neighborhood, but instead I have the distinct impression that *I* am the one who's travelled – in a mere instant – partway across our Solar System. With one brief look I've become a Martian, a quietly spectacular event.

Outwardly all appears the same: I am held together nicely by my navy suit with the flared skirt and tailored jacket, my white silk blouse trimmed in delicate lace, and the fashionable navy hat with sleek feathers and contoured netting.

We are already living the future with our first cup of morning coffee, our table set for breakfast on the rustic sunlit porch of a tiny house atop the mesa.

We pretend nothing has changed, as if we are still in civilized Boston, an illusion requiring elaborate preparations if we are to maintain it – arranging for cigars, French claret, water crackers, fine china, silver and table linens to be shipped here from what used to be home. If the cigars are too dark they must be returned and exchanged for lighter ones. If even the length of the soup ladle is incorrect, it must be returned, the handle reconfigured and sent again to us. It is my job to insure that all these things happen exactly as they should.

Are you comfortable enough? you ask me, not knowing I have already embraced the change. *We are somewhat out of our natural element, are we not?*

A shiny black crow alights nearby, struts and caws with a coarsely uncivilized voice. He makes a horrible ruckus when approached by another one, outfitted in more muted tones. They flit and complain to each other, hopping from tree to tree. Each time the first one moves, the second one follows suit, and a newly grand uproar ensues. Once they recognize each other, all the fuss ceases. It's as if they must take time to protest the proximity of the other – yet they're drawn together nonetheless and, once connected, are determined to travel in tandem.

I think the birds are us in another guise, our real selves away from the city and the proper manners we must adopt when there. Here we shall be ourselves, loud when we wish, subdued when we realize this is what we have been searching for, though not our final destination. Soon one of us will flit to another more distant perch and call out to see if the other will follow. But for now, we shall inhabit this place you have built, and it will more than suit my present needs. And though accommodations are not much better than a nest in a treetop, I shall not complain.

Down below I hear the low whistle of the next train arriving and wonder whether all onboard have experienced a similar transformation. I think not. For most, travel is simply a way to get from one place to another. Most are not provided with what I have been given: a rare opportunity to reorganize my soul, and a decent salary paid monthly to support the effort.

-2-

```
The quick brown fox jumps over the lazy dog. [return]
The quick brown fox jumps over the lazy dog. [return]
The quick brown fox jumps over the lazy dog. [return]
```

A t last Letha was making progress in her YWCA typing class. She could not see the keyboard on the Underwood typewriter clearly, but she'd memorized it. Now her fingers jumped effortlessly from one key to another as she listened to the words flowing into her ears from the Dictaphone. She enjoyed making fingertip contact with each typewriter key, pushing confidently, hearing the clickety-click of each metal letter rising to make an imprint through the carbon ribbon onto the paper, recording perfect letters in an even row. She was picking up speed, but her typing teacher, Miss Virginia Dawson, demanded more.

"Girls," Miss Dawson had warned her class today, "I'm sorry to tell you this, but there are precious few office jobs for secretaries out there, and you may be assured that these will go to the fastest typists."

When the session ended, Letha covered her typewriter, removed her eyeglasses, wrapped them in tissue, and stored them in her skirt pocket. Her eyes were stinging and watering; she needed to rest them.

Miss Dawson stood by the doorway, watching each girl depart.

"Oh dear," she began as Letha approached, "Your eyes are red and swollen. Have you been crying?"

"No, ma'am, it's just eye strain," Letha replied. "I need better eyeglasses."

"If that's what it will take to make you a better typist," Miss Dawson advised her, "then I'd suggest that you get them before our next class."

"Yes, ma'am," Letha said, moving past her teacher into the hallway.

"Well, then," Miss Dawson replied, as if the matter were closed.

Letha hurried to her room upstairs and collapsed onto her bed. She closed her eyes, sensing some relief at last.

She listened to girls giggling in nearby rooms, to whispered conversations in the hallway, to automobiles passing in the street far below. She heard slow, labored footsteps climbing the stairs, approaching her closed door. A sharp rap, and Letha's eyes sprang open. She made herself close them again.

"Miss Broussard?"

Letha recognized the voice of her typing teacher, Miss Dawson. She heard a swishing of stiff fabric, the creak of an arthritic knee joint, and then the softest sliding sound inside her room. Outside, the knee creaked again, the fabric rustled, and the footsteps slowly departed.

Letha opened her eyes to see a crisp white sheet of typing paper lying just inside the door. She forced herself up and into her eyeglasses once more. She picked up the paper and held it at arm's length. The brief message was typed perfectly.


```
Dear Miss Broussard:

It occurs to me that a girl like you may
not have the resources needed to purchase
new eyeglasses. My nephew, a dispensing
optician, can help you. Please tell him
that I have sent you over. He will fit you
with new eyeglasses and charge them to
my account. You may repay me after you
secure employment.

Yours truly,
Miss Virginia Dawson
```


A calling card was attached:

Mr. Vernon Dawson
Vision Specialist
Kenmore Square in Boston

Letha spent two weeks talking herself into taking the underground trolley to Kenmore Square where she now stood, shivering in her thin cotton coat under the giant eyeglasses mounted over the doorway. She whistled nervously for fifteen minutes before convincing herself to push open the door. When she did, little bells above the door jingled to signal her arrival.

"I'm here to get my eyes tested," she called out.

Vernon Dawson, vision specialist, was summoned by the bells from a room in the back. He advanced to greet his visitor, and once she'd introduced herself, he seemed to know already why she was here.

Letha noted that he was a tall, trim, blue-eyed man, decidedly handsome, but she couldn't gauge how old he was; he could be thirty or fifty.

He ushered her into a darkened room in back and sat her down in a tall padded chair.

He pointed to an eye chart hung on the opposite wall. "Can you read the letter on the top row?"

"It's an E," Letha announced confidently.

But the letters beneath the large "E" increasingly shrank as she continued reading them out loud. They blurred and disappeared into the white paper before she could identify them all.

"Did I pass the test?" she asked, though she knew she'd failed miserably.

"You did just fine," he reassured her. "Now please excuse me for a moment."

He disappeared into another room. Just when Letha thought he'd abandoned her, he hurried back with a round light fastened to the center of his forehead. He approached, holding a spoon-shaped instrument in one hand.

"An ophthalmoscope," he explained. "It lets me look inside your eyes."

He held it clumsily in his fist; his hand was shaking.

"Will you tell me what you see?" Letha asked nervously. She'd never had her eyes examined like this before, and, sensing his unease as he approached her, her own anxiety increased.

"Of course," he said. "Now please hold very still."

He leaned in, pressing one hand against her forehead to steady it.

Letha had never been this close to a man who wasn't kinfolk. She could smell tobacco on his breath and could tell he was a dedicated pipe smoker.

He turned his head directly toward Letha, the light on his forehead invading her left eye with its brilliance.

"What color is it?" she asked.

"Mostly reddish."

"Is it moving?"

"Only when you fidget, ma'am."

He shifted his light and shone it into her right eye, refusing further comment.

Sensing that this was an excruciatingly silent and solemn occasion, Letha shushed herself and held herself very still until the light moved away, releasing her.

Vernon Dawson removed the light from his forehead, sat down at a table, and turned on a goose-necked lamp. He pulled a white piece of paper in front of him, took a pencil and drew a nearly perfect circle. Inside he sketched a series of nervous lines, networked and converging close to the center of the circle. He handed the paper to Letha, adjusting the lamp so that light fell on his drawing.

"Can you see this?"

She stretched her arm to hold the paper at a distance; she thought she could make out faint hints of lines in a blurred circle but could not be sure.

"Hold the paper here," he repositioned her arms to a more comfortable position, closer to her face, "and keep looking."

Letha spent what seemed like the next hour looking at the paper while Mr. Dawson had her try on every pair of eyeglasses he had for sale: black ones, white ones, silver ones, gold ones, and some made from tortoise-shell.

"Tell me what you see," he'd say each time he changed the eyeglasses.

Sometimes the lines he'd drawn on the paper were more distinct, and he put the corresponding eyeglasses in a separate tray. Later he would put these on her again, asking, *Do the circle and lines look better or worse?*

Her eyes were burning with the strain. She was beginning to get a headache and told him so.

"Then we are finished for the day," he announced, moving away from her. "But I'd like to ask you to return next Monday for more tests."

She returned the next week, and weekly thereafter, to Mr. Dawson's optical shop. Each time she left with a new treatment: salves and ointments to calm the irritation in her eyes, soothing drops and creams she must apply morning and night. There were exercises to improve her seeing; she must insist her eyes perform these promptly at four-hour intervals. And there were flat polished stones that she must balance on her closed eyelids while sleeping or resting. She never questioned the treatments, even though she never realized any results from using them.

Each time she visited, Mr. Dawson looked inside her eyes. And each time he put the light on his forehead and approached with his ophthalmoscope, she quizzed him for details. But he said nothing during these examinations, except to shush her when she tried to converse. Eventually he leaned even closer, and closer still, until he turned off the light on his forehead and kissed her hard on the lips.

She closed her eyes; her breath caught itself in transit; her stomach flipped over. She'd never been kissed like this, so suddenly and ferociously.

"I will look for you next Monday at four, then," he said as he stiffened, stood, helped her into her coat and ushered her out the door. He was trying hard not to smile.

And that – according to my mom – is the story of how Letha and Vernon, the improbable couple that became my parents, first met.

"Why don't you have a picture of him?" I'd asked my mom courtless times. It was maddening for me not to know what my own father looked like.

But each time I asked, she'd shake her head. "I just don't," she'd say, then proceed to describe him from memory.

"He was handsome, clear-eyed, with good teeth, and the tiniest hint of a smile even when he frowned," she said. "You smile like that sometimes, when you're trying hard not to."

"You could be making all this up," I'd always accuse her. With no proof, she might as well be.

"No," she'd say defensively. "He was real."

She could tell me what he liked for dinner (roast beef in gravy, with string beans and corn on the cob). And how he combed his hair (parted on the left side, patted down with Brylcreem). And what tobacco he used to fill the pipe he smoked (Prince Albert). But none of these details made him any more real to me because I couldn't see him for myself.

When I was older, in high school, I'd take the Green Line to Kenmore Square, get off and walk a few blocks to the storefront where my mother said the optical shop used to be. But the giant eyeglasses she'd described to me were long gone. Now it was a jewelry store, diamond rings instead of eyewear displayed in the window. One time, the jeweler had stepped out onto the sidewalk to ask if I were interested in trying on some of his diamond rings. I said yes, just to gain entry, and then stood at the counter, tapping my foot impatiently, while he brought tray after tray of sparking rings out for me to consider, as I looked all around, seeing nothing that suggested the store had ever been an optical shop. When it seemed the jeweler had grown weary of my indecision, I declared that I liked the ring I'd just tried on: a massive diamond rising up in the center of a row of smaller ones.

The jeweler took my hand and gently slid the ring from my finger. He slowly put it away in a little velvet box and said, "Now, Miss, all you have to do is find yourself a man who'll get you this ring."

I left the shop, my cheeks burning with shame. We both knew that I'd never bother him again.

- 3 -

I t is easy to sense the dangers inherent in this pursuit of clear vision, the subtle disturbances in the air that serve to cloud the mind, confuse the eye, upend a splendid smile and set a troubled frown in its place.

You have done your best, building this place high on a remote mesa in the Arizona Territory, hoping to escape earthbound air currents so easily stirred up by those living in more civilized places. Even so, you cannot be satisfied with your own efforts, traveling halfway around the world in your relentless search for good seeing, but finding none better, eventually you and your telescope return to the mesa.

You name this place Mars Hill, in honor of the planet whose mysteries you will unravel here. To construct the round dome, you hire local workmen, bright and industrious brothers whose sign outside their Flagstaff shop boasts:

Makers and Menders of Anything

Supports of cedar are sunk into the earth, stabilized and prepared for the walls and the finial: a glowing white edifice built somewhere else, dismantled, transported in pieces by rail, and then upon its arrival in Flagstaff, dragged to the top of the mesa and carefully reassembled. Once the finial is in place, you realize it is too heavy; it must be removed and the foundation must be made stronger. The critical juncture between the fixed walls and the dome, rotating on beveled steel rollers, is made smooth enough for the repeated adjustments it must endure.

When time erodes the heavenly view, it must be re-engineered. An itinerant Englishman named Harry has been hired as dome porter and is paid fifty dollars per month to accomplish this task. When heavenly sights move out of range, Harry is called upon to drag the roof with its tall narrow window to a new position, a noisy and difficult task.

The heavy roof seems to have a mind of its own. Sometimes Harry – who is slight yet solidly built – pulls the rope and the roof stubbornly holds on to its current position. Sometimes it lurches forward, past its intended destination, and poor Harry must hurry to change direction and drag it partway back.

We all must wait for Harry to complete his task because there is no more seeing until he does. Sometimes precious dark-sky minutes slip away before we can once again engage in our own less strenuous work of observing the heavens, while Harry, now briefly relieved of his duties, goes outside for a smoke.

The centerpiece of our new dome, the instrument of seeing itself, must be on a sturdy mount – iron sunk into a deep well filled with the finest Portland cement. The glassmaker's enlarging glass is perfectly fitted within the tube positioned at the portal, all elements locked in unyielding position. Stabilization is a necessity in this line of inquiry. When the object of the view is so distant, even the slightest jiggle of any component can produce gigantic waves of distortion and periods of miserable non-clarity. It is a situation you cannot tolerate, and yet one you cannot always control.

When unsettled, the air outside the dome cannot be calmed by any amount of money, and the heavenly view cannot be improved by even the most skilled craftsman's labor.

Tonight I left the dome feeling intense gratification, even though I'd not seen any of your canals. The atmosphere had not cooperated and the seeing had not been much above average – although you'd claimed to have observed for yourself a canal not previously seen on the surface of our red neighbor, and had sketched it with enthusiasm in the viewing log: a bold, straight line running diagonally from northeast to southwest, just above the equator.

Don't you see? you'd asked me, gesturing not to the view through the telescope but to the drawing you'd just made. You add your initials to finalize the heavenly event.

Harry stands outside, staring at the ground. He does not concern himself with the views in the sky, only the adjustments he must make to the roof to facilitate our seeing. I think he studies the earth beneath his feet as seriously as we study the stars and planets above our heads.

I watch as he stoops to pry something from the dirt. He rubs it clean on his coat sleeve and places it in his pocket. I approach to ask him what he's discovered.

He pulls a smooth, flat stone from his pocket and holds it in his palm so I can see the primitive dancing creature carved on its surface. He transfers the cool stone to my hand, turns and walks away.

"Proof there's intelligent life on Earth," he calls back to me, punctuating his announcement with a short, hard laugh.

GOOD SEEING

-*4*-

Vernon Dawson knew he need look no further.

The moment Miss Letha Broussard had stepped into his optical shop and he'd gazed into her wide-open, honey-hued eyes, he'd been seized by powerful romantic feelings that had by now grown to obsessive proportions. A middle-aged bachelor more by chance than determination, he had not anticipated this development, but welcomed it nonetheless. Each Monday afternoon when she came to be examined, he'd mask his emotions with stoic professionalism, keeping conversation to a minimum, eventually relaxing into a weekly routine of observing, sketching and writing accounts of what he'd seen, and suggesting another treatment when the previous one had proven ineffective.

He had no immediate kin in whom he could confide: no mother or father, no brothers or sisters. An orphan, he'd been adopted as an infant and raised by his Aunt Virginia. Aunt Virginia didn't know much about the family he'd lost. She'd kept a newspaper clipping and showed it to him once he was old enough to read and understand. There'd been a train accident, it said. Aunt Virginia said the accident had claimed his parents' lives, but because he'd been left behind with a member of the household staff, he had survived.

"What household staff?" he'd ask. Fantastic fleeting notions that perhaps his family was wealthy were followed by more practical musings that there might somewhere be someone who knew more about his origins. But Aunt Virginia shook her head side to side, signaling there was no more information to be gotten, and no point in looking for it.

Vernon had not made a decision to become a dispensing optician. Rather, one day he'd seen the giant eyeglasses hung over a storefront in Kenmore Square, a "Help Wanted" sign in the window. He'd walked inside, looked the owner in the eyes, offered a firm handshake and had been hired instantly. He'd easily mastered the task of fitting customers with suitable eyeglasses or spectacles, and his gentle nature pleased even the most uncertain among the clientele. The owner, upon his retirement a few years later, had offered to sell the business to Vernon for a more-than-reasonable amount. Vernon sometimes wondered whether Aunt Virginia had accomplished all these things in his behalf with her behind-the-scenes maneuvering.

"I believe I have fallen in love with Miss Broussard," he feverishly confessed one evening as he and his aunt dined at a modest but respectable restaurant near his shop in Kenmore Square. He could no longer contain his raging emotions nor keep them secret.

"I have kissed her," he continued. "Perhaps that was inappropriate behavior on my part."

Aunt Virginia did not seem surprised by this news. She finished eating her crème pie as she considered her response.

She used the white napkin she'd kept in her lap to pat her mouth, then cleared her throat and inquired: "And do you know whether the young lady has feelings for you?"

Vernon set down his coffee cup so abruptly that a little wave of brown liquid sloshed over its rim onto the tabletop. He'd never considered until now Miss Broussard's feelings for him, whether she'd been pleased by his impulsive act, whether she'd enjoyed the kiss, whether she would welcome another.

"I am working to improve her vision," he explained to his aunt. "We have not spoken about feelings."

"A kiss makes a powerful statement, indeed," Virginia opined, and Vernon did not disagree with his aunt's wisdom. On the contrary, he understood now that because he'd initiated the kiss, the burden was his to discover if mutual feelings existed. But how to do this – he had not a clue.

Vernon had no strategy; he'd formed no plan beyond convincing Miss Broussard he could help her – if only she'd come back to see him again. Over the past few weeks he'd given her the creams, salves and drops he'd purchased from the druggist across the street to treat the irritation, meanwhile trying to fathom the underlying cause of her vision problems. He'd refused to accept money for any of the treatments.

"It's just something to try," he'd tell her. "It may not work, so of course there's no charge." Although there would have been, if she'd had the money to pay for them.

But lately he'd begun to sense his own desperation. As a dispensing optician, Vernon was not supposed to test and examine eyes, but his attraction to Miss Broussard was so intense that he'd become committed to diagnosing and improving her vision. He'd never used the ophthalmoscope he'd purchased from a mail-order catalogue until she walked into his store; now he could not keep himself from looking inside her eyes each time she arrived. Even this minimal bit of optical intimacy felt intensely romantic and overwhelmingly sensual in both his mind and loins, and he'd attempt to calm himself by sketching on a piece of paper what he'd seen. He'd extended the number of appointments, postponing the moment he'd have to decide which of the hundred-or-so pairs of eyeglasses in his shop would help her see best, because he knew that once he fitted her with eyeglasses, he may never see her again.

But the determined Miss Broussard was not willing to be patient with his prolonged examinations and ineffectual decision-making.

"When can you get me a pair of glasses so I can see?" she begged him the next Monday afternoon. "And how much will they cost me?"

He looked back over the notes he'd written and explained the results as best he could to his insistent patient. Each time she'd seen the letters on the wall and the drawing in her hands best with a different pair of eyeglasses. Each week she'd needed a stronger pair; her eyesight was deteriorating. He could put her in eyeglasses, but these would need to change again soon, as her condition worsened.

"But that...I mean, I couldn't pay you for even one pair, much less a series of eyeglasses." Letha put on her coat and hat, eyes stinging with both fatigue and tears, and prepared to leave, knowing she had no cause to return, until she was gainfully employed. Even then, with the money she was determined to send to her family back in Louisiana, there would be precious little to spend on pair after pair of fancy eyeglasses.

"Miss Broussard," he stood, she thought, preparing to see her out, but instead, "could you…I need," he fumbled for words, finally finding them. "I am prepared to offer you a job as my assistant."

- 5 -

My mom fell in love with her boss. My Great Aunt Lulu fell in love with hers. How'd I end up working for a jerk like Dr. Dick?

When the earlier Mars Mariners had been launched, scientific hope was high that the pioneering space explorers might find and photograph some evidence of life on the red planet during their brief fly-by encounters. If not Martians, then some sign that Mars could support life in some form: water past or present, tolerable temperatures, a potentially breathable atmosphere.

I hadn't thought much about Mars before starting my job two years ago as a temporary darkroom assistant at JPL, but now it was hard to avoid. Even the coffee mugs on every desk were emblazoned with the ♂ symbol.

There were many teams at JPL. I'd been assigned to the "image processing team," who would support the "science team" in its efforts to see and understand details of the Martian surface as recorded and transmitted back to Earth by the two Mariners now closing in on Mars.

Because I'd taken a photography course in college and knew my way around a darkroom, I had no trouble performing my assigned duties; in fact, I enjoyed working alone and sometimes kept the "do not enter" sign on the darkroom door even when I didn't need to. That's why I was so surprised when Dr. Dick barged in unannounced one afternoon, flipping on the overhead lights, catching me peeling and eating an orange instead of developing his precious negatives.

"No more hiding out in the dark," he barked. "Get over to Personnel."

I'd been promoted to a permanent, full-time position as "image analyst." I'd be trained to use the "video film converter," an amazing instrument with the ability to transform the pictures on a television screen into actual photographs. I'd never even seen this device; it was attached to the IBM computer in an area that was off-limits to all but a few of the computer scientists on the image processing team.

I should be thrilled to get a "man's job," the ladies in the personnel office told me after I'd signed the papers re-classifying me and upping my salary substantially.

"The men get paid more," they explained, "because they work with the computer."

When I got back from Personnel, Dr. Dick was waiting to give me a quick tour of the new area where I'd be working. My former "office," the darkroom, was a closet-sized space at the end of one hall with a table outside for my prep work. Now I followed Dr. Dick happily through a much more expansive area equipped with wide metal desks and vast rows of crisp florescent lighting overhead – I'd already been assigned a real desk!

"Once the Mariners reach Mars and transmit their data," he explained to me between long draws on his cigarette, "we'll turn the real-time batch around in thirty-six hours."

He stopped to pull the top page from a stack of papers, and the others attached to it followed, unfolding accordion-style. On each page were orderly columns of printed numbers.

"The real time data comes in raw, like this."

"Where from?" I asked him.

"From Mars." He grinned and re-folded the papers into a neat stack, ready to move on, pausing first to stub out his cigarette in an ashtray conveniently placed nearby. "From the Goldstone tracking station out in the Mojave, actually, but they get it directly from Mars."

"I don't get it."

He frowned. "You don't have to get it, Miss Dawson. Our programmers take the numbers and load them into the IBM," he pushed on a glass door and ushered me inside to demonstrate, "like this."

He'd already lit up another cigarette. Smoking was not permitted in the computer room, the sign on the doorway announced, but Dr. Dick apparently did not read the signs, or else did not care to obey them. Wherever he was, he was smoking, and no one cared stop him.

Until now I'd only observed through the glass doors the floor-to-ceiling racks housing the IBM computer that nearly filled the room. Now I watched up close, mesmerized as Dr. Dick fed a page full of numbers into a slot attached to the huge machine, pressed several buttons in a sequence, then flipped a small switch upwards. The computer blinked, swallowed the paper and began its electronic digestion.

"What's happening now?"

He sighed. "Again, not something you need to understand. We work efficiently here, Miss Dawson, on a need-to-know basis. Anything more slows us down. Got it?"

"Yessir."

He'd moved already to the other end of the giant wall of a machine, where a small black-and-white television screen displayed a nondescript landscape in soft shades of gray that were nearly overwhelmed by static, the kind you see on TV when the station won't come in clearly. I reached instinctively for a dial underneath, hoping to improve the image, but Dr. Dick grabbed my arm and stopped me.

"You're not watching television, Miss Dawson," he scolded me. "This computer cost millions and you're not allowed to just play with it."

"Sorry."

"What you're looking at is raw data recorded by the first Mars Mariner back in 1965."

"That's Mars?"

"I'm trying to make a point here, Miss Dawson," he snapped back, his patience growing thin.

"And what's that, sir?"

Dr. Dick paused before answering to pull a red-and-white pack of Winstons and a slim silver lighter from his shirt pocket, firing up yet another cigarette and taking a deep draw. He closed his eyes as he inhaled, briefly satisfied, before he released the smoke into the computer room.

"It's not Mars until we call it Mars," he chuckled. "You'll see."

Within weeks after I'd begun my new job, the straight-laced scientists in the Spacecraft Operation Control Center watched as two Mariners, launched only days apart, approached Mars, then endured the breathless wait to see if the cameras they'd packed inside (to perform their critical "television experiment") would operate as planned. When the data began its slow trek across millions of miles back to Earth and the teletype machines jumped to duty, they whooped in delight and traded all manner of hand-slaps; some even performed dance moves in the aisles, poorly.

The frenzied excitement didn't last long as each Mariner in turn flew past Mars and then kept going, but during the precious few minutes of the close encounter, each had performed perfectly, recording over a hundred pictures and sending them back to Earth, the information in each image taking an agonizing eight-and-a-half hours to arrive.

"Now it's our turn," Dr. Dick announced.

The rocket scientists needed detailed pictures to study and write papers about, and Public Relations needed dramatic pictures to show the rest of the world, but detail and drama were the very things lacking on Mars. The surface of the red planet had such low contrast, it was nearly impossible to distinguish a mountain peak from a hole in the ground – until the computer scientists on the image processing team got out their slide rules and went to work. Feverishly they'd write algorithm after algorithm, feeding each into the IBM and waiting impatiently – sometimes for hours – as the computer processed their instructions and then displayed the results on the television screen. The TV images were most often disappointing, sending them back to their slide rules to write yet another algorithm and start the whole process all over.

Once Dr. Dick and the computer scientists were satisfied with the image as processed by the computer and displayed on the television screen, they called me into service. I'd been trained by now to operate the video film converter, a nondescript box-like unit whose electronic magic (which I had yet to fathom – I only knew which button to press) recorded the pictures from the television screen onto 70mm photographic film that I'd take to the darkroom, process and print up as high-resolution 8 x 10s – nothing less would do for the fussy scientists.

The prime rule of image processing, I learned quickly, was not to add any information. We had to work with what the cameras onboard the spacecraft had recorded. Only the computer scientists were allowed to adjust the raw data, and then only within strictly defined parameters: the removal of residual images and transmission noise, geometric corrections, and carefully controlled contrast enhancements. Neither was creativity permitted in the darkroom. I was not supposed to filter, dodge or burn; I had to print exactly what the film converter had recorded.

Each time I emerged from the darkroom to present them with new photographs, they all professed their delight, but I don't think anybody was really impressed with the close-up pictures of Mars. Our "red" neighbor was colorless, desolate and barren, with no signs of life anywhere. Privately I wondered why we'd gone to all the bother of sending such expensive space hardware to photograph this bland and uninformative world – and why we were planning to do it all over again.

IMAGE PROCESSING

-6-

I t didn't help that NASA's most spectacular achievement, landing Apollo 11 on the moon, occurred just days before the two Mariners sailed past Mars. We'd seen the astronauts on live television: two poorly defined figures in bulky spacesuits climbing down from the lunar lander and bounding about the low-gravity surface, hefting big moon rocks as if they were pebbles, planting a stiff, wired version of the stars and stripes that would never wave and flap on this airless world, before heading back to a hero's welcome on Earth.

"Men in space are sexier than metal in space," the Mariner science team joked, and I had to agree with them.

The low-resolution television image from the moon's surface was no better than the ones the Mariners would record of the Martian surface a few days later, but we all knew that Neil Armstrong had a kind face hidden behind the reflective helmet of his spacesuit, and a strong albeit static-y voice that had delivered his well-rehearsed line, "That's one small step for man, one giant leap for mankind."

While the astronauts had returned triumphantly to tickertape parades and an official visit to the White House to shake hands with Nixon himself, the dutiful Mariners competed their mission, then sailed on toward the sun. No glory for them, just the raw data they transmitted back to Earth and our careful treatment of each unremarkable part of it.

It was up to my team, apparently, to fix up Mars as best we could and fashion a happy ending for the Mariners, even within the nearly impossible restrictions of image processing. Our exemplary work was critical, Dr. Dick never tired of explaining, in keeping all the bucks from going to Buck Rogers. The bigwigs over in administration depended on our properly enhanced photographs of Mars as they worked feverishly to persuade NASA to keep funding its unmanned planetary missions, despite the Apollo-fueled man-on-the-moon madness.

That's why I'd have to run each new set of photos I printed by Dr. Dick to get his approval before delivering them up the hill. His office, at the opposite end of the hall from the darkroom, was Spartan clean and orderly; his desktop held neatly arranged in-and-out trays plus the cigar box that used to hold his smokes but now housed his Juicy Fruit gum

– he'd just announced his determined quest to stop smoking and was using the gum as an oral substitute. His walls were adorned only with his framed diploma – a doctorate from Cal Tech – and an 8 x 10 photo showing him shaking hands with Spiro Agnew during the vice president's visit to JPL last year. Spiro Agnew!

This afternoon he was busy playing with the new Polaroid camera he'd ordered so the computer scientists could take instant pictures of the television screen when they couldn't wait for me to finish the darkroom work. It's like they were going to come all over themselves if they couldn't get their hands on a picture right away, but they hadn't yet figured out how to rig the camera to the computer.

"Smile," he pulled me toward him, aimed the camera at both of us and pushed a button. The flash bulb stunned me momentarily as the camera clicked, whirred and spit out the picture – only it wasn't there yet. Dr. Dick placed it on his desk and we both watched as the gray-toned image gradually came into being – me, frowning, holding a big envelope containing the photos I'd just printed, and him, grinning broadly for the camera.

While we waited for the photo to resolve itself, he popped a few sticks of gum into his mouth.

"Want some?" he asked, holding the pack of gum toward me.

"No thanks."

He put the gum back into the cigar box, judged the photo as completed, then took a lipstick-sized squeegee from his desk drawer. He held the photo in place by one corner and passed the device, which contained a foul-smelling chemical fixative, over its surface.

Pleased as a magician who'd just performed his finest trick, he lifted the corner of the still-wet Polaroid photo and presented it to me.

"Trade you." He reached for the envelope of prints I'd come to deliver. I stood there tapping one foot impatiently as he opened the envelope, pulled each photo out and studied it intently. I was not allowed to leave until he'd signed off on each print.

While he examined the photos I'd printed, I took the opportunity to examine Dr Dick in the Polaroid photo he'd taken. He was much taller than me, with a blond crew cut and a silly grin, not a type I'd ever go for – too tall, too nervous, not enough hair, and he didn't seem interested in romancing me (not that he should be), unless tormenting me counted and it didn't.

"Miss Dawson," he looked up from one photo with a devious grin, "you do know the prime rule of image processing, don't you?"

"Of course, sir," I replied. "Adding information is not allowed. I didn't add anything."

"But removing whatever you don't need is just fine," he fired back, then added, "We do have a dress code here at JPL, you know."

I looked down at my outfit: tan slacks with what was surely an inoffensive navy blouse buttoned nearly to my neck, and sensible brown shoes. I was wearing those dangly peacock-feather earrings, but my hair had grown out enough to cover them.

"Is there something wrong, sir?"

He was holding back his laughter. "I hear the braless look is in," he finally spit out with a huge guffaw as I raced from his office.

"You can take it all off for all I care," I heard another guy shout; a series of wolf-whistles followed me as I hurried back to my desk, angry and embarrassed.

I was surprised and a little dismayed soon after my run-in with Dr. Dick, when I woke up one morning to realize I'd dreamed about him.

I've come to his office to turn in my latest prints, but he's not there, so I decide to take some pictures with the Polaroid camera sitting on his desk.

Brazenly I open desk drawers and look inside manila folders, snapping instant photos of whatever I find there. In my mind I'm collecting little pieces of Dr. Dick himself, an activity that seems overly intimate and slightly arousing. When I open the cigar box on his desk and find not his Juicy Fruit gum but instead his stash hidden there, I'm quite shocked, but there it is: a sizeable amount of weed, plus a small, stylish pipe.

"Want some?" he asks. He's standing right behind me; I hadn't heard him enter.

He's back in his chair and we're smoking now, passing the pipe back and forth across his desk wordlessly, holding the smoke we're inhaling as long as possible. I think about his face, about how handsome he is, but hadn't noticed until now. He coughs once, twice, a sure signal he's a novice stoner (that and the fact that he calls it "Mary Jane"). Then he smiles at me as if I were somebody different, not the employee he loves to antagonize.

Then we're in the downstairs lounge, with the big U-shaped leather sofa. All the men I work with are sitting there, watching me intently. I'm wearing a miniskirt and fishnet hose, and in the next instant I realize they all expect to have sex with me, one by one. I jump up angrily. I didn't know this was going to be a fuckfest, I say, hurrying to the door.

I was sure I'd parked nearby, but now cannot remember where. I walk around and around, but my Karmann Ghia is nowhere to be seen, so I head back toward Building 168.

Upstairs, Dr. Dick is waiting for me in the IBM room. He's smoking again and for no good reason I've undressed to my bra and panties.

"Adding information is not permitted," he chuckles, leaning toward me, exhaling cigarette smoke into my face, "but removing what you don't need is perfectly fine."

"I'm wearing a bra," I inform him proudly.

"Not for long," he replies confidently.

-7-

Each morning before leaving for work, Letha examined herself in the full-length mirror downstairs in the YWCA lobby. Wearing the newest pair of eyeglasses her boss had provided at no charge, she was pleased to see herself both fashionably and clearly.

Now that she was earning a modest but regular salary, she'd been able to purchase a new outfit – a contemporary frock to replace the faded, outdated dress she'd worn daily, rinsing it out nightly and ironing it each morning for the past few months. She'd also bought new patent-leather high heels, seamed silk stockings, and a new girdle to hold them up.

Letha had learned how to choose an appropriate foundation garment in a free class (that also included free tea and cupcakes) held one Sunday afternoon last month at the YWCA, titled, "Are Your Garments Correct?" Even so, the girdle chafed at her waist and the new heels were hard to walk in. Nevertheless, she'd seen girls who worked in other offices in Kenmore Square trotting around in them, and she was determined to follow suit.

At first Mr. Dawson didn't notice – when she'd taken the mail into his office, he'd barely looked up. But when she returned later that morning to go over the mail orders with him, he removed his reading spectacles and took a good, long, admiring look at his suddenly well-dressed secretary.

"It says here the universe is expanding," he said, setting on his desk the scientific journal he'd been reading.

"I'd suspected as much," she answered with a tired smile. Her eyes had become irritated again, and she'd been rubbing them, although she wasn't supposed to.

"New dress?"

"Yessir."

"Very nice. I like it."

Letha lingered in the doorway to see if Mr. Dawson needed anything else, but he simply returned to his reading.

She softly closed his door and walked back to the reception area, where she went to work straightening the papers on her table, and tidying the rows of eyeglasses displayed underneath the glass counter.

Mr. Dawson approached silently from behind, surprising her, as always, turning her toward him, wrapping his arms around her, kissing her passionately for a long, long time, pausing only to profess his love for her, eloquently and repeatedly.

Always embarrassed after having this fantasy, Letha sat quietly in her chair until her boss emerged briskly from his office, already wearing his overcoat, fedora in hand. He crossed through the reception area on his way to the entry door.

"You mustn't stay too late," he cautioned her. "I can't pay you overtime, you know."

They laughed in unison as he departed, and the tinkling bells above the door joined in.

She put on her own coat, a modest little brown thing (she had a new woolen one on layaway). She stuck her feet into the uncomfortable high heels (which she kicked off when there were no customers in the office), held her breath and reached under her skirt to quickly adjust her too-tight girdle before closing up the office and hurrying to catch the underground trolley back to the YWCA. In the universe of foundation garments, it seemed a little more expansion was needed.

Back in her room at the YWCA, Letha sat in the dark, unloosed from her girdle, barefoot and already in her nightgown. The other girls who lived here had gone downstairs for dinner, and most had stayed for swimming, for glee club practice, or for evening calisthenics.

In the blessed silence, she endured the latest treatment Mr. Dawson had prescribed, attaching a suction cup to each of her closed eyes and pumping them with the little rubber pump she held in one fist. As she pumped, the pressure on her eyeballs increased, until they felt as if they were going to burst. She quit pumping, rested for three minutes, then began again.

She saw the stars after the second or third pumping cycle: tiny lights sparkling in the dark inside her eyelids. She'd never noticed stars in her eyes before. She kept her eyes shut tightly and looked up and down, then side to side, mesmerized, trying to see them all, but they went on forever. Perhaps this was part of the treatment. She must remember to tell Mr. Dawson about the stars. What would he think about that?

She'd gratefully accepted his offer of employment, as much from girlish infatuation as grown-up financial need. Ever since he'd kissed her, she'd waited anxiously for another kiss, and had fantasized about that kiss even more.

But there had been no further attentions on his part. Instead, he acted stiffly and formally in her presence, even though she thought she'd caught him looking longingly at her when he thought she wasn't looking at him. He must have decided logically and rightfully against a romance, that he needed a reliable secretary more than a paramour.

Letha was determined to be the best secretary imaginable but, in her weaker moments, allowed herself to think of ways she may be able to catch his eye again.

Tonight she felt more confident. The stars that had just appeared in her eyes were, she decided, a potent sign that another kiss would soon follow.

Course Correction

- 1 -

This part of Texas – its panhandle – is flat, bland and deserted, with only an occasional roadside scrub brush or dead stunted tree in the distance to interrupt the unremarkable view that, unfortunately, goes on forever.

I drove all night and so will have to stop soon or else risk falling asleep at the wheel. I force myself to sit at attention and scan the bleak horizon ahead, searching for relief in the form of any interesting feature. But there is none, and Amarillo is still fifty miles away.

I've been up and down the radio dial several times – nothing but static. I turn it off. To fill the silence I sing the chorus of Aretha Franklin's "Natural Woman" several times ("you make me feel, you make me feel, you make me feel like a natural woman"), hoping words to the verses would follow, but they don't, so I just *la-la-la* the rest, comforted at least by the fact that no one can hear my tuneless and spiritless rendition.

With the midday Texas sun bearing down, even the air conditioner on high seems to blow warm. I crank open the window to freshen the stale air, but the rushing wind makes too much noise, so I crank it up again.

I've been through all the minute body adjustments I could make while driving: leaning forward to arch and cool my back, lifting my sweaty butt an inch above the vinyl seat and then lowering it into a slightly different position, moving both clammy hands to nine-and-three instead of ten-and-two on the warm plastic steering wheel. None offers even the slightest relief. My sunglasses keep sliding forward on my sweaty nose. I should have put on cutoffs at the last rest stop. I should have drunk more water.

Something is building inside me – more than irritation, impatience or boredom. I'm stuck on a featureless highway that will never end, with infrequent road signs announcing cities and towns that seem impossibly remote, like places I've dreamed about but cannot locate anywhere in my waking life. There is no destination in sight. Great Aunt Lulu's journey may have been transformative, but mine is boring me to death.

I must have closed my eyes for a moment, just long enough to create the spectacle I see up ahead: My Karmann Ghia flipped upside down on the road, steam rising from it, my own bloodied form wedged against the collapsed roof of the tiny car.

I've always feared having an accident in a desolate place like this, where no one will notice for hours. When they finally find me there'll be no one to call. Not even Dr. Dick.

At least I can stop driving now, and sleep.

In the next instant I gasp and force myself awake. The startling illusion of my highway accident vanishes like one of those watery mirages sometimes appearing like a puddle on the road. In its place shimmers a cluster of signs insisting that Amarillo is just ahead:

> **The Cowboy Motel**
> **Earl's Esso Service Station**
> **Shoney's Big Boy Restaurant**
> **Rexall Drug Store**

I drive past closely-built ranch houses, barns and silos, and roll down my window to hear the distant roar of a farm tractor at work, filtered through the wind blowing my hair in my face. I grab a loose strand and put it back behind my ear, but it escapes once again. I don't care. I realize I'm pleased by the distinct animal smell coming from herds of tightly packed cattle along one side of the road. The fenced-in cows go on and on, stopping abruptly at the city limit sign.

> **DO NOT PASS**
> **SLOW TO 35**

I remove my foot from the accelerator and allow myself to coast.

> **Welcome to Amarillo, Population 147,500**

The sign is proof: I'm no longer alone.

Within minutes, the landscape changes again: an improved view featuring cozy white houses with shade trees, wide yards with swing sets, a German Shepherd sniffing a fire hydrant, all visible portents of civilization. Suddenly I'm craving entry into this community; I want to belong somewhere, and this place holds promise. At a stoplight, I fix a smile on my face, close my eyes and summon a good mood I keep in reserve: *I'm sitting in a wide, wooden swing on a generous front porch, the swing chains creaking pleasantly as I urge the contraption back and forth while sipping iced tea from a tall, frosted aluminum glass.*

The car behind me honks impatiently, and the driver yells out his window, "It ain't gonna git any greener, lady!"

"Screw you!" I holler back, taking off in a hurry.

Giving in to road weariness, I get a room at the Amarillo Howard Johnson. I turn on the air conditioner, fall into bed, and sleep for eight hours straight. Around midnight I get up and shower, put on clean jeans and a white t-shirt, and walk over to the 24-hour restaurant.

The night air seems considerably cooler.

Just inside the restaurant door I buy a pack of "Eves" from the cigarette machine. I'm not much of a smoker, but there's little else to do here: No drinking allowed in this tee-totally dry county.

The Book of Great Aunt Lulu is tucked securely inside my purse. There will be no more leaving it behind. As annoyed as I am by the confusing style and chaotic contents, I've come to believe that there must be a reason why this book is in my hands now, and I'm determined to discover its significance.

I pull it out, place it on the counter in front of me and open to a random page. I light one of the pretty flower-trimmed cigarettes and take a weak draw without inhaling, lest a coughing fit overtake me. I order coffee and begin reading:

I've discovered of late that my vision has been compromised, and let me warn you that yours, too, may be less reliable than you think. You say your own vision is acute, that you see details where others do not. You claim that the preciseness of your vision depends not on sensitivity, an overabundance of seeing that may, in fact, blur the details. Visual acuity is more perfect; with it you are able to see not more, but more clearly.

Think of your own eyes, you explain to me. If your visual sensitivity were suddenly increased, more light would rush in providing the object of your gaze with grand illumination, but in the same instance, details of the object would be lost in the unforgiving brightness. On the other hand, if your visual acuity were to suddenly increase, blurred objects would become sharply focused, perhaps to the point of specific identification.

I concentrate on seeing, as you have instructed me. I steady my eyes, focus them and gaze, but the view keeps slipping. I see a spotted cow in a pasture, a worn rocking chair on a shaded veranda, red wine in a stained glass, a train slowing as it approaches a quaint station in Flagstaff, Arizona. The view shifts again. I'm on that train; the brakes squeal; I'm already at the station. The wine glass has been washed sparkling clean by a member of the household staff.

We have arrived. I see myself relaxing in a rocking chair in the lobby of the Bank Hotel, sipping a glass of fine French claret while waiting for the carriage to carry us up the hill. We brought the wine with us from Boston. We drank it there as well, the same glass, the same vintage. In the distance the spotted cow bellows as she gives birth. The cow's name is Venus.

"I just found out I was named after a cow!"

I slam the book closed and announce this to the gangly man with long unkempt hair seated near me at the coffee shop counter who just asked my name. He seems disappointed "Venus" does not refer to the goddess of love.

"No," I tell him, "not even to the planet."

I explain how my mom used to tell me I was named for one of Great Aunt Lulu's friends back in Arizona, but she'd never mentioned the bovine part.

"That's a hoot!" he says.

"More like a moo," I reply.

He cackles again, obviously easily entertained.

"I'm Jorge," he tells me, although I hadn't asked. He grins a slightly crooked but pleasing smile that angles down one side of his face, as if he'd suffered a mild stroke. His cowboy hat, a gigantic brown dome trimmed with a colorful Indian-weave band, occupies the seat between us.

"And who's that?" I ask him, pointing to the hat.

"Margarita," he answers flatly.

"Your hat has a name?"

"That's only the beginning."

Over a second cup of coffee, he introduces me to his worn dusty boots Ellie and Nellie: "They take me places I never imagined going," he says wistfully. And to Frances his silver belt buckle: "Keeps me in check," he chuckles. And to Cinderella, the silver trimmed western bolo he wears around his neck: "So close to my heart," he sighs.

"Why do you name your clothes like that?"

"Gotta have somebody to talk to," he answers. "And you din' show up til just now.'

I return my book to the safety of my no-name purse. "I need to find a telephone," I say.

He leans over to put one hand on my arm. "Whassa hurry?"

I distinctly smell liquor on his breath but hadn't noticed his slurred speech until now. "I could gitcha drink," he offers.

"Oh, yeah?" I challenge him. "Where you gonna find me a drink around here?"

He opens one flap of his red leather vest, pointing to a thin silver flask hidden inside. "Betty Lou," he promises sincerely, "serves up the berry vest."

Jorge follows me to my motel room without being asked – and without being sent away. I take both him and Great Aunt Lulu's journal to bed. I read a few pages out loud while he listens patiently, sipping occasionally from his flask:

Night and day find themselves oddly inverted here on Mars Hill: the stars overhead our shimmering work lights, the sun our brilliant night lantern. We have taken charge of the illumination, however, with electrical lamps able to brighten all our rooms and thick curtains hung in all our windows, allowing us to decide between light and dark, no matter the hour.

"But this next part," I explain to Jorge, "is written on top of the part I just read – like this."

I turn the book sideways and continue reading as he feigns full attention, meanwhile creeping his hand along my forearm on its way toward my breast.

The afternoon nap will become commonplace here, a necessary preparation for staying up late. We pull the curtains to darken the room, welcoming the privacy that accompanies the darkness. You lie on my bed, hum a sweet tune, and stretch out one arm to pull me toward you.

"What wonders we shall see when we peer though the telescope this evening," you explain to me, "have already taken place on a distant world. The light illuminating them is now on its way, making an orderly progression through the heavens, preparing to present the vision to those who will look at the 'now' but will see the 'then.' The time needed for the light to reach its destination varies, depending on the distance it must travel. What do you think of that, Miss Lulu?"

"If there are in fact beings living on other worlds," I reply to you, "then it's possible we may watch them at play, though by now they are actually having their dinner, or we may be dining while they have already put themselves to bed. They may declare war while we nap, make peace before we awake. Our dinner bell may signal their nightcap, our evening glass of absinthe their goodnight kiss."

"Kissing can, in fact, be done at any time of the day or night," you tell me, and you then proceed to demonstrate this scientific fact, quite nicely.

Your pocket watch counts time audibly on the bedside table. Nearly two hours will pass before I am awake again. As always, you and your watch will have vanished. You will be in your own room, dressing and grooming yourself, preparing for the darkness that will soon envelop the mesa, our version of dawn, the beginning of our workday.

Your watch, if resting on a Martian's bedside table, would be of no use at all in keeping time! You would be early for dinner here, much too late there. Time, it seems, is a curious and mischievous imp when it strays so far away from home, and will never reveal the truth of the moment, even if asked politely.

"What do you think of that?" I ask Jorge, who has been stretched out silently and yet hopefully beside me.

"I think it don't matter one doodad," he finally says, handing the flask to me. "There's a little bit left."

I sip and grimace. He takes the flask back and screws the top on before putting it on the nightstand. He's losing patience with me, and even more so with Great Aunt Lulu.

"Now shut up," he whispers sweetly, "and put the book away."

He gathers me in his Texas-sized arms. "Lemme show you how we do kissin' in these parts."

Not all my boyfriends are imaginary. I'll have a new one to tell my mom about, I note, before remembering she's dead and no more boyfriends, real or imaginary, would be necessary, and no more Sunday afternoon phone calls would be possible.

I must still be in mourning, but I don't feel like it. Most likely because I'm too busy getting laid.

Jorge and I hung out all day yesterday and I decide to stay another night in Amarillo. We go to his trailer – a long, rusted contraption parked on cement blocks anchored to a barren patch of land and surrounded by old tires, machine parts and a pack of skinny brown hound dogs emerging from underneath to sniff my busy crotch relentlessly. Inside, a classic male mess of a place: stale cigarette smoke, piles of clothing, empty soda cans and Jack Daniel's bottles, old *TV Guides*, a dirty saucer full of ashes, rolling papers, a few prepared joints, and a ripped Naugahyde recliner aimed at the color TV set front and center in the tiny living room.

I plop down in his chair, and then wince. I lean forward and remove the soiled ashtray I just sat on. It looks like an old engine part he's re-engineered.

"Ford V-8 piston," he informs me proudly.

"You got a phone?" I ask him.

He comes over and kisses me on the mouth before answering

"Now who you gotta call?" he asks me. "Ain't I enough man for you?"

"You sure are a handful," I answer him truthfully.

He'd been very well endowed, I was pleased to discover, and somewhere along the Chisholm Trail, he'd actually learned a little something about foreplay.

"You got to go to the bathroom," he tells me then.

"No, I don't."

"That's where the phone is," he explains, turning on the television. With a hum and crackle, the big set pulses to life. He fiddles with the tuner to bring *Wide World of Sports* into view and then cranks the volume to an insanely high level.

I get up and he claims my place in the recliner.

"Why is your phone in the bathroom?" I holler over the tinny roar of stock cars racing as I push open the bathroom door.

"'Cause," he hollers back, "that's where I do my business!" Then he laughs. "But it don't work."

I stop in my tracks.

"I din' pay my bill so they cut it off. You got to go down to the corner, cross the street, turn left and keep goin' till you see the Esso station. They got a phone booth there."

He lights up a joint and takes a long drag.

"Want some?" his voice pinched from holding the smoke in.

"No thanks." I grab my purse. "Guess I'll be seeing you then."

The hound dogs bark up a storm for a good thirty seconds when I walk out the door, then slink back into the cool darkness underneath the trailer.

I jump in my car and speed down the dirt driveway, kicking up dust, and never once looking back – not even as I pass the phone booth at the Esso station. The phone call can wait, trumped by my sudden need to put some distance between Jorge and me.

If there's one thing I appreciate more than foreplay, it's what I call the "afterglow," the little things a lover can do later on that keep you both in the moment. I can't explain afterglow, but I know when it happens. It's like the physical bond that's established when the two of you are going at it shifts to another plane and then keeps on going. You feel attached to the other person still, even if he goes off to work, or you do. I'm pretty sure men don't go much for the afterglow. It's rare, in fact, to find one who knows about it.

Jorge, I'm sad to say, didn't display much of the afterglow, unless the tip of the cigarette he lit up after sex counted. And it didn't.

I'm already on the interstate, heading west toward the state line. I'll find a phone in New Mexico.

Sky High

$$- 1 -$$

$$\mu \, \pounds \neq \infty \, f \approx \, < ! \, ! \, ! >$$

E ven when we have ceased our travels, our words continue to dress themselves up and venture out on their own. We send them to places we have not the time nor inclination to go ourselves. They are good and ready travelers, never complaining about the difficulty of their journeys – trains that run late, seats that are uncomfortable, fellow passengers who behave rudely.

Our words most often travel in groups. Each morning we prepare the necessary letters. Once you have signed them, I address and seal the envelopes and place them in a sack to be carried down to the eastbound train by four each afternoon. Always more letters arrive with the train, most demanding responses, creating an endless loop delayed three or four days, the time it takes the Express to get from here to Boston, or from Boston back. All the accoutrements we need to duplicate a high-styled Boston existence, whether French caviar or Cuban cigars, can be got by sending a letter. It's just a matter of time and transportation.

Of late I've acquired an able assistant to help me prepare the letters, a brand new Hammond typing machine so advanced it can almost create the correspondence on its own, an exquisite little device built of thin silvery parts more air-like than metallic, encased in a hinged wooden box so I can carry it with me wherever I am needed. Its alphabet is arranged circularly around a tall upright cylinder that can be removed and another one inserted, enabling the letters to take on varying characteristics: curved and cheery, solid and stately, large and full of importance, fancy with tapered tips and decorative flourishes.

But changeable letters are not the most amazing function of

my new typing machine; it serves another purpose that I have yet to comprehend and utilize. Its keyboard features not only the letters of our alphabet, but also scientific symbols that seem magical to me because I must still master the meanings of them all. Each time I push an unknown key and its mysterious marking appears on the white paper wound onto the carriage, there's a brief sense of wonder about what I may have just written. I imagine a tiny spark emitted as my message is released into the universe, where it will travel far in search of someone who understands its significance.

If my more mundane letters to Montgomery Ward in Chicago or Thayer's in Boston are answered and the products they request are delivered, then surely my odd scientific messages also will garner eventual results.

Someday I shall receive a reasoned reply from a being on some distant star or planet. Perhaps the message is already on its journey, a tiny pulse finding its way through the heavens, destined to arrive at my writing desk, where my hands are poised over the silvery keys, ready to respond.

My fingers twitch, tingle, sparkle and dance over my new keyboard, in praise of the Hammond's unprecedented ability to send unknown messages across the universe. I am writing in a language I do not understand and corresponding with creatures I have yet to encounter.

I press another key to begin the marvelous cycle once again.

-2-

####!!!!!#####

Not two months into her new job as Vernon Dawson's assistant, Letha made a serious mistake.

"Get us one of these, Miss Broussard."

Mr. Dawson had not been specific in his instructions, but instead had pointed to a picture on a page in a mail-order catalog he'd placed in front of her, too close for her to see it clearly, even with her powerful new glasses.

She filled out the order form and mailed it off, not realizing until three weeks later, when the unusually large package arrived, that she'd ordered a telescope instead of a stereoscope! The package was too large to hide, and so of course Mr. Dawson spied it as soon as he walked into the little reception area.

"What's this?" he asked, using his pocketknife to slit the twine and edges of the box, revealing a long brass tube.

Letha cowered at her desk, waiting to be fired.

Instead, at the end of the workday, her boss had carried the shiny new instrument up the stairs to the roof of the building. A moment later, he went back down and led his bewildered secretary to the roof. He guided her eye to the aperture of the telescope.

"Look now," he urged her, "and tell me what you see."

"I...I don't see anything," she confessed. Inside the lens it was all darkness. Was this another test for her problematic vision? If so, surely she'd failed it.

"Are you certain?" He took a look for himself, fiddling with the knobs outside the tube. "Now, please try again."

"Actually, I've been meaning to tell you," she said truthfully, closing her eyes and pressing on her eyelids the way the suction cups had done, "when I do this, I see stars everywhere. What do you think of that?"

Her eyes were still closed when she felt Mr. Dawson grabbing her around the waist and holding her so tightly she nearly lost her balance.

"I think you are full of stars," he agreed joyously, planting a passionate and energetic kiss on her lips.

Letha held her breath, waiting for what must surely come next. She was not disappointed: "I've been meaning to tell you," he whispered her own words back into her ear, "that I have fallen in love with you."

Letha kept her eyes tightly closed, terrified but thrilled, her heart pounding more than when she'd attended the thunderous fireworks display on the Common last 4th of July.

Vernon breathed sweet, warm words into Letha's face: "Open your eyes."

But she could not take her eyes off the stars she saw inside. They swirled madly, spilling everywhere – a glorious universe expanding past the confines of her eyes, sparkling above a fanciful and faraway place where, she'd already decided, she and Vernon would live forever.

Midway through New Mexico and I'm pretty stoned, thanks to the skinny joint I stole from Jorge. Words from my great aunt's journal haunt me because there's no logical order in them, no arrangement I can find that makes sense, no indispensable truth emerging from the lines I've read backwards, forwards and sideways, piecemeal and continuously.

Each evening we prepare ourselves as for a religious experience, freshly scrubbed and agreeably scented creatures approaching the sacred place as a cathedral built on a hill, slowly ascending the steps in thoughtful anticipation of the visible blessings awaiting our arrival.

You already know what you will see here, the vision fixed in your mind, blank circles neatly drawn in the logbook you carry under your arm, ready to be filled with sketches you are poised to reveal to the world, spectacular evidence that we are not alone in this universe.

Yet, as you pause here outside the dome just after sunset, waiting for Harry to fetch the key that opens the padlock on the door, you must also know the implications your announcements will have, the international uproar they will create, and the eventual schism they will rip inside our little group now living peacefully on Mars Hill.

I stopped long enough to grab a burrito in Albuquerque – the pot-induced "munchies" demanded it. Then I jumped back in the car and kept driving, the city now stored in my memory as a soft brown blur of adobe structures – houses, stores, hospitals, even fire and police stations – mixed with new chrome and steel offices and malls, someone's shiny but non-matching idea of urban renewal, all topped at one point by the incongruous sight of large colorful balloons rising into the clouds, tiny people riding in gondolas tethered beneath them. I saw signs announcing the city's annual balloon festival but figured I was high enough already, so I headed straight into the sunset, speeding now to outrun the darkness I can see approaching in my rear-view mirror.

Radio reception between cities has been dismal, but just now when I switch on the radio, there's no static at all. I turn the dial from one end to the other. My radio has gone out for good – an eerie silent accompaniment to the color fading quickly from the sky ahead, with nighttime chasing me from behind, and my great aunt's unorganized words struggling to coalesce into meaningful prose but persisting as nothing more substantial than the hot air used to lift the Albuquerque balloons.

The journey toward any worthy goal contains within it a frozen moment in which past, present and future are fused into one that offers a brief view of the completed event. It is like the pause just before a rose opens, its imminent splendor already evident, or the moment just before an accidental fall, the knowledge of its certain and painful outcome caught up in the very moment of falling.

I'm stepping carefully alongside the rustic house we laughingly call our "mansion", but a rounded stone lies in my path and no one will be there to catch me when I trip. I will remember always seeing the redness and feeling the pain, and even though the rose bush is not yet planted, I make my slow way toward its fullest blossom, each labored step on wooden crutches I do not yet possess.

To prolong this timeless moment would be to know the future as effortlessly as we know the past.

The house seems big and empty without you; I know this before you present me with a perfect rose you've plucked from the garden, before you climb into the carriage, before the horse steps carefully down the hill on a narrow and twisted roadway to the station, where an impatient Express train prepares to deliver you to a distant shore. There you'll board a luxurious ocean liner that will transport you ever further, to European capitals where you will deliver your grand news. Your eventual return has been promised, but not guaranteed, and I've been abandoned in a house that's far too large for one person alone.

My footsteps echo through the dark hallway. I can hear myself breathing. Time is caught up in the air constantly circling the mesa, sometimes settled, other times so disturbed that it howls its way down the chimney and out the stone fireplace, ruffling the pages of books in bookcases lining the silent room. In unsettled times the past may intrude upon the present, and the future may disturb the very past it soon will become. Even my mood is at the mercy of invisible currents of air.

I have not tripped and fallen at all, but I most certainly will. I know, as clearly as I know in advance of the momentous events approaching, the loneliness I will feel once they occur, without your wise and familiar presence. I pull my handkerchief from my sleeve and quickly blot my eyes before you notice.

"Here we are, sir." Harry hurries up the stairs, key ring in hand. His delicate British accent tickles the chilly night air as he unlocks the heavy door, pushing it inward, then stepping aside.

In your eagerness to observe the heavens, you rush ahead, forgetting to offer me your arm as a gentleman should.

"Step carefully, ma'am," Harry whispers from behind me, placing a supportive hand on my elbow as we enter the darkened sanctuary.

-4-

n her later years my mom was almost blind, but her memory never faltered and she repeated the same family anecdotes when I'd call a truce and travel back East to visit her each humid Boston summer. We'd open all the windows to encourage whatever cross-draft came our way. She'd sit on the sofa in one of her voluminous sundresses, bare feet propped on the coffee table, fanning herself with both hands, pausing to take a drink of the superb iced tea she'd learned to make in New Orleans, so perfectly brewed that we never used sugar or lemon. I'd relax in the old platform rocker nearby, where she claimed my father used to sit while reading the evening paper. I'd rock and fidget, waiting for one of her stories to begin. Always the same, nearly down to the exact words, as if the truth were grand enough on its own, without any embellishment.

Great Aunt Lulu, my mother told me, was caught up in the biggest celestial controversy of the past century: the brazen idea that there were canals on Mars constructed, apparently, by intelligent beings. The canals had shown up earlier, in Italy, as posited and admirably drawn by the astronomer Giovanni Schiaperelli, but it was Dr. P, Lulu's boss, who'd made the most convincing case for them the world had ever seen. A wealthy Bostonian, he'd searched the American West to find an ideal site for the observatory he'd build, equip, name for himself, then use to propagate the world with bold ideas based on his observations. Observations, some claimed, that were inspired more by artful thinking than by disciplined scientific procedures.

Eventually the professional astronomical community divorced themselves from his claims, refused to publish his manuscripts, and worked behind the scenes to diminish his reputation as a scientist, even as the public embraced him. He loved the public attention, but what he really craved was verification from other astronomers, which he did not get. Even some astronomers who worked for him began to doubt his theories; when he'd find out, he'd promptly fire them, then lock up the whole place until he was sure none of his papers had been pilfered. Once, he lost the key and had to wait a week for his personal locksmith to arrive from Boston.

"Lulu always laughed as she told this story," my mother confided in me, "and yet it seemed to make her sad as well. She kept a scented handkerchief with her always, and dabbed at her eyes whenever she spoke of Dr. P."

Great Aunt Lulu and Dr. P had most certainly been on discretely intimate terms. She was dedicated to both him and his work, traveling on astronomical jaunts with him to Mexico, Northern Africa and more times than anyone could count to his nascent observatory in the Arizona Territory.

I never believed one word of this story because none of it was in *The Golden Book of Astronomy* I'd read as a child. There was no Dr. P pictured anywhere among its colorful pages. There were no Martians working or playing on the beautifully illustrated surface of the red planet.

But globe-trotting Aunt Lulu was real, my mom insisted, fervently committed to her story. She'd come to live with my parents in their modest Back Bay flat during her final years, before I was born. Her glory days long past, her astronomer boyfriend deceased, she was destitute and alone, with dementia closing in.

"There was nowhere else for her to go," my mom explained. "So of course we took her in. She was a handful toward the end."

Aunt Lulu had lived in the tiny spare room that eventually became my bedroom. There, she'd rarely slept, telling stories about Dr. P and his Martians, and repeating herself endlessly, as my mother and father took turns keeping her company.

I couldn't bear this part of the story, and always interrupted.

"If he was so rich, why didn't he leave her some money?" I'd ask. "Why didn't he take care of her?"

My mother shook her head sadly, as if not wanting to tell the next part, but she always did.

"Eventually he married an uppity woman who lived in his neighborhood up on Beacon Hill, and she'd have nothing to do with Lulu. When Dr. P died suddenly - brain hemorrhage - that woman fired Lulu before his body even cooled. Took all the money to build him a fancy mausoleum. Cut Lulu off with nothing. Wouldn't let anybody in the family even mention her name after that."

I'd heard this tale so many times I knew exactly what was coming next.

"Now that's a love story for you," my mother whispered into the air above her head.

"You and I are the true Martians," you assure me. "We are the same."

But I think there are distinctions even among the Martians, especially those of us living here on Mars Hill.

We women, for instance, are drawn to the view we observe in a looking glass, and we hold precious the belief that what we see there is real. Each morning before breakfast I pin up my hair, not from the memory of my fingers lifting and twisting each strand, but because I see myself in my mirror, arranging the strands one by one, pushing each comb into place, anchoring each swirl with hardworking hairpins. I'm here and yet I'm there, also. Who would argue that what I am observing is not the actual truth?

I think a man would never admit to such a sustained interest in the looking glass view, and yet what else is the telescope you spend your nights staring into but an enormous version of the same?

So it is when you look through the finely-tuned looking glass of your telescope and observe a red planet with markings you say are waterways. You must know the channels are indeed waterways because you see yourself reflected there among the Martians, moving stubborn red soil with a steam shovel, laying tracks, welding a framework inside deep crevices, constructing the canals, directing the water as it flows through networked routes from snow-capped pole to arid equator, delivering nourishment to parched land and living creatures all along the way. You see in your own reflection evidence of life on Mars.

And yet there are doubters who do not believe your extravagant claims, who dare dismiss as mere fancy your detailed sketches: crisscrossed patterns of lines, a finely engineered network that could not have been formed by forces of nature. You have observed not only canals of late, but also double lines on the Martian surface, suggesting that some canals have been built in pairs. No one else has seen them. Even among your own staff, there is unvoiced dissent ready to erupt at any moment. You need an ally – one, you are certain, who will reflect your own findings.

You ask me to look and to tell you what I see. You sit me in the viewing chair on the platform mounted high into the air. Positioning the delicate eyepiece of the long tube just in front of my right eye, saying, "Look now."

My vision shifts when I look, as always. I blame this on the air currents, constantly plotting to spoil our evenings in the dome. The canals, if that's what they are, appear in ruins, straight lines collapsed into soft wrinkled curves, no longer able to hold water. If there were any water present, it's long since run off and disappeared.

"You must stay with it," you insist.

So once more I press my eye against the eyepiece and keep it there. You call encouragement to me from down below, telling me what to look for. "Over time," you remind me, "the air will stabilize, but only for an instant, and you must be ready."

Why must I wait for one instant when I prefer experiences more durable? Yet I hold myself still, inhale a deep breath and decide to keep it there. If the air inside me is still, perhaps the air all around me will follow suit.

"Why did you hold your breath so long?" you ask. You tell me I fainted and fell from the viewing platform, but there is no pain, because you caught my fall.

"What did you see just before you fainted," you persist. "Did you see a double canal?"

I saw you, as I plunged toward your arms.

I really don't want to be in the middle of nowhere at night, but I've become obsessed with the little green mile markers and their glowing numbers counting down as I approach the Arizona border. Once the number gets under twenty, I know I can't stop. In fact, I'm speeding up just to make the markers seem closer.

But just as I'm about to leave New Mexico forever, a brazen heifer steps slowly and carefully onto the interstate, right in front of me. I slam on the brakes, skidding onto the shoulder of the road.

The cow has second thoughts, turns away from the road and ambles off into the darkness.

I find myself trembling, weak-limbed and gasping for breath, all signs I shouldn't be driving. So I turn off the ignition and climb out of my car. I light the remainder of the pilfered joint, inhaling deeply and holding the smoke in, determined to calm myself down by softening the recent memory of my near-disaster.

I exhale slowly, preparing to take another hit with the next breath, but then pause to inhale the quiet air around me.

You can't trust the air, Great Aunt Lulu had written, but I still don't know why. Don't we depend on the air for our very existence? Don't we have to trust the air with every breath we take? Shouldn't I inhale some more of it right now?

I'm breathing comfortably in my own bed, covered by familiar yellow quilts. You tell me to lie still while you go fetch me a drink, but I'm up already, stepping carefully across the dark red soil in the garden, pulling weeds, setting bulbs in snow-patched dirt, the mud on my shoes already tracked through the hallway all the way to my sleeping room. You are there, waiting for me, presenting me with a clear glass of water delivered from polar ice caps millions of miles away.

I've just set out the jonquils, I tell you as I remove my muddy shoes and stockings. I pull out my combs and my hair tumbles onto my shoulders, but you are there to catch it, asking me again what I saw. But I cannot answer because it's still changing. I see us together in the mirror on the wall above my dressing table. You are encircling me with your arms, pulling my blouse away from one shoulder, leaning in to kiss my bare skin.

We lie side by side on my bed, as close as double canals. I curve myself to match your every move, each of us reflecting the other. I listen to you whispering close in my ear what you say I saw, but still I cannot be sure.

I watch you napping on my bed. You have promised to remain here with me, and I have promised not to tell. I cover you with a soft quilt before I tiptoe away.

As the days pass, I shall gather a sunny bouquet of jonquils from the garden and arrange them in the alabaster vase on my little bedside table. This is what I want you to see when you open your eyes. But what if you awake and see something else? What becomes of the vision I have prepared for you?

- 6 -

'm way stoned, lying on the hood of my car, staring into the shimmering extravagance of the night sky. There's no moon tonight, but a billion stars are scattered above me like tiny pinpricks in a black blanket. All the stars look alike, and I'm lost among them, the sparkling brilliance of one duplicated in all others.

I have no idea where my Great Aunt Lulu's Mars is located, but I decide to search the heavens for any object colored even slightly red. Soon I locate what I think may be the red planet, but even as I stare at it, the color seems to fade away. Again I try, my view fixed on a red light I think must be Mars, but once again the color drains. I think about how far away the object is I'm trying so hard to see, and what all might lie between me here on this lonely highway and whatever is there on the surface of Mars that had so enamored Lulu and her stargazing sweetheart.

A hefty breeze kicks up, reorganizing the air above me. The red planet remains determinedly elusive.

As privileged observers of the heavens, we have an obligation to share the abundant riches we enjoy. Our door is always propped open and visitors welcome. Nearly every clear night, some curiously brave citizen from the town below makes his way up the winding road, asking to see the sights never before witnessed in these parts. No one is turned away. But visitors must be patient, standing sometimes for hours in the dark. Only one person at a time can gaze through the narrow tube holding our looking glass. We patiently await his description of what he has observed, sometimes a sight so difficult to express in words we must often sit through quite a long period of silence.

This person must also draw with the greatest accuracy possible the sight he's seen. There is a book for this purpose. Perfect circles have already been entered, using an engineer's template. The circles must be filled, and notes attached: Who filled the circle; when and under what conditions, the last being the "seeing scale" we have implemented here, ten being the best, a rare and joyful occasion.

Whenever my turn comes around, I climb eagerly into the seat, press one eye against the eyepiece, and am instantly blessed by a glittering array of stars and planets in a far-away celestial neighborhood. There is nothing in the world like this vision – a vision that so removes one from the present moment and places one in another so remote that I can no longer think of myself as sitting in a chair under a dome built on a mesa in the Arizona Territory.

Then a stark epiphany, that the opposite event must also be possible, that distant beings spend nights gazing at faraway worlds, seeing us, not as flesh and blood, silk and taffeta, pretty or plain, but as awe-inspiring displays in their own heavens. That I might look thusly to inhabitants on some other world cannot help but lift the spirit. To far-away folk, I'm a glowing object in the night sky, and the stain on my blouse from the soup I spilled at dinner matters not at all.

Seeing and being seen are compatible events. Even as I remove my eye from the eyepiece, rise from my seat and leave the sanctuary, others on distant planets mimic my activities. The afterglow of the glorious vision I've just witnessed is so lodged in my head, it illuminates my dark pathway back as I make my way back to my sleeping room. I think with pride how my own magnificence must linger in the minds of those inhabiting faraway worlds.

A series of soft bumps, and I'm brought back to Earth instantly. Two hard eyes gaze at me from the porch railing, frozen in time. I approach slowly, in wonder, and a small gray fox with ruffled fur materializes around the eyes, trapped where she is, as I'm blocking her way back into the trees. We gaze at each other, eyes locked, until I back up a few steps, she sees the escape path and leaps toward it. The heavenly event has just been repeated here on Earth, the seeing and the being seen, each one working its way toward some small understanding of the other, our shared vision offering us both a brief glimpse into universal and mutual meaning.

In my room, I remove my skirt, blouse, shoes, stockings and undergarments, then put on my nightgown, take down my hair and look at myself in the mirror. In doing so, I realize it was the fox, not the stars, that has captured my imagination. In seeing and being seen, I recognize in the fox a living, breathing replica of my curious self, while in the stars I imagine some other version of myself, perhaps, but one I cannot, as of yet, fathom.

-7-

Mired in the profound stupidity that comes with being far beyond wasted, I'm looking at something that can't be seen and yet seeing it perfectly: a vast sheer air-curtain between the heavens and me, like someone's cosmic laundry hung out to dry. When the wind catches it just right, the curtain lifts and for a tiny instant I can see forever, before the wind shifts and the curtain falls, limiting my vision once again.

I'm thinking about my mom, surely by now on the other side of the sky-high curtain. I can almost hear her clicking her tongue, can see her frowning as she looks me over, a little disapprovingly, as always. My wardrobe, my habits, my easy disregard for my own security. She must be so far away by now, and yet I can't shake the notion that she's nearby, still checking up on me.

"Have you seen my cow?" a thin voice punctures the darkness.

An elderly woman with long gray pigtails stands beside my car. I think she's Navajo. I jump when I see her; I hadn't heard her approach.

"What color?" I ask, propping myself up on one elbow.

"She's white with some brown, I've been told."

"Your cow nearly wrecked my car." I say, and sit up. "Ran me off the road."

"But where is my cow now?" The woman does not seem concerned about my own condition. I point toward where the cow had disappeared.

"You were studying the stars," the old woman tells me matter-of-factly.

"I was just looking at them." (Studying, I'm proud to say, is something I haven't done since dropping out of college.)

"The Coyote stole them from the woman and threw them into the sky," she explains somewhat sourly.

I'm not in the mood for a lame fairy tale, but the woman is intent on delivering one.

"The woman," she continues, "was arranging the stars. But impatient Coyote, he had to have it his way. That's why the stars are scattered across the sky. You won't see order there, no matter how hard you look."

As if that explains everything.

She wraps her generous cloak tightly around her shoulders, grasping it with both hands to her chest as a sudden burst of chilled wind encircles us. The swirl of dust particles caught up in it sting my bare arms and face.

"Where is my cow?" she asks again, stepping closer.

Even in the darkness, I can see the finely etched lines on her cheeks and forehead. I look into her softly clouded brown eyes. She's looking past me at nothing and at everything simultaneously. I realize she's blind; my mom had had the same bearing, never letting on how impaired her vision was, moving and behaving throughout her life as if she could see perfectly.

"This way," I say, taking the old woman's arm and pointing it toward where I'd seen the cow disappear. She nods and steps confidently into the swirling darkness, gone as suddenly as she'd appeared.

In Heaven, as on Earth, the curtains had parted briefly, allowing Letha a rare opportunity to bridge the formidable divide and to occupy both regions simultaneously.

She was dead but still living, a peculiar sensation, not at all unpleasant. Her breathing was regular and calm, though possibly more nuanced than usual: She was finely tuned to the inner workings of her body, and could feel thin rivers of blood coursing through her veins and arteries, though she could not detect a strong enough heartbeat to propel them.

Floating freely above the Albuquerque hot-air balloons buoyed, as they were, by substantial currents of air, Letha tried stretching her legs far enough to touch the ground below her, but encountered only vast pools of nothingness. She tried stepping across the void, but made no forward progress.

From her sky-high vantage point, she'd watched her daughter driving down the deserted highway much too fast and far too recklessly. She'd witnessed the near-collision with the wandering heifer. Now, she observed Venus splayed on the hood of her car in the middle of nowhere. Couldn't her daughter sense the dangers all around her? And she'd seen the girl smoking a marijuana cigarette – that most certainly was not the way she'd been raised!

I did not tell my daughter everything, Letha sighed. *Far from it, and now I think I may have failed her. The secrets I've kept are too big, their implications too profound. I*

was only trying to protect her when she was young and still playing with her paper dolls.
I told her easy stories with partial truths and happy endings while she sat on the floor
cutting out the fancy outfits with her little-girl safety scissors.

They'd grown more distant as Venus matured and hid inside her schoolbooks or the occasional Nancy Drew mystery she devoured in a day. Sharing intimacies became more difficult until, finally, revealing anything new became impossible.

"Venus–" Letha would begin, but the girl would squirm and offer a little fake smile, her ever-ready signal indicating she did not want to be bothered by any of her mother's overdue revelations.

It's too late now for anything I say or do to make the slightest difference, Letha thought sadly.

She'd heard that death was like this, a gradual disengagement from earthly concerns, but wasn't ready to separate herself entirely from Venus: There was unfinished business.

Letha knew her daughter's uncertain future lay ahead of them both, beyond the giant puzzle pieces of Texas, New Mexico, Arizona, but the harder Letha looked, the less she was able to see: The tenuous systems of nerves, blood and oxygen powering her eyes, brain and body were about to be overtaken by fatigue. Yet she was determined not to spend her afterlife napping: As she closed her eyes for what she promised herself would be a briefly restorative moment, she wondered how long this eerily sensual part of her afterlife would last, when the cosmic curtains might part again, and what, if anything, she'd see when they did.

The wind has calmed, but the air still feels heavy with the dust-specked curtain that must wait for another current to move it out of the way. There can be no seeing without clear air, and no clearing without unsettled air. There seems to be something I'm not getting, but am getting close to. Something I need to see for myself before this trip ends, before I go back to work. Something I *have* to see, only it's not yet visible to me. And I only have one more state to go. I'm tempted to stay where I am, contemplating this contradiction until the curtain shifts again.

Instead, I'm back in my car, crossing the state line just as rosy dawn reveals itself in my rear-view mirror. I begin to relax as the mile markers start all over.

I'll call my boss from Arizona, I decide. It's a big state; there's plenty of time.

Opposition

- 1 -

The long-anticipated celestial event has taken charge of our nights and holds captive all imaginations on Mars Hill. We call this planetary visitation an "opposition," but this is entirely the wrong word for times when we clamor for Martian views. The word suggests that everyone is at odds, each positioned as far from the others as possible, hugging the edges of the parlor like a reluctant guest who does not want to dance. And yet it is during these times — when the Earth and Mars move nearest each other — that we converge under the dome in celebration of the rare planetary intimacy and the extraordinarily close views it allows us: Mars, as large as a full moon! Even Harry takes his turn at the eyepiece.

Opposition is a volatile state, however; a short, precious time during which we watch in awe as you grab the heavenly knowledge displayed before your eyes and fashion it into novel concepts you will soon scatter like stardust on a public easily entranced. You will be properly feted, honors and awards will be bestowed on you, but you must also endure the occasional denouncement of all you proclaim, for one cannot travel in such a sparkling orbit without attracting the attention of the naysayers who seek to discredit your findings. Just one of these attacks, properly placed, has the potential to bring your journey to an abrupt halt. You will limp homeward with your wounds, and I will prepare hot tea and nurse you and your ideas back to health, all the time preparing for the next opposition, and for the entire cycle to commence once more.

Two years and two months must pass before we gather here again to welcome the red planet into our neighborhood, a span I have decided is quite too long. Yet the train already belches smoke and cinders, and soon will whistle its loud and extravagant farewell as it pulls away from the station.

You have come to my room to bid me a quieter and more private good-bye before you climb into the buggy that will deliver you to the train station. I have stayed awake nearly all night to make sure your notes are properly typed and organized inside your valise.

Your arms surround my waist. I see us together in my looking glass: you in your starched shirt, woolen vest and trousers; me in my silk blouse and the brown skirt I like, the one with the pockets. My eyes look tired, but yours are sparkling clear, I observe, and your chin projects confidence.

"Get some rest," you whisper.

Your tender kiss and the brush of your finely groomed mustache linger on my lips, but you are gone already.

As always, when I am left alone in my looking glass, I find myself all the more difficult to see, and this time you have contributed to my diminishment. I am a neophyte, you said in your own words, the ones I typed last evening, sitting at my desk while you stood over my shoulder, dictating. I'd never heard this word before, but now, before your buggy even reaches the train station, I run to the dictionary, turn its thin pages and locate the word with my finger:

Neophyte: a novice, a beginner, a recent convert

You will proclaim these words in new lectures we have prepared, the ones you are on your way to present to audiences in Boston and throughout Europe. You will explain that my own vision is as a blank slate, as if there's nothing there, a situation that serves your purpose nicely, because what I see when I look through the telescope is not colored with prior knowledge or viewing experience.

You see a newly forged double canal on a distant planet. "Look," you say to me, "do you see it, too?"

What am I to say? The soft dark line crossing a dime-sized red orb may be a new canal; it may be two canals running side by side; or it may be something else altogether: a mountain ridge, a deep valley, an enlarged dust mite lodged on the looking glass of the telescope.

"A very slight hint from the eye goes a long way in the brain of the one," you have written and I have typed, "but no distance at all in the brain of the other."

You are as much admitting that we humans are designed to experience the same event in varied ways. Surely it follows that we must be faithful in how we describe our own peculiar visions.

"Keep looking," your order delivered softly, yet with authority.

I must not stop until I see the canals, even though you have by now departed, and the red planet, inching away from us, shrinks slightly each day, showing itself by night as a progressively smaller disk, its markings less distinct, making their identification less possible, until all of Mars is a smudge, save for its white polar caps, and only a fool – or a neophyte – would keep looking.

Once your lectures are delivered, the newspapers will write widely and glowingly of them, the book publisher will come calling, and soon I shall be known as a neophyte in the eyes of the world: a beginner, as if all my years of seeing amount to nothing at all.

~ 2 ~

W here have you been?" Dr. Dick demands when I call him the next morning from a phone booth in downtown Winslow.

"At my mother's funeral," I answer with the obvious, which seems to irritate him even more.

"I know your mother died, for Chrissakes," he explodes. "But that was weeks ago. Did you fall in a hole?"

"It's been six days," I counter, then add, "You told me to take some time." But he seems to have forgotten his largesse.

"I need you back here ASAP!" he shouts. (Dr. Dick is fond of saying ASAP.) "We're running geometric distortion tests on the new IBM."

"I hope that means next Monday?"

"Miss Dawson?"

"Yessir?"

"Do you even want this job?"

I pause to think. "Want" is such an emotionally charged word. I can't put it with "this job" and come up with anything I feel even a little bit positive about. Especially geometric distortion tests.

"Yessir, of course I want this job."

I feel my temporary freedom dissipating in the hot dry air outside the phone booth.

"Then say goodbye," he says, "hang up the phone, and get your shapely little butt back to work."

"What is it you do there?" my mom used to ask.

Although I'd tried, I'd never been able to explain my duties at JPL clearly enough for her to understand.

"The cameras on the Mariners take pictures in space," I'd say, "but they come back as numbers. We take those numbers and make pictures out of them."

"Like a paint-by-number?"

My mom and I used to do paint-by-number together when I was a little girl. She struggled in her thick glasses to fill in the tiny numbered areas, her diligent but imperfect efforts balanced by my sharper eyes but less steady hands and less precise brushwork. It was amazing how the bits of garish color eventually coalesced into a finished painting of a tropical oasis or snowcapped mountain range you could put in a cheap frame you'd bought and hang on the wall. My mom had done just that. I'd grown up surrounded by sloopy paint-by-number art.

"Not exactly," I told her. "The scientists load the numbers into the computer and it turns them into pictures. Then I take the pictures into the darkroom and print them out so they look really nice."

"So you're an artist?" my mom tried again.

I'd begun to think of myself that way, and of the photographic documents I churned out as my own creations – though Dr. Dick had warned me about this over and over, each time with considerably less patience.

Even with the scientists' best algorithms, the computer's tireless calculations, and my best toe-the-line darkroom work, the resulting pictures remained less than spectacular. I wanted badly to fix them up, even though I knew "subjective enhancement" was not permitted.

I was rarely satisfied with my photographs. Sometimes I kept working with the images in the darkroom long after I'd turned the properly enhanced versions over to the scientists. I'd dodge and burn details, trying to achieve more drama. Mostly, I was frustrated that the so-called "red planet" displayed only gray tones. So I brought in a photo-tinting kit I'd purchased at an art supply store and, one evening, stayed late hand-tinting the bland Martian landscape into gloriously colorful re-creations using brilliant reds, crisp yellows and rich browns. Mind you, I did all of this on my own time.

I'd begun my color-tinting experiments – or "tampering with the truth," Dr. Dick called them when he found out – innocently enough and out of workplace boredom. But when I compared my own creations to those of the scientists and computers, I realized mine were far superior, and tacked one example up on the wall by my otherwise unadorned desk so I could admire it from time to time.

Dr. Dick called me into his office for a talking-to. "What you have done is decidedly unprofessional."

"It was just for fun," I defended myself. "I wasn't going to send any of them out."

"We have high profile visitors coming though," he said, and gestured at the photo of Agnew and him on the wall behind his desk. "We can't afford any hint of inconsistency with our data."

I squirmed in my chair, sure I was about to be fired.

"You work for the government, not for Van Gogh." He wagged a long index finger at me, then pulled it back, as if he'd gone too far with this particular harangue. He knew I'd studied art in college and probably assumed I considered all art and artists as sacred. I do not.

"Consider this a warning." He put both hands palms down on his desk in an effort to keep his anger in check. "If you deviate again from prescribed routines, I'll be forced to terminate your employment here."

"Got it," I said.

I scooted back to my workstation, threw my paints and brushes into the trash can, pulled my offensive "artwork" from the wall, folded it, and tossed it into the dark cavern of my shoulder bag. Then I fumed and pouted for the rest of the afternoon.

"I'm not an artist," I answered my mom, recalling the troublesome tinting incident. "I'm an image analyst."

"Well, that sounds more important."

At last my mom seemed satisfied with an answer I'd provided to one of her unending string of questions. But I knew she was already primed to ask me another, more annoying one.

"The young man you work for, your boss, what's he like?"

I knew what she was thinking: *Good husband material.*

"He's OK, I guess."

"Sometimes," she pushed home her point, "the thing you're looking everywhere for may be right in front of your nose."

"He does tend to get in my face a lot," I told her.

- 3 -

The air here is unusually unsettled, a constant rearrangement of the unseen currents encouraging the worst temperaments in otherwise placid creatures. I hear the changes before I see them, a rushing vortex of air circling the mesa, creating in its wake a time ripe for disruptive events that threaten to undo all we have accomplished here.

Predictably, the public has fallen in love with you. But your fellow astronomers have been more than merciless in their criticisms, and you have fallen ill with neurasthenia from the frequent need to defend your beliefs. The grand speeches that created the uproar have ceased for the time, the lecture circuit abandoned. The doctor has advised absolute peace and quiet, far away from the turbulence here, as the necessary cure. You will not return to Mars Hill to practice your astronomy – and I shall not see you – for a very long time.

Even without your guidance, I continue thinking about the stars and planets because I cannot stop. My thoughts are less precise than yours; I begin each morning without a coherent theory, but always with a vague and fragmented idea that seems to have crept into my head as I've slept. By the end of the day, I try to either coalesce my notion, or else dismiss it and wait for another to announce itself. I realize, of course, this is not scientific protocol, but I am a secretary, not a scientist, and it is the method that works best for me.

This morning when I put on my woolen wrap and stepped out into the chilled air, trying to coax my unorganized thoughts into some useful direction, I startled a lean brown jackrabbit and followed him as he sprinted across the meadow and disappeared into the trees. There, I nearly collided with the most unlikely apparition: a planet that had been captured, shrunken and mounted on a tall pole, all features removed from its surface, its very identity lost forever.

There stands Mr. A. E. beneath it like a warrior, his shovel held like a weapon in his hand. He's removed his suit coat, has hung it on a tree branch and he's sweating, even in the crisp autumn air. There is a dirt patch on one knee of his pants that will require careful cleaning. He notes my approach, but does not acknowledge my presence.

In your absence, your assistant, Mr. A. E., considers himself chief planetologist, and as such, he has decided to pursue his own theories. This is all his doing: miniature planets placed all around us, stuck to poles, unable to wander, as they are expected to do, across the night sky. I cannot help but inquire of him: *Why?*

"It's grand theatre," he explains to me. "The planets remain in their far-away orbits; these are the actors who perform as Mars and Venus in my drama. There is no danger in pretending these are distant planets brought down to Earth. See, I have scaled them down to match the illusion we see through telescopes."

It's all off, I want to complain. The illusion does not work.

Yet he points the telescope at one of his planetary creations, then at another, sketching madly in his notebook details he cannot possibly be seeing. If there's nothing to be seen, then why enter such copious notations? If this is Mr. A. E.'s best attempt at drama, I must say I've experienced far better on a bad night of theatre at the Exeter, back in Boston.

He does not invite me to join in his observations. I watch from a distance as he peers through the long tube. His sketches cannot be accurate; his theories cannot be proven. His planetary theatre can only be a waste of a supposed scientist's precious time, and I leave him alone with his folly.

Twilight, back in my room now, at my writing desk with my open journal. I must sketch out this morning's scientific notion before the curtains fall, as they must. There is no applause, only a thin insect hum in the air around me. I swat the annoying fly. The air stops moving as the dead insect falls silently to my desk, caught between blank pages as I close my journal and put down my pen.

The moment has passed; the notion I'd hoped to nurse toward respectability has not defined itself. I shall not write it down.

OPPOSITION

Shifting Itineraries

- 1 -

One state away from home, but the closer I get, the less inclined I am to continue. Arriving back in Pasadena would signal the end of a journey that has not yet delivered on the promise I've imagined it has made to me: to offer some enlightenment, to suggest some direction in my aimless life.

My irritation with Dr. Dick and the Dicklings – as I collectively call all the men on the image processing team – has only grown while I've been away, but my frustration encompasses everything "JPL." I'm not a "career girl" and image processing is definitely not my chosen career. It's just that I haven't come up with anything better yet. I have no more interest in making more photos of Mars than I have in going there myself.

I'd landed at JPL randomly and had never thought to leave – until my mom died. Maybe this interruption is her gift to me and the book she'd asked Uncle Ollie to hand over an unusual inheritance: the ultimate guidebook to steering one's course in an entirely new direction.

According to the chaotically written Book of Great Aunt Lulu, what comes next might be anything at all – although lately Lulu's been no help, fretting over her precious Dr. P more than making good use of the glorious opportunity she has been given, in his absence, to chart her own course through the heavens:

I've written a letter to you about Mr. A.E.'s absurd activities with his artificial planets, but in the afternoon mail I received instructions from your brother, back in Boston, not to disturb you while you are away, recuperating in the hushed luxury few can afford. Another letter not sent. You shall not hear of this mutiny. Instead, you will convalesce, folded between the finest linen sheets, without disruption, your own undefiled theories as company enough, while I shall endeavor to think more clearly for myself about all matters both Earthly and celestial.

But I'm no more clearheaded in my thinking than Great Aunt Lulu. I can be anything in the universe, I tell myself, but what do I want to be? So far I've only been able to determine the things I do NOT want to be. I do NOT want to process and print more images from Mars. I do NOT want a career at JPL. I do NOT want to put up with any more boorish behavior from Dr. Dick and the Dicklings, but the moment I'd spied the star-spangled notices hung all around the cafeteria last month, I knew I was in for another round of cajoling, coaxing and demanding pressure to participate in another senseless beauty contest.

I do NOT want to be "Queen of Outer Space," most definitely.

The name of this year's event has changed, as has its stated purpose. But everything else remains the same – except,now, tickets cleverly printed on used IBM computer punch cards would be sold, and the proceeds donated to charity.

"You'll be feeding and clothing poor children," the Dicklings encouraged me this time.

"I'll buy a ticket," I told them, "but I'm not entering your stupid contest."

There are additional incentives, they reminded me. This year's winner will get a Las Vegas weekend for two (hint, hint, wink), a prized photo session with a *Playboy* photographer, and a "space memento" (rumored to be an actual moon rock).

As before, they were relentless. One had already sketched what he thought my costume should look like: slinky and shimmery, my nipples visible through the top. He'd drawn my body comic-book style, with big boobs and long legs (made me look fantastic, but I'd never admit it).

"No way," I told them, even when they pushed an entry form right under my nose.

The Dicklings were not ready to retreat. One threatened to publish in the JPL newsletter a sketch he'd drawn if I refused to enter: Venus outfitted as the "great galactic ghoul," the fanciful creature lurking in space, purportedly responsible for all mission failures. As the despicable ghoul, I'm bulbous and bloated, with lightning bolts shooting from both eyes.

"Leave me alone," I said. I grabbed the hideous drawing, crushed it, tossed it in my wastebasket, and shooed them away. But I could tell we weren't done with this yet.

"The position was described to you as a 'man's job?'"

A few days later I sat across the desk from a young man in a K-Mart suit who was busy writing careful notes on a yellow legal pad. I'd looked up the "Equal Employment Opportunity Commission" in the phone book, called, and made an appointment. Now, facing the reality that I was ratting on my boss and the scientists I worked with, and the fact they would not be happy about this, I found myself sweating and nervous. Nevertheless, I kept offering the inquisitive young man details, which he kept writing on the legal pad. My "statement," he called it.

"And they entered you in a beauty contest without your consent?" He shook his head as if he could not believe what he was hearing, what I was saying. "What happened when you refused?"

"I was ordered to meet with the Director of Protocol." She was a tiresome creature named Miss Evelyn Pruette.

"Miss Dawson." Miss Pruette frowned at me from across her wide desk, steel gray eyes looking up from the file she'd been reading. She was dressed in a smart navy business suit, its tailored lines softened by the lace trim on her white blouse. Tiny pearl earrings and a JPL service pin on her lapel completed the ensemble.

"I see you are dressed as we like to see our young ladies when they appear for work," she smiled, extracting a sheet of paper from the file; stapled to it was a Polaroid photo someone had snapped of me just as I'd arrived at the beauty contest last week.

I'd decided to enter the competition after all and had worked hard at fashioning my outfit: Inflated balloons tied around my boobs, waist and hips, all covered with an oversized beige leotard to make me look huge and lumpy. Enormous sunglasses hid my eyes, and I'd attached twisted clothes-hanger lightning bolts to the frames, extending outward from each eye. I'd applied long fake nails to each finger and had painted them black. Then I'd taped a thin pointed devil's tail to my butt.

As the Great Galactic Ghoul I felt all-powerful, in full attack mode, as I lumbered out of the ladies' room and into the cafeteria decorated with an appropriate cosmic theme especially for the contest. Predictably, a hush descended over the assembled crowd and all eyes fell upon me. Suddenly I realized I had no idea what to do next. Beyond the horrified looks on their faces when they first saw me, I had not imagined anything further.

"What do you have to say for yourself?' Dr. Dick demanded, once he'd regained his composure. He approached, taking me by one arm, leading me toward the door, red-faced and embarrassed as if he were somehow responsible for my bizarre appearance.

Determined to stay in character, I replied with pure gibberish, more like high-pitched space chatter than human conversation.

"You take the cake," he fumed, ushering me out onto the patio.

"What happened then?"

The E.E.O.C. man encouraged me to continue with my recollection, quickly stifling a smile. "Did you win the contest?"

"No," I told him. "I was, uh, reprimanded."

Dr. Dick had escorted me to the employee parking lot and had waited while I tried to figure out how to get in my car with all those balloons underneath my leotard. My Karmann Ghia was too little, even with the driver's seat pushed all the way back.

Finally, Dr. Dick lost all patience. He pulled a ballpoint pen from his shirt pocket, clicked it open and started poking me with it, trying to pop the balloons.

The E.E.O.C. man stopped writing. "He *attacked* you?"

"He burst my balloons."

"There was physical contact?"

I nodded yes.

Again he began writing ferociously, coming to the bottom of one page and quickly flipping it over to write on the next one, without even a pause.

"Did he threaten you?"

"Uh…he said, 'Don't show up here again until you learn to dress appropriately for the workplace.'"

"That sounds like a threat to me," the man agreed.

But I had left out the next part of my story.

Just before I'd climbed into my car, deflated, I'd looked Dr. Dick in the eyes and he'd looked me in the eyes and we'd both burst out laughing.

QUEEN OF OUTER SPACE

- *2* -

I t seems as if Miss Spring will take her good time in arriving here on Mars Hill – there is still snow on the ground and yet there are changes in the air.

Mr. A.E. has written, not to you – that is forbidden – but to your brother in Boston, with the results of his experiments. The clean-faced artificial planets, when viewed through the same telescope you used to find the canals on Mars, have revealed networked lines where there are none.

The problem, he writes, is in the instrument itself, and in the way you have stopped down its eyepiece to get a clearer view of the distant red planet. A smaller aperture creates a less diffused view, a brighter image – but what is the image you see? Mr. A.E. speculates that what you have observed is an optical illusion, one he has easily recreated with the unmarked, artificial planets. He mistakenly concludes his letter with his own assessment of your work:

"The man, I fear, is more poet than scientist, seeing what he wants to see, then charming the world into frenzied agreement."

Mr. A.E. does not imagine that your brother will choose to disturb you with this alarming news, or indeed that this news, no matter how gently delivered to your bedside, will encourage you to rise up at once, wash your face, shave, dress yourself in a crisp new suit, and become an astronomer once again. Until you are well enough to travel, you will be working in your Boston office.

Mr. A.E. has been dismissed. I have been instructed by your brother to lock your office and allow no one entry until further notice. I am not usually left alone here, and normally your journeys are brief, long enough only to deliver your lectures or to collect some new honor. You step into your office on State Street, my friends there have told me, say hello, turn around and walk out again – as if you cannot wait to get back to Mars Hill.

But this time I have waited impatiently through another Martian opposition, and still you have not returned.

Last weekend's snowstorm was fierce: wind howling across the mesa, penetrating closed and shuttered windows to create an unrelenting chill throughout the little house where I am staying. I could not get down to the train station for several days, until the storm subsided and the snow began to melt. Only today have I been able to send for the mail that surely has accumulated by now.

I am not disappointed. At last you have written me a letter saying you will return. You include three pages of handwritten instructions describing how the place must be arranged in advance of your arrival.

Rooms must be added to the "Baronial Mansion," rugs laid and windows draped. Each addition will need radiated heat and electrical lighting. "The brothers who built the dome will be able to accomplish all of this," you tell me.

A Regina music box with changeable disks is being shipped from Chicago. When it arrives, I am to place it on the sideboard table in the dining room and set it in motion to make sure it has survived the trip and works properly.

Finally, a milk cow must be purchased, and a barn built to house her.

"Re-employ Harry," you tell me, "if you can find him, and ask him to look after the cow."

Your news brings me almost more joy than I can bear! You will return, not just to the mesa and the dome, but to a larger and more comfortable home filled with joyous music and fresh cream for our coffee each morning.

Your private rail car, cleaned and attached to the rest of the slumbering cars in the train yard at South Station, has been roused, and is waiting to bring you back to Mars Hill, back to me.

- 3 -

This is what I have to look forward to when I get back to work: Dr. Dick will grouse and fume, then once the new Mariner reaches Mars and begins transmitting data, he'll start issuing non-stop orders, interspersed with the suggestive commentary he finds so humorous. Plus, any day now he'll find out about the discrimination complaint I've filed with the E.E.O.C. and then all hell will break loose.

I'm sure that's why I'm dawdling on a street corner in downtown Winslow just after calling him. I'm sure that's why, when I see the sign for the meteor crater, I decide to drive out there and take a look. Even staring at a big hole in the ground sounds better than going back to work at JPL.

"We're closed today."

How can you close a meteor crater? Pull a giant tarp over the whole thing?

"I don't see how that's possible," I reply.

But the smiling woman in a "meteor crater" t-shirt and Bermuda shorts who meets me at the door of the Visitor's Center seems confident about her information.

"I'm sorry." She lowers her voice, offering me privileged information in partial appeasement. "NASA's running tests here today. We have to restrict access. Could you come back tomorrow?"

I'm about to whip out my JPL employee identification badge to show her that I work for NASA, too. I could tell her I've been sent here on official business, but then she might get on the phone and talk to Dr. Dick to confirm this, and I'd be in so much trouble. I don't need any more trouble with Dr. Dick.

I turn and walk back toward my car, anticipating the heat that will blast me when I open the door. I unlock it and toss my purse inside – but then, impulsively, I close the door and turn around. I quickly step over the chain holding the "road closed' sign. I glance over my shoulder to make sure the woman at the Visitor's Center has not noticed, then I head off in the opposite direction.

I spend the afternoon strolling leisurely around the ragged rim of the crater, stepping cautiously in my flip-flops along a dirt path lined with boulders, occasionally scaling one of the big ones to peer down into the crater's depths.

Spread out before me is an enormous version of the dilemma I'll face as soon as the Mariner reaches its destination. Mars is pockmarked with craters just like this one – big empty holes – and the new Mariner is determined to photograph every last one of them. Instead of sailing past the red planet like all the earlier Mariners, this one will lower itself into orbit around Mars, point its two television cameras toward the Martian surface, and busy itself in a sustained and dedicated search for evidence of life there.

With each orbit producing new images it's only a matter of time, the scientists at JPL reason with confidence, before Mars reveals its secrets.

"No place to run, no place to hide," they chortle, anticipating the Martians' upcoming plight, their cosmic unveiling.

For me it'll be a workload nightmare: more images than ever to analyze, more photographs to print, more ways than ever for Venus to do Mars.

My dismal reverie is interrupted when I hear the *putt-putt* of a golf-cart-sized engine. Edging closer to the rim of the crater, I watch in wonder as an oddly constructed open-air vehicle – like a car chassis but with thick wide tires and a skinny radio antenna – seems to do the impossible: It scales the nearly vertical side of the crater, crawling across the uneven rim, and pauses to idle right in front of me.

I just stand there, not sure what to do. Then I notice the Apollo patch on the driver's blue jumpsuit. And the driver. He's about my age, dust-colored hair blown every which way, wearing big aviator sunglasses. I can't place him as any astronaut I've seen on TV.

He'd obviously learned nothing in astronaut charm school: He stares rudely at me for a good half-minute, looking me up and down without speaking, nodding in approval when his eyes come to rest on my boobs. I realize I've sweated so much that my t-shirt is near-transparent.

"Get in!" he finally yells over the noise of the sputtering engine. "You're not supposed to be here."

"Aren't you're supposed to be on the moon?" I shout back at him.

"Not until I learn to drive this moon buggy," he replies with a deep-throated chuckle.

"Can I drive it?" I ask.

"Can you drive a stick?"

I nod yes.

He grins and jumps over to the passenger side and I climb into the driver's seat, push my left foot on what has to be the clutch and shift into what is hopefully low gear. We crawl forward, back toward the main road where I'd parked my car. Just before we reach the "road closed" sign, I spot a dark blue, unmarked van. Outside the van, a figure completely covered in a padded silver suit with a bulbous white helmet steps carefully in giant clown boots across the rocky ground, bending awkwardly to pick up a stone in his path, putting it in a shoulder sack he carries.

"It's NASA, those bastards," the man sitting next to me shouts in my ear. "They crawl all over the place, like they own it."

"I thought *you* were NASA."

"I'm security detail."

"Is this really a moon buggy?"

He laughs long and hard. "The Lunar Rovers are electric," he explains between guffaws.

"Stop right up there," he says.

The woman from the Visitor's Center is waiting beside my car.

"Now get outa here," he shouts as I stop and climb out. He jumps behind the wheel, turns the cart in a wide circle and drives away, raising a trail of dust.

The woman steps toward me. "Miss Dawson?"

She knows who I am. Must have traced my license plate number with the Highway Patrol.

Frowning, she holds out a plastic cup of water. I nod in answer to her question, take the water and drink it down. I hadn't realized until now how exhausted I am, and how thirsty.

"We were worried about you, out there all alone."

Who is this "we" she's referring to?

"May I see your NASA identification, please?"

That can only mean one thing: She's talked to Dr. Dick – and I'm in big trouble.

"It's in my car, I'll get it."

I'm thinking I can jump in, start the car, drive fast and get away.

But she's one step ahead of me, and reaches into my car for my shoulder bag. She rifles through it and finds my NASA employee badge. And she's not done yet. She pulls a folded piece of paper from the depths of my handbag and examines it intently: It's the Mars photo I'd improperly enhanced, the colorful hand-tinted one that had nearly gotten me fired.

"Nice work," she judges it. I can't determine her level of sincerity.

"Thanks."

"And did you manage to get the photos Dr. Dickson sent you here to shoot, or do you need to come back again tomorrow?"

I'm speechless. Dr. Dick had covered for me?

She doesn't wait for an answer. "If so, please do check in with me before you go wandering about. We are liable for any mishaps, you know."

Dr. Dick had covered for me!

"And, Miss Dawson?" The woman hands me my badge and my artwork, then steps aside, clearing a path for me to make my escape.

"Yes, ma'am?"

"The next time you come here to take photographs, make sure you bring your camera."

She's correctly judged the depths of my deceit, but is releasing me from all its ramifications.

The sun is near to setting when I pull onto the interstate, accelerating and shifting into second gear before realizing Dr. Dick is riding beside me in the passenger seat. The gearshift is between us and I know he'll be impressed when he sees I can drive a stick. As I prepare to shift from second into third gear, my foot slips; I can't find the clutch and the gears make a nasty grinding noise.

"Stop the car," he orders me. Embarrassed, I pull over while he gets out and walks around the front of the car to the driver's side. Meanwhile I've stripped down to my bra and panties, evidence enough that I'm dreaming.

"You must be in a hurry, ma'am."

I need to wake up now, really I do.

Dr. Dick has vanished and in his place a stiffly outfitted highway patrolman looms outside my window. I hand him my driver's license before being asked. He turns on his flashlight to look at my photo, then shines the irritating beam right into my tired eyes.

"Ma'am?" His voice, more insistent.

"I'm sorry, sir." I struggle my way to full consciousness, working to maintain my composure. No way I can let him know I've been driving while asleep at the wheel. I take a quick glance down to make sure I'm wearing all my clothes, and am pleased to see I'm fully dressed.

He parks the flashlight under one arm as he writes the ticket, rips it loudly from his ticket book and hands it to me.

"If you're tired, ma'am, I'd suggest you stop up ahead in Flagstaff, get some rest before you get back on the road."

"Yessir, I'll do that."

He waits while I start my car and pull slowly and prudently into the sparse interstate traffic, imagining my mom observing the scene from some heavenly perch, clicking her tongue and shaking her head.

"She comes by all her waywardness honestly," she must be lamenting.

My mom had always been solid as a rock, tight as a tick, reliable as a well-wound clock – but, sadly, she had not managed to pass any of these admirable qualities along to me, her undisciplined and contrary daughter.

"Freedom's just another word for nothing left to lose," I sing tunelessly as I drive the last few miles toward Flagstaff, struggling to stay awake.

Some people, my mom included, have described me as a free spirit, but I don't feel that way. I have a full-time job; I pay my bills on time; I sent a monthly check to my mom in Boston as long as she lived; I keep my clothes freshly laundered and always have edible groceries in the refrigerator. I even remembered to pay my rent in advance before I left for New Orleans.

In fact, I'm just the opposite of a free spirit. I envy the hippies I've seen in magazines and on TV, their very lack of concern for grasping the bigger picture. I can't dance around barefoot in a meadow and not worry about what's going to happen to me when it gets cold or rains, or if I turn my ankle or step on a bee, or what I'll do when everybody else pairs off and I'm left without a partner for the night and don't understand why. I must have inherited this unwavering sense of responsibility from my mom, who refused to give up after my dad disappeared, working whatever office or retail job she could find to keep us going - the position mattered less than the regular paycheck she earned by performing its required duties. She could type, take dictation and make change in almost any kind of business.

"Just don't make me read the fine print," she'd tell every new boss with a proud laugh, "and we'll get along all right."

By the time I was old enough to notice or care, her eyeglasses had grown so thick that her eyes, seen through them, appeared distorted, far away and miniature. Because that's the way I always saw her, I mistakenly thought her eyes really were shrunken – due perhaps to an accident, or a deformity she was born with – and reasoned this was why she couldn't see very well. And why she'd never found another husband after my dad took off for some reason she either didn't know or wasn't willing to reveal.

"I don't know where he went," she'd say every time I asked.

"Didn't you go and look for him?"

"You were a tiny baby then."

"So it was *my* fault you never found him?"

We'd eventually drop the subject, silently agreeing to keep my dad's disappearance a mystery, each of us privately sharing the blame.

As far as I knew, my mom never even had a boyfriend after my dad left, and she definitely was not the type I'd ask for advice about men. The deplorable example she'd set was reason enough not to trust her with my love life.

I'd learned on my own to give men a wide berth, waiting to see what they promised and, more importantly, what they actually delivered before considering any commitment on my part. I was spectacularly unpopular in high school, not even scoring a date for the senior prom, and pretending hard that I didn't care. My first actual lover, a boy in my freshman photography class at BU, turned out to be gay, another warning sign I interpreted as evidence the male gender was not what it professed to be. After our darkroom encounter – the first time for either of us – he'd jumped up and rushed out the door. He never came near me again.

My mom had constantly hoped that a good and dependable man would show up in my life and provide it some direction, as women of her generation fervently believed men were supposed to do. If I'd known she was going to die so suddenly, I'd have at least made up something to tell her about Dr. Dick and me. We were dating, we were in love, we were engaged, maybe even secretly married. (We'd have to keep it secret; there was a no-nepotism rule at JPL).

In reality, I'm hardly even friends with Dr. Dick. Yet, here I am heading west, driving just over the speed limit, hurrying toward our inevitable, dreaded reunion. He'll fuss and flirt – both superficial acts on his part – and I'll ignore all his theatrics and get back to work.

I wonder if perhaps I'm destined to become a replica of my mom, with a clear instinct for taking care of my practical and financial needs but never having a clue as to how to fulfill my less tangible ones. My dad must have been the free spirit in our family, but he'd left without passing any of his knowledge along to me. I realize I'm missing him terribly – but how can I miss someone I never even knew? How can I judge his contributions to my character?

Drive, don't think, I remind myself, lighting a cigarette I don't want and pushing harder on the accelerator, forcing my eyes to stay open and my mind to stay alert for just a little while longer.

Flagstaff, a green sign promises, is just twelve miles away.

_4_

11 March 1903 (the day of your return!)

Our tenuous but vital connection to the civilized world arrives and departs according to a schedule we've all memorized, and yet the times posted inside the train station might just as easily be fiction. Rainstorms or blizzards, animals on the tracks, a bent or broken tie, a washed-out bridge...any of these events may delay the train's arrival, and though Dr. P owns a considerable portion of the railroad and pays for his own private car, even his abundant resources cannot make the train run on time.

Waiting for a train that is late is like delaying the remainder of one's life. Surely the time spent waiting could be spent much more judiciously. The stationmaster tells me the train is late this time because the engineer was found drunk on liquor and was thrown off the train at Omaha. With no one to operate the train, the Omaha stationmaster (himself a retired engineer) was recruited. But he was not used to the modern instruments onboard and so refused to travel faster than twenty miles an hour, lest there be an accident for which he'd be blamed.

The heavens are much more timely. We know precisely when Mars will come around again. I think the Martians must revel in the knowledge of their superior punctuality, observing, perhaps, as you creep across the great plains, inching your slow way toward me, while I languish on a hard wooden bench at the Flagstaff station, waiting for a snail-paced Express train that may not arrive tonight after all, perhaps not until noon tomorrow.

When I can no longer hold my eyes open, I send the carriage back up the hill and take a room at the Bank Hotel just across the street from the station, insisting that the clerk wake me the moment he hears the train approaching.

I lie stiffly wrapped in my clothes, since I brought no nightgown, and do not want to wrinkle my only outfit. I've removed my hat and have placed it on the bed beside me, but keep my hair pinned up, ready to rise and greet you at a moment's notice. I'm on my back, eyes closed, hands clasped across my stomach, and realize I must look like a nicely prepared corpse on display. Death, we have been taught, is timeless. There are no train schedules, no drunken engineers running late, no scrambling to reorganize our lives, to smooth our skirts, to pin on our hats, when plans go askew. This is why the dead look so much at peace.

Without you it's as if I *am* dead, and yet I am not at peace. My throat tightens, my forehead creases at the thought of you so distant. Perhaps, I muse, the train has jumped off its tracks, abandoned its schedule, and has ventured into uncharted territory. Perhaps this time you have actually managed to travel all the way to Mars!

I wake to a distant train whistle, a knock on my door. A quick look in the mirror and I am standing on the station platform to greet you as you step off the train in your Eastern finery. You have brought nothing from Mars, but present me instead with a delicate lace collar you think will nicely accentuate my neckline.

Look, I quietly shout to the Martians, *he's returned to me!*

We are reunited in my small but tidy room upstairs at the Bank Hotel, no longer corpses on our backs, now turned to face each other, fully alive, in no hurry for the carriage that will arrive in the morning to carry us up the hill, where we will live in concert for the rest of our lives.

June 1937

Vernon could not believe his good fortune to have met and fallen in love with Mrs. Letha Dawson, née Broussard, and she with him. To have proposed to her, and for her to have accepted.

The newlyweds sat side by side on the train carrying them to their weekend honeymoon on the Cape. He placed his hand on hers, gently, and she turned to look into his eyes – which always unnerved him. Her soft hazel eyes were so beautiful, yet so flawed, and he feared she would never be able to see as she should: clearly, perfectly, completely.

From the moment she'd first pushed open the door to his optical shop, tinkling the bells overhead, fate had placed her vision in his hands, and he was fast running out of ideas for improving it. He feared she'd leave him if he ever admitted to failure, that she'd go elsewhere in her dogged pursuit of clear vision. He resolved to never stop trying, as long as he lived. He'd write letters to every vision specialist, subscribe to every scientific journal, search out every new optical product, investigate every promising eye treatment, and attend every lecture presented on the topic. He would never give up.

Letha had awakened from a light sleep when she felt his hand squeeze hers. She searched his troubled blue eyes silently, wanting to tell him not to worry so much, that even with her limited eyesight, she saw far more than he'd ever be able to imagine. She saw things swimming in his deep-set eyes that even he did not know, things that had not happened yet, things that might not happen at all. She saw disturbing events still off in the distance, beyond the low, curved sand dunes giving way to the gently wave-tossed Atlantic Ocean now visible outside the train window. But she could not say for certain whether these events would ever occur. Her particular kind of vision, she'd decided privately, was one of possibility more than actuality.

Letha could not fathom how to put these thoughts into words that would make sense to her husband, words that would tamp down his worries and smooth the wrinkles on his forehead. But she could also see that nothing untoward would happen here, not now, not on their honeymoon.

The flowers Vernon had presented to her earlier this morning – a tidy corsage of golden mums and yellow rosebuds – were pinned to the lapel of the little brown suit she wore, inserting a sweet fragrance in the otherwise stale air of the passenger train. Her new silk undergarments rested on soft skin she'd bathed, powdered and scented early this morning.

She inhaled deeply, leaned her head against her husband's sturdy shoulder and closed her eyes. Soon, she thought, she would discover the pleasures that lay beneath his crisp navy suit, his starched white shirt, and his diagonally striped, perfectly knotted tie.

She smiled as she put away all distasteful notions, determined to ignore everything except this moment and the next, and to enjoy the perfection of blue skies and wedded bliss as long as both would last.

-6-

Edna happens while I'm not looking, while you are looking elsewhere – at a stately, well-dressed creature, taller and thinner than me, wearing an extravagant diamond necklace instead of a simple lace collar.

You move toward her unthinking, not intending more than a polite hello and perhaps light and vacuous conversation – until she asks you about your work. She is mesmerized by your Martians, how you have discovered them, what you think they are like. She has never heard your stories before, and her soft lips smile, her green eyes sparkle: She is new to you. You touch her elbow, guiding her to a private corner, where you plant a simple kiss on her blushing cheek. She grasps your left hand, feels no ring there, and then, emboldened, she leads you outside, away from the crowded party.

You were nearly a country away and hours ahead of me; there was nothing I could have done to prevent the event to which you have just confessed, as the sun rises outside the window of a rented room at the Bank Hotel.

"It was nothing," you tell me. "She's not even very pretty. Her nose is much too long and her eyes are too close together. I took the poor girl shopping," you explain, "in the hope that a new wardrobe would improve her appearance."

The next day and I'm dead again, locked inside my sleeping room, weeping privately into my cheerful yellow counterpane. Our carefully plotted future is in shambles. Yet the sun has just risen above Mars Hill and you appear outside my window, tapping gently on the glass to awaken me.

"I'm planting a vegetable garden," you tell me, motioning to a newly roped-off square of nearby landscape that lies flat, with freshly turned earth. "Melons and squash, beans and sweet peas. I brought the seeds with me from back East."

"What about flowers?" I ask.

"Jonquil bulbs and rose bushes are on the way," you assure me.

The table is set for breakfast on the veranda, and you invite me to join you. The coffee is strong, the thick cream we pour and stir into it is rich and fresh. Hot scones with melting butter and marmalade are soft and sweet in my mouth, as are your words describing our future here: observing by night, gardening when the sun is high overhead – both, in your estimation, serious and ongoing pursuits.

"Just as the astronomer must spend time with the heavens in order to observe and comprehend the stars and planets," you explain to me, "the gardener must spend time with the seedlings, encouraging them to grow tall and straight during the warm summer months."

I realize there is a commitment inside your declaration to grow a garden. You will remain here, tending the plants as they grow, instead of hurrying down the hill to the train station, packed and primed for another departure. I gradually relax into this knowledge of a fixed future, an agreement among us, the sun, and the soil, to raise your plants to proud maturity.

Then why? I have to know about Edna.

But, for once, you have no ready answer. You sip your coffee and gaze evenly into my eyes.

"Edna is the past," you tell me, "and we are here now." You take my hand in yours with a gentle squeeze designed to reassure me, but instead I squeal in distress.

Edna, I realize, is the name I've given the splinter I got in my finger yesterday when I ran my hand across the rough wood of the newly fashioned door jamb. Surely she'll fester and grow more painful, unless I find a way to remove her.

-7-

Flagstaff and Route 66 are one and the same for several miles. The railroad that brought Great Aunt Lulu and her Dr. P here so many years ago fuses with them both, running straight through downtown. Passenger trains must still pause at the quaint Flagstaff station, but these days many more visitors come by car.

Just across the street from the train station, Main Street, all lit up in the spreading darkness, looks like a tourist trap to me. I don't want to eat at the Grand Canyon Grill, nor do I want to shop at the Pow-Wow Trading Post. I slow for a look but prudently avoid stopping.

Mars Hill must be around here somewhere, but I've already convinced myself I don't have time to poke around in the dark for a look-see. Instead, I'm going to do the reasonable thing (unusual for me). I'll stop at the first cheap roadside motel I see. I'll get a good night's sleep, then drive straight home. I'll be back at my desk tomorrow afternoon. Dr. Dick will be surprised and pleased, though he'll mask it, as he does any emotion that might be remotely considered "girly." He'll sit me down and deliver a new string of instructions, all in preparation for Mariner's arrival in orbit around Mars. He'll flirt, maybe. I'll ignore him, most determinedly. When the letter about my complaint to the E.E.O.C. arrives, I'll pretend I have no notion of how this happened – one of the Dicklings must have done this as a joke. He'll laugh it off and everything will get back to normal – or at least JPL-normal.

Just as I'm about to leave Flagstaff behind me, I see emerging from a row of trees on a hill just west of the city, a round white structure that can only mean one thing. And in that instant, my whole get-back-to-work-in-a-hurry plan falls apart.

I turn off the main drag and head up the hill.

The gently curving and rising road leads eventually to a pair of stone gates. "Lowell Observatory," announces the column on one side of the road when I turn my headlights on it. Its twin column on the other side displays a series of symbols I take to stand for the planets, although in truth the only ones I recognize are Mars (man, the JPL coffee mugs) and Venus (woman, the cow, and me). The last planetary symbol, which I take to stand for Pluto, looks like the initials "P" and "L" written together: Lulu's "Dr. P" – the astronomer Percival Lowell himself!

As I pass through the stone gates, something like a near-subsonic roar pitches itself audibly upward and intensifies. I shift into a lower gear and keep climbing, rolling down my window to listen to the faint but vaguely unsettling sounds outside. It has to be the air I'm hearing. The constant rearrangement of the atmosphere circling Mars Hill. Great Aunt Lulu had described it in her journal.

The road – and the noise – end abruptly as I reach a parking lot and stop my car. The top of the mesa, unlike the route leading to it, is a flat tranquil sanctuary, so much so that closing the car door becomes a noisy and momentous event.

Faint lights are just beginning to emerge in the fading sky on this warm summer evening that seems just perfect for stargazing.

The walkways are crawling with people: families with kids staying up late, younger couples clasping each other's hands, older ones holding each other up as they navigate the spreading darkness.

"Is it always so crowded here?" I ask the man walking behind me.

"Didn't you read this morning's *Sun*?" he asks. "Mars is closer tonight than it's been in fifty years. They're staying open late so we can all have a look."

His grand news delivered, he takes a series of long-legged steps to outpace me, to hurry ahead of me in the long line that has organized itself into a busy but tidy queue leading up a gradual incline.

The opposition!

I'd forgotten all about it. The Sun and Mars aligned on opposite sides of Earth, creating a relatively close encounter between the two planets. I'm headed to the same telescope to observe the same cosmic event at the same time of day as Great Aunt Lulu would have, stepping carefully with her hand on Dr. P's arm, the familiar anticipation mounting as shadows deepen and the tiny lights in the sky prepare to grow enormous.

The evening of the first day since your return, and you have never been more attentive. After dinner you open the new music box and set it in motion with a playful waltz. You bow and take my hand, and we dance round the parlor, out into the hallway, through the front door and underneath the first few stars revealing themselves in the twilight. Your handsome face so close to mine, your blue eyes shining. You are an excellent dancer, quick and graceful, with just the right amount of pressure to turn me and move me in any direction you please, without my having to do a thing except relax and follow your every move. My usual clumsiness evaporates; I am graceful while on your arm. Dancing has become a pleasure instead of a chore, as the music box sends its magical melody out through the open windows and door of our newly grand mansion.

So recently you have been dancing thusly through Boston and New York, through London and Paris, always with someone on your arm. If you can charm me so easily, then haven't you already enchanted half the women in Europe?

Edna, the splinter in my finger, squeals as we take our last turn before you detach yourself, climb the steps and enter the dome.

"I must get to work now," you say, and kiss me goodnight.

You close the door, and I am left alone under the stars.

You will spend this night reunited with your true love – not Edna, not me, but rather the tantalizing planet whose rosy countenance always delights, whose graceful movement through the heavens never misses a beat.

It's dark now, really dark. No flashlights or other illumination allowed near the dome. Nothing to interfere with the heavenly view.

As the line gradually creeps forward and my eyes adjust to the darkness, the white structure suddenly looms up ahead. Great Aunt Lulu had called it a dome, but this round building with an oddly flat roof looks more like a giant upside-down bucket, more utilitarian in appearance than the stately and inspiring edifice she'd convinced me I'd see here.

I stand in line for a few more minutes, then lose patience and leave to wander around behind the building. Sure enough, there's another door – with no line – and it's unlocked. I open it and step inside.

In the dim, orange-hued lighting I can make out the giant instrument positioned diagonally and pointing toward a narrow vertical slit near the top of the tall room, just as Great Aunt Lulu had described it. And there's the viewing chair where he'd sat her down to look for the Martian canals.

Before I can get any closer, a man approaches, dressed in an old-fashioned three-piece suit, something a proper Victorian gentleman might have worn. He's using a polished cane to support one leg as he walks. He's short; I note we are nearly the same height.

"I'm sorry, ma'am, but you'll have to use the front entrance like everyone else."

His moustache is neatly trimmed and he looks at me with clear blue eyes. I know exactly who this is – or at least who he's pretending to be, albeit with a highly questionable Boston accent.

I'm inside the so-called dome, standing face to face with Dr. P!

-- *8* --

Not just any Martian opposition, but a rare perihelic opposition – a super-close approach by the red planet – had inspired Charles to dress up tonight in vintage clothing that had once belonged to Observatory founder Percival Lowell.

Charles adored Lowell and claimed the maverick astronomer as his own personal hero. The first time he'd sat in the observer's chair perched high up inside the dome – the same chair Lowell had used – Charles had felt electricity running up and down his spine. Since he'd come to work here and had taken the opportunity to examine the historic photo albums stored in the Observatory archives, he'd begun fashioning himself in the founder's image, often wearing a Lowell-esque red beret while observing in the historic dome or lecturing to students who'd come here on afternoon field trips.

But the two men had far more than a wardrobe in common. Charles shared Lowell's desire to impact the staid world of institutional astronomy with independent and possibly mind-bending findings. As a newly assigned member of the International Planetary Patrol headquartered here, Charles was to network with astronomers in observatories worldwide in a concerted effort to cover the heavens, collectively observing the same celestial objects with the same instrumentation to create an ongoing and complete portrait of each object over time. It was the modern global version of Percival Lowell's concept of kinematic viewing: consistency of one viewer using the same instrument with the same settings over time. That way if a change were observed, the observer could say with confidence that the object being studied had undergone some change, since all other elements had remained the same.

Charles could not believe his good fortune, that he'd been hired at Lowell Observatory not as an astronomer, but as the next best thing: a planetary observer. He looked, saw, photographed and reported to the astronomers, who then reasoned and explained what he had seen. It was the looking that was most important, he told himself. Each time he put an eye to the eyepiece, it was with the anticipation that something unforeseen might come into view, a feature never before observed, a discovery he could use to advance his own budding career as a planetary visionary.

Like others in the astronomical community that now stretched as far as South Africa, Chile and Australia, Charles had been anticipating and preparing for this evening's event for two years and two months. The Martian approach culminating tonight would provide a compelling drama, and he'd dared cast himself in the starring role – as Lowell himself.

While the calm, clear but very warm evening of the opposition passed, Charles dutifully photographed the red planet, using three different color filters, once every half hour. In between, he invited a few from the crowd that had gathered outside to enter, guiding each one in turn toward the eyepiece of the big telescope where Mars hovered, shimmering in its rosy glory.

He stepped outside the stuffy dome every so often, desperate for fresh air, using the polished cane he didn't need to navigate along the line of visitors still waiting for a turn at the historic telescope. He greeted each one with a smile and a gentlemanly bow, feeling himself slipping easily into a familiar role, his Midwestern twang carefully nursed into an upper-class Boston accent.

"Welcome to my Observatory," he told each and every visitor. "I trust you'll enjoy your visit."

Children giggled and adults whispered about the man in the strange, old-fashioned get-up. But Percival Lowell persevered.

-9-

shift my weight from one foot to the other to keep myself awake. All I have to do is stay alert long enough to take a look at Mars through the big telescope – once the guy playing Victorian dress-up will allow it – then drive down the hill and find a place to sleep, like I'd promised the highway patrolman who'd stopped me.

But I won't go downtown where tourists, I'm sure, are willing to pay exorbitant room rates to lie in a antique bed with real goose-down comforters and handmade quilts. I'll drive a little ways out on Route 66 where I'm sure to find a Motel 6. I'll pay my six dollars for a room, lock the door, turn the window air conditioning unit up to high and fall asleep. I'll wake up refreshed and I'll drive straight home. No more delays, no more roadside diversions. This is the last one, I swear.

Surely I'll be able to explain this most recent side trip to Dr. Dick as vital research that will help me analyze and process the next batch of Mars data, the pictures the new Mariner will soon transmit. Wouldn't he want me to see Mars as it really is, big and red and glorious? Wouldn't he actually appreciate this extra little effort on my part? Wouldn't he let me know how pleased he was?

And exactly how would he do that?

Damn. I always get horny when I'm tired. One expertly self-administered orgasm always clears my head and helps me think clearly again. But that, too, will have to wait.

By the time I get to the steps leading to the Observatory front door, it's well past midnight. I reach the front of the line just as the little man dressed up like Dr. P steps outside and announces, "I'm sorry, ladies and gentlemen, but we're going to have to close now. Mars is about to set and will no longer be visible. You're invited to come back tomorrow night."

He turns and disappears inside the dome as the few others still waiting voice their disappointment and begin walking down the hill to the parking lot.

But I'm not going anywhere. I have to see Mars tonight. I'm running out of time.

"You can't close until I've seen Mars!" I shout in his direction.

I feel myself erupting in slow motion, my brain expanding beyond my tight skull, spewing its pent-up lava flow of anger in all directions. The rest of me is about to collapse, rag-doll style, but I manage to regroup just in time to storm the building. Furiously I rush up the stairs and into the round darkened room, my flip-flops spanking the hard wooden floor. The oddly dressed man turns to stare at me.

"I'm sorry, ma'am, but the view has deteriorated."

He busies himself by turning knobs and flipping switches as if none of my considerable distress matters. I put my hand on his arm to stop him. My fingernails actually penetrate the sleeve of his fragile wool jacket.

I stand my ground. "I'm not going away until I look through your telescope."

"OK, look then," he sighs and nods toward the giant instrument. "But you should hurry."

I race to the viewing platform, scurry up and step toward the telescope. Because the planet is so close to the horizon, the far end of the telescope is positioned nearly horizontally; I'm forced to climb up high to get there. I put one eye to the eyepiece and look inside, prepared to be thrilled. But there's only a smudgy, dime-sized sphere in there. How anyone could see canals and Martians on its surface is beyond me.

Keep looking, he'd urged her when he'd sat her in this exact chair on this very platform.

I keep staring, as if willing the details to appear, but see only rosy softness.

So that's it. No reason to linger any longer. Time to get back to work. The Martian spell has been broken. I'm ready to leave. The fake Dr. P was right: Nothing worth seeing here.

Then, just before I remove my eye from the eyepiece, for a split second the blurriness resolves into distinct features, dissipating so quickly I could not be sure what I'd seen, nor could I put the bizarre vision into any words I know.

"I saw them," I say under my breath.

But the Lowell impersonator hears me. He drops his cane and rushes up the viewing platform toward the eyepiece, pushing me aside in the process.

I'm instantly off balance and know I cannot recover. I fall clumsily from the chair, my head knocking against the platform, onto the uneven floor, tumbling down to the lowest level next to the telescope mounting.

I yell and grab the ankle I've landed on. I feel a thick substance oozing from my nose, and touch it to discover that it's sticky – then smell the distinct metallic odor of blood.

"Why didn't you catch me?" I ask him, just before everything goes black.

Dr. P was supposed to catch me when I fell.

Stranded

~ 1 ~

Each day's end signals our transformation from businessman, typist, handyman, gardener – duties best accomplished when the sun is shining – to nocturnal creatures whose fancy and exuberance come alive as darkness approaches.

I watch the changes from my window: The setting sun casts dramatic shadows across the mesa, and on Harry who trudges up the hill from the barn down below. He wipes his forehead with one sleeve of his wrinkled jacket. His tie is undone, dangling like a loose string around his neck. His ill-fitting trousers hang too long over his mud-covered shoes; he must remember this time to wipe his feet before he comes inside.

Harry's duties have been expanded. He not only serves as dome porter but also feeds and cares for our growing animal family – two horses, a mule and Venus the cow. Dr. P has agreed to this because he knows that whatever will make Harry happy will keep him from running off again.

Harry has been here and left so many times that I've lost count. Dr. P considers him an honest man and a hard worker – when he's not intoxicated – and therefore continues to employ him whenever he shows up again. Each time he is rehired, Dr. P insists on giving Harry a small increase in salary, thinking this will encourage him to stay put. Harry is making nearly sixty dollars a month by now! I think Dr. P's hired hand has devised a clever method for making himself more money.

Between tending to the animals and the astronomers, Harry has precious few hours for other pursuits. Perhaps during his absences, he spends time searching for whatever pleasures he cannot find on Mars Hill – as does Dr. P, regrettably, with his various Ednas. I suppose this is a man's natural inclination, never to be satisfied with what he has, always looking to acquire more. As if what we have here is not enough!

Harry stops to speak to Dr. P, who is busy watering his bountiful garden: the spreading hills of cantaloupe vines and tall tomato plants already weighted with small green spheres.

The two men gesture and chat, a study in contrasts: the one wealthy and well schooled, driven in his scientific pursuits; the other coarser in appearance and personality, his life's aspirations less specifically defined. Both, however, have an inner drive I do not possess: a man's need to venture farther, to experience more, to build an expansive life that knows no bounds.

As for me, I sit comfortably in my rocker and look out my windows as the daylight fades above the magnificent mountains, anticipating the dark sky wonders that soon will be delivered to our doorstep. I cannot imagine anything else that would be necessary for my perfect happiness, except for all of this to last forever.

-*2*-

June 1937

The startling letter had arrived just prior to the wedding date Vernon and Letha had chosen. It was written on a fine linen weave with engraved letterhead. Letha read it twice before interrupting Vernon with the urgent request.

"Sadly, I can no longer provide support for your aunt under these conditions, and must ask that you act promptly to make alternate arrangements for her care."

This was an aunt that Vernon had never heard of, perhaps a real blood relative, not an adoptive one like Letha's former typing teacher, Aunt Virginia Dawson.

The author of the momentous news claimed to be the younger brother of an astronomer who'd long since passed away. The newly revealed aunt, a Miss Lulu Leonard, had been the astronomer's secretary; her health was failing, and she'd declared Vernon Dawson to be her next of kin.

"I will see her onto the train on Tuesday of next week," the letter concluded, as if the matter were settled.

Going and coming.

The trek down the hill. The crouching, heaving stream engine that soon will turn its wheels eastward. We've come to accept this journey as insignificant, something we endure without question, a part of our jobs, our daily lives. Yet each time I climb aboard with some degree of fear, because I do not know what the journey holds in store. There is a route, there is an expectation, but there is no guaranteed outcome.

I wish for the journey to be instantaneous, to blink my eyes in Flagstaff and open them in Boston, for Mars Hill to lie next door to

Boston Harbor. I no longer enjoy the duration of the travel, only the moment of departing and the moment of arriving, because those two things are certainties; they are printed in the train schedule.

Being taken somewhere seems odd – what if I want to go elsewhere, or wish to pause to take in a splendid view along the way? But I am not in charge of this journey. The tracks have been laid, the rail routes established and people are waiting at the other end to greet those arriving or to climb on board and begin their own journeys.

As with light that travels through the long telescope tube – and even farther, from the tube into the heavens themselves – there is nothing that can be accomplished along the way. Duration might be better spent in contemplation than in anticipation. You tell me it takes a quarter hour or more for light to travel between Mars and Earth. How to spend those fifteen minutes? How to endure them? How to adjust them to suit my own convenience?

Moreover, who instructs light on the details of its journey? Must it always take a direct route, or can its itinerary change? What if it notices a brilliant star off to the left and wants to linger in its luminous presence before continuing on to the red planet? Will the Martians object to a change in schedule? Will we?

We assume the light will behave itself and do exactly as it's been instructed to do, like a mother bird who has brought up her children properly, and expects good behavior to continue, even though the fledglings have left the nest.

But I think the light knows no bounds and, if the opportunity arises, may chart its own course, bend and branch at will, telescope be damned. Who among us can train such a cosmic force?

Observers are as passive as travelers. We have no power over what we see, only the manner in which we see it. We sit under the dome, open the roof, rotate and point the giant instrument toward the heavens. We fiddle with focus and aperture, thinking we are in charge of the view just because we decide when to put an eye to the eyepiece and what settings to employ. What fools we may be!

I've seen Mars! I've seen Venus! As if we invented the view. We are the recipients only. Then who does direct the spectacle?

I am being taken somewhere new, helped on board the train by the older gentleman who looks so much like you I almost called him by your name. He settles me into a seat, clasps my hand briefly, and then departs.

I finger my lace collar as the train begins to move. I cannot remember where I have been and do not know where I am going. I can only trust that you will be there to meet the train when it arrives, as I have been there to meet you so many, many times. You will escort me in your fine carriage up the hill, guide me into our mansion, and welcome me home properly, as a gentleman always does.

Tell me what you've seen, you'll inquire.

Whatever answers Vernon thought he'd receive from his newly discovered aunt so far had only produced more questions.

When her train had arrived at South Station, he'd climbed aboard to find her, having no idea what she looked like. Nearly everyone had already left the train; an elderly woman sat alone, gazing out the window.

He approached her. "Miss Lulu?" He didn't feel comfortable calling her his aunt as of yet.

She turned to look at him and giggled, an improbably girlish sound coming from so old a woman, then offered him her gloved hand. She had very little baggage for him to carry, only her handbag, a soft-sided fabric valise, and a small wooden case that seemed heavy for its size.

"My typewriter," she explained. "There will be letters, you know."

Vernon balanced her bags in one arm and with the other took her elbow and gently guided her toward the train exit.

"I've been looking forward to meeting you," he told her, "ever since I found out about you."

"Found out what?" she inquired sweetly.

"That you exist," he answered, helping her descend the steps onto the train platform.

"But I've always existed."

They began the long trek across the cavernous South Station waiting room. But with each forward step she seemed to be losing patience with him, finally fretting out loud, "You know how upset I get when you leave me for so long a time. It's like you forget all about me."

"Ma'am, we've never met, until just now."

She stopped walking and turned to look directly into his eyes. Vernon noticed for the first time that she was a tall woman, nearly his height. Her eyes were dark brown, only a little faded with age, but as strikingly vacant and unfocused as those of a newborn.

"I'm sorry, sir," she stepped away from him. "I've mistaken you for someone else. Someone who left me a long time ago."

She pulled a white linen handkerchief from one sleeve of her coat and dabbed at her eyes until she felt better.

- 3 -

must have gone in and out of consciousness. Sometimes I saw stars overhead, other times a black, featureless sky. Eventually my eyes focus on what appears to be Saturn, a gold-toned orb surrounded by softly glowing rings, hanging from a polished dome.

We've entered another building, My head is still spinning, but I've come to rest on a butter-soft leather sofa, tucked underneath an exquisite quilt made of colorful patches, each one featuring a carefully embroidered heavenly object. The planet suspended above me is a round golden chandelier graced by delicate, circular rings.

After I'd fallen from the viewing platform, he'd carried me to bed and now has gone to fetch me water. When he returns, I sit up cautiously, sip first and then take a greedy drink. He takes a clean white handkerchief from his pocket, pours some cold water from the glass and hands it to me.

"Here, press on your nose with this."

I do, and soon the bleeding stops.

"Ma'am, do you know where you are?"

My head aches. My ankle throbs. I can't think clearly enough to place myself anywhere, but looking around this dimly lit space, I can tell I've left 1971 behind – or else I haven't gotten there yet. Everything in this circular room recalls a previous era. Front and center is a small but exquisite telescope, polished bronze, mounted on a matching tripod, surrounded by other intricately constructed, polished-to-perfection brass-toned instruments I'm unable to identify. An ornate circular staircase made of rich dark wood leads upward to another level, this one lined with curved wooden bookcases filled with leather-bound texts.

I think I've climbed those stairs before; I've opened some of those books. I can almost quote the words I've read inside. Yet the more I struggle to place myself in what seems familiar territory, the more its identity remains stubbornly out of time, out of place.

"Is this the Baronial Mansion?" I ask.

He looks sharply at me, as if I've inquired about some top-secret place I have no business calling by name. Then he sits down slowly next to me and puts one hand on my forehead softly but firmly, as if to check the functionality of my brain, perhaps even the condition of my soul.

"The Baronial Mansion no longer exists." He nods toward the stately double doors leading outside. "It was falling apart, a real fire hazard. They had to take it down."

He speaks solemnly, as if a loved one has passed away and he is troubled to be the one who must reveal this fact to me.

"Then what did you do with all my things?" I ask him, suddenly alert.

Our residence here, the spreading, ramshackle structure we call the "Baronial Mansion," has grown admirably from a four-room observer's house where we dared spend a cold and perilous night when we were too tired to take a cart and horse to a comfortable hotel down the hill, into a spacious, warm, well-lit and fashionably dressed edifice I'm increasingly inclined to call our home.

My room has two grand double windows, one facing the dramatic mountain range to the north. A door opens onto the covered veranda where a breakfast table is set on warm sunny days. I have a fireplace, a writing desk, a comfortable bed covered with multiple quilts topped by a soft yellow counterpane. I have a spacious bureau and a built-in corner closet to accommodate the clothing I must still mail-order from Thayer's in Boston. There are no fancy clothing stores for women in downtown Flagstaff, nor for men, providing you the perfect excuse for ordering your suits from a London tailor, then traveling across the ocean for a custom fitting. Once, when you arrived there, all the tailors were on strike, "forcing" you to spend additional time visiting various capitals throughout Europe before returning to London to claim your new wardrobe!

Your elegant suits reside in your own closet in a corner of your room, which is all done up in robin's egg blue, the color with which you have chosen to surround yourself here. Your personal stationery has the same tint. It is the color of your deep-set eyes.

We even have a new tennis court, and I have been presented with my own tennis racquet, my initials already carved into its handle. One afternoon when I have just returned from practicing my tennis stroke all alone (I must at least be able to lob the ball over the net before I take on a partner), I find a new photograph perched on my writing desk. You must have sat for it while you were away, recuperating from your neurasthenia; your eyes are clear, but clouds linger just behind them. Still, you are handsome in your natty three-piece suit, leaning on your polished walking cane. I wonder briefly whether this pose was before or after Edna, and whether she has an identical photograph sitting on her own desk back in Boston. And then I remind myself of my new rule: There will be no more thinking about the Ednas.

Something else is new about the Mansion. Because the house sits perched on the north side of a hill, facing the mountains, it has a lower level we have previously used only for cellar storage. When the new rooms were added, a passageway was carved out of the cellar, running diagonally underneath all the new rooms, with narrow stairs and a trap door fashioned at each end. The passageway is lit with brass sconces mounted on the walls like any above-ground hallway, but its purpose from inception had always eluded me, as there are adequate hallways on the main floor for traveling between rooms, even to the new lavatory and photographic darkroom built at the opposite end of the Mansion.

A discrete tap on my door in the middle of the night solves the riddle of the underground hallway.

"May I come in?" you inquire when I open the door.

You are not dressed in one of the new suits you've been showing off, but instead in a silken nightshirt and household slippers, a new look, I must admit, and one never seen in the daylight hours. I am in my nightgown and my hair is down, a mess, I fear, but you gather the tangled strands with one hand and place the other hand on the nape of my bare neck, drawing me close as we step inside my room and you close the door.

"May I?" you ask as you sit beside me on my bed.

Of course, I can refuse you nothing.

Only after you began appearing just outside my door at all hours of the day and night did I at last understand. No one was to know you were not in your own room. Our intimacy would continue but on your terms; our ongoing liaison was to be kept strictly secret, and you'd built an underground passage to assure discretion.

The household staff has grown in number, as there is more to be managed of late. We have also hired a new observer, Mr. V.M., imported from Indiana to replace Mr. A.E. as your assistant. Mr. V.M. lives here now with his wife, a Flagstaff schoolteacher. More people moving about day and night, passing each other in the hallways, always ready to interpret the comings and goings of others as eagerly as we observe and interpret the events we see on Mars.

My room, your room, our minds and souls newly connected by a passage deep underground that makes the impossible possible: You are asleep in your room, and yet you are here with me.

"We can stay here as long as we like," you tell me each time you visit. "No one will know."

DARK PASSAGE

-*4*-

Everything has changed. My sleeping room is tiny, and there is nothing to see out the window except the tall brownstone building next door, stubbornly dispelling the possibility of any view beyond it. I am not accustomed to such limited vistas. Sitting on the uncomfortable narrow bed made up with stiff starched sheets and a thin faded counterpane, I listen to the sounds beyond my room: harsh engines and motors, loud voices on the street below, and now the distinct sound of typing just down the hall.

I've been replaced! It's because of the splinter in my finger, I realize. It never healed, and now it's infected to the point where I cannot type. That must be one of your Ednas I hear typing your letters.

I get up and creep barefoot down the hallway to investigate.

She's sitting at the dining room table, my exquisite typing machine set in front of her. Her speed is admirable; she never looks at the keys as her fingers fly over them, pressing, releasing, with only the slightest pause to return the register.

"You must stop typing now," I say out loud as she comes to the bottom of the page, pulls it from the carriage and prepares to insert a new sheet of paper. "I have my own work to do."

"Beg pardon?" She stops typing and looks at me, sternly and a little surprised. Then, "Oh, I'm so sorry if I've disturbed you."

She's older than I thought she'd be, not at all smartly dressed, and wearing not one piece of jewelry. Her nose is too long, her eyes are close set, and there are wrinkles crossing her forehead and surrounding her pursed mouth. She's not even put on rouge or lipstick today and her hair is piled on her head haphazardly, combs stuck into it in a most unorganized fashion. If you could see her now, there'd be no question about which one of us you'd keep.

"Where's Dr. P?" I ask her.

"Your doctor isn't here," she replied, "but he said you should stay in bed and rest as much as possible. You're most likely all worn out from the trip you just made."

She stands, smoothes her skirt and takes my arm to escort me back to my bed.

I understand. You'll visit me in my room, using the new secret passage you've just had built. No one will know.

I close the door, fix myself up by looking in the little hand mirror on the table beside my bed, and lie down to wait. I'll doze, as I always do; you'll wake me gently. I'll pretend to be cross with you, but you'll calm me with your arms surrounding me, your lips gently pressing my forehead, my cheeks, my mouth.

"Edna's in the past," you'll tell me, lying close beside me on the narrow bed, as the sounds of typing fade away. "This is now. This is real."

Aunt Lulu had been deposited in the little back room in Letha and Vernon's flat. She was not feeling up to the wedding ceremony and could not be left alone afterwards, so Aunt Virginia agreed to stay with her while Letha and Vernon took their brief honeymoon. When they returned, Virginia was in quite a state, proclaiming Lulu a thoroughly disagreeable being.

"My duties here are finished," Virginia had declared. She left in a huff, and never came back to visit.

After that, Letha, Vernon and Aunt Lulu had settled into the only routine that made sense. Letha stopped going to the optical shop so she could stay with Aunt Lulu during the daytime, and Vernon cared for her at night. Bedroom intimacy, when the newlyweds managed it, was now a hurried and mostly joyless event.

"I want to go home," Lulu began begging right away. "I need to see Dr. P."

By "home," they thought she meant the New Jersey town in which she'd been born, according to the astronomer's brother. And by "Dr. P," they thought she was confusing the name of the physician who'd been hired to check in on her twice weekly.

"I'm fairly certain she's in her final days now," the doctor had told Vernon at the end of his last visit. "Her mind is nearly gone, but she will not let go easily. I'm sorry."

"Tell me about home, Aunt Lulu," Vernon suggested the next time she asked to go there. He sat by her bedside late each night, holding her frail hand and searching her dark eyes for whatever secrets they might reveal, but her tired gaze offered little or nothing. The doctor was right; there was not much time left.

"I'm the only one who ever left home," she told him. "I didn't want to, but you were dead and she sent me away."

"Who was she, the one who sent you away?"

"That horrible woman, lived around the corner from you on the hill. Why did you marry her? Nothing good ever happened to anybody after that."

Vernon's mind raced to process the new information. "We're not talking about New Jersey, are we?"

"Don't be silly. You know where we live."

"In a house…"

"Not a house," she corrected him. "We live in a mansion."

"A mansion, then," he repeated her words slowly and carefully. "A mansion in…"

"Not in, on," she spoke so quietly he had to lean in close to hear her.

"A mansion on," he attempted, "a hill? Beacon Hill?"

"Mars," she whispered.

"We live on Mars?" His face was close to hers; he could feel her labored breathing.

"Mars Hill." She kissed him on the lips and fell asleep. The busy movement visible beneath her wrinkled eyelids and the relaxed smile on her face told him she was dreaming already.

Someone has been kissing me in the dark, revving the passion deep inside. A pulsing, pleasingly throbbing current invades my soul, building its intensity like a massive musical scale sliding upwards, its sharp notes nearly bursting from the restraints of measure, beat, pitch and melody.

"*Don't stop,*" *I scream.*

Just as the orgasm is primed to overtake me, I hear a thin voice pleading:

"Ma'am, please open your eyes."

The fake Dr. P wakes me with a firm shake, both his hands on my shoulders. The moment passes; I'm still unsatisfied.

"We should get you to the hospital," he says.

The imposter is wearing your clothes, attempting to speak in your voice, trying, as the others have, to convince me that I have to leave now. He wants to send me away, but this time I'll not go. Not without putting up a fuss. I know where I belong.

"You said we could stay here as long as we like," I remind him.

"Ma'am, I think you're confused."

"Leave me alone." My head is heavy and spinning again.

"It's the prudent thing to do," he tells me. "You hit your head and lost consciousness." He circles my shoulders and with some effort eases me into a sitting position.

"I don't need to go anywhere," I protest. "I just need to rest."

But before I can close my eyes again, he's shaking me more insistently. His touch is demanding, not tender, as he pulls me closer. I resist his efforts. If he takes me to the hospital, I'll never get to come home. I'll be stuck there forever. But he seems to be gaining strength while I'm losing it; he's already got me standing up. He's walking me toward the door, out into the cool Arizona night. I take a deeply labored breath and then I'm Venus again – the blue jeans, blood-stained t-shirt and noisy flip-flops all the proof I need.

"You couldn't possibly have seen Mars," he insists, guiding me toward the parking lot. "It had already set."

"I didn't say I saw Mars," I correct him.

I know what I'd seen, but could not say. Not canals, something else I couldn't put into words. I'd seen movement clarify itself – not in crisp detail but rather soft-focused in its necessity to keep the view evolving, almost like a double-exposure in a photograph, or a page written on once, then turned and written on again. I'd seen a salmon-colored sky over a barren, rock-strewn desert existing simultaneously with glassy blue avenues of water spreading in all directions at once.

I'd seen a vast storm approaching and in advance of it, where the air was still calm, I'd seen them: two defiant, finely dressed Martians strolling arm in arm, climbing to the peak of a rock-solid mountain, looking over the improbable landscape below like a miniature couple on top of a unevenly stacked wedding cake. And it was all there and gone in an instant, replaced by a black void. Just as I slipped from the viewing platform, Mars must have slipped below the horizon, into darkness.

A Blemish on Mars

– 1 –

There has never been such intense and sustained joy on Mars Hill: forty-five consecutive nights of good seeing so far, an Observatory record!

During this opposition, activity inside the dome has been relentless: views rarely witnessed, rarely documented, and rarely discussed with such complete agreement among our group. Distinct canals, some of them double lines, robust clusters of oases at canal junctures; we can almost see the creatures responsible for such features – canal builders, water tenders, gardeners and farmers, all noble and hard-working Martians.

When we are not observing them, we invent and tell each other stories about the Martians – what tools they use, what nourishment they need, what lives they live. Looking and seeing over time cannot help but inspire us to create scenarios with compelling characters and a dramatic story that keeps unfolding. You call it "kinematic seeing" to reference, I think, the new invention I've yet to observe, the one called cinema: moving pictures in which you watch someone's story going on before your eyes as if you are there, too.

The Martian marriage must be built on a mutual commitment to survive the difficult circumstances of their lives, I begin my story and then stop it abruptly. I can tell from their uncomfortable shifting about that none of them has ever imagined a Martian female alongside the Martian male.

"It may not be that way at all on Mars," Dr. P politely disagrees with me, and I sweetly remind him that we are spinning tales which are not necessarily truths.

"Stories," he declares, "must have some factual component."

"As does mine," I stand my ground. "If the Martians have survived to this day, and if they are to survive into the future, they must have some way of coupling and bearing young ones, as we do here on Earth. Otherwise, who will maintain the canals? Who will benefit from the water they transport across the planet? Who will visit the shaded oases in the company of a pretty young Martian in a fancy outfit?"

There is no retort this time, only sustained silence eventually interrupted by a small but distinct chortle coming from somewhere overhead. Have the distant Martians heard my story and come in person to renounce it? But it is only Harry standing on a platform near the top of the telescope, preparing to nudge the roof into a new position.

Perhaps it is because my limited observations are more glance-like (there is so much competition to be at the eyepiece) that I have not yet developed an acceptable scenario about the Martians, one in which they fall in love, marry and raise children, all the while racing to protect their families from the harsh elements on their native planet. Surely the Martian women must be as strong and resourceful as the Martian men.

"It's a fine story you tell, ma'am," Harry compliments me when I step outside the dome for a breath of fresh air. Inside, you are still watching your own undisputed Martian tale unfold: desperate, drought-stricken creatures digging long troughs in the red dirt beneath their feet to direct the scant remaining water, frozen in polar ice caps, to all parts of the parched planet.

Harry sits on the top step. He has removed his eyeglasses and has lit up a cigarette. I notice for the first time that he has striking blue eyes, nearly as blue as yours, but not as deeply set. They hug the surface of his face casually and appear somewhat impish, like those sewn onto the face of a rag doll.

"I prefer to live my own life," he says, somewhat arrogantly, about the scientific work going on inside, and the stories being told there. At any moment he may be called to reposition the dome so that the celestial work can continue. He says he doesn't mind. He says he likes it here. Before this, he was in the Merchant Marine.

"Always in motion, always in danger," he declares, "is no way for a sensible man to live."

He gestures toward the dirt below our feet. "This is solid."

I find myself sitting next to Harry on the steps, rightly surprised to be holding a lit cigarette. (I was not proud to admit that I'd ever smoked and was quite sure I had quit the filthy habit.)

Harry and I inhale in unison and look at the stars sprinkled generously across the sky.

"On long sea voyages we did the same thing," he says. "Entertained ourselves with fantastic tales. None of it was real. It was our tedium alone created the drama. We filled the skies with our stories, where there were only stars."

"But Mars is distinctive from the stars," I reply. "A planet has the potential for life built into it, with its land and waters and air in the sky above."

"So you've seen the canals with your own eyes, Miss Lulu?"

"I've seen features that might certainly be canals, as have you."

"It's a rightly big step from 'features that might be canals' to entire civilizations who build and use them."

"I suppose so, but that is not to say the Martians do not exist."

Harry rises from the top step, takes me by the arm and stands me up beside him.

"If there are indeed dramas in progress up there," he indicates the heavens with a sweep of his arm, "it doesn't mean we have to spend all our bloody time looking at them. Where's our own drama, then? And what if they're watching us, and all they observe is us, watching them! We'd be pitiful, boring creatures in their eyes, wouldn't we, now?"

Harry's unaccustomed talkativeness is short lived; he's summoned to adjust the dome, and is up and gone before I even try to answer his perfectly reasonable queries. Where's our own drama, indeed?

He's tossed the stub of his cigarette in the dirt below, where it still emits a glow, like a tiny red planet at my feet. Within moments the roof begins to creak as it is encouraged toward its new position. I drop my cigarette beside Harry's and step on both, extinguishing them at once.

-2-

'm close to fainting from the pain in my head and can't bear to touch my left foot to the ground. I have no idea what happened to me or how long it's been since I looked through the telescope, but as this strangely dressed man leads me hopping on one foot toward the parking lot, I know exactly how long Dr. Dick will put up with any more delays on my part.

I finger the keys in my pocket. If I can just get to my car I'll be able to escape.

But the man is instead steering me toward a white van decorated with the blue "Lowell Observatory" logo.

"Thanks for everything," I say with fake gratitude as I try to pull away, "but I've got to be going now."

He ignores me, so I stop, look him in the eyes and explain exactly why I have to get back to Pasadena: my job, my demanding and impatient boss, the Mariner spacecraft closing in on Mars, all the work orders that will soon be piling up on my desk.

"Oh, you work at JPL," he smiles as if he's put a long-sought piece of my jigsaw puzzle into place. Then he changes his mind and removes it again, deliberately, to postpone the puzzle's completion. "There's no hurry, then."

"Of course there is. I might lose my job." Obviously, the fake Dr. P doesn't know the real Dr. Dick.

"No, you won't. There won't be anything for the Mariner to see." He seems sure about this.

We're at the van; he's opened the passenger door.

"Step up with your good foot," he cautions me, pushing from behind.

"Aren't you forgetting the entire planet Mars?"

He closes my door, hurries around the front of the van and climbs into the driver's seat.

"Nope. Spend all my time with the little red enigma." He points to his forehead. "Mars is in here," he says, "always."

"Oh yeah?" I challenge him. "What's it doing in there right now?"

He turns the ignition key. The van's engine roars to life. He looks up through the windshield at the sky above and grins knowingly.

"It's preparing, ma'am, a huge surprise for all those scientists you work with at JPL."

Charles made his remarkable discovery while on routine planetary patrol.

A few weeks ago when he'd guided the big telescope into place, adjusted its settings and peered through the eyepiece, he'd seen that a small portion of the Martian surface, just below the equator, appeared slightly fuzzier than the rest of the planet's features.

"Far out," he whispered to himself.

Any planetary aberration, no matter how small, is worthy of detailed examination. He fiddled with the focus, trying to adjust the questionable blur, but it remained stubbornly soft.

"That just doesn't make sense." Charles was fond of talking to himself through the long, solitary nights he spent under the dome.

He photographed the anomaly and entered the event in his logbook that night and the next. But on the third night the fuzzy spot did not appear.

"Weather," he said to himself, not waiting for an official astronomer's explanation. "Short-term change is always weather."

The Martian atmosphere, unlike Earth's, was thin, and when heated by the sun, could produce occasional spectacular wind-driven events: thick, swirling, yellow clouds of dust created as the storms lifted small particles from the planet's surface into the air, suspending and carrying them for miles before releasing them.

Mars and Earth were approaching an unusually favorable opposition and NASA's most ambitious Mariner mission to date was in transit to the red planet, preparing to photograph its mysterious terrain in great detail.

A major dust storm occurring at exactly the same time as Mariner's arrival – too much of a coincidence? Or perhaps, Charles mused, Percival Lowell had seen more through this very telescope than he had admitted: intelligent beings working feverishly to protect their identity from encroachment by their nosy earthly neighbors? Working up a storm – ha!

Charles realized the gift he'd been given by the two-night dust storm he'd just observed. Conditions were ripe for another one, perhaps larger and even more problematic for the tiny, vulnerable Mariner spacecraft. No one had yet mentioned the possibility. If he could predict an actual weather event that would occur just as the Mariner reaches Martian orbit – and be first to do so – perhaps he'd give the scientists at JPL time to devise an alternate plan.

No one would dare make such a prediction – would he?

Of course, if he were wrong he'd be the laughingstock of the scientific community. But if he were *right*, he might well become part of the Martian lore alongside his hero, Percival Lowell.

Charles carefully removed the pages from the logbook referencing the atmospheric disturbance and his jotted addendum: *possible large dust storm forming?*

He'd wait until he could corroborate his newly found smudge with synchronized views from the other telescopes stationed around the world. He had a little time, but not much. Most likely, the same weather event had already been observed and photographed by distant telescopes, and the photographs were on their way to Flagstaff, where resident astronomers would develop and print them, and determine exactly what they'd all seen.

- *3* -

Our weeks of sustained good seeing have been tarnished by something unforeseen, a small but annoying blemish appearing just south of the Martian equator. The others briefly discuss its cause, but mostly complain when it grows larger the next night, appearing as a blonde smudge that blurs a significant portion of the southern hemisphere.

Mr. V.M. has retired for the night, and you have lain yourself down to sleep on a quilt you've spread on the floor of the dome, saying, "Wake me if anything changes."

The view is exclusively mine for the moment. Harry helps me into the viewing chair and watches as I put my eye to the eyepiece. I think perhaps it is a woman's notion that blemishes must be examined and then taken care of. Careful cleansing lest an infection take hold, a generous amount of thick lotion to soften and soothe the offender, and finally a thick application of pressed powder to conceal its stubborn presence. Eventually, with sustained patience and sanitary care, the blemish will vanish of its own accord.

At first I study the Martian blemish as I would study one on my own face, as something that must be visibly diminished lest the men lose interest in looking. But then I remember the glassmaker's advice on how one should view the Martian surface: *Look not at it, but on it.* "On" is more than the surface itself; it contains whatever the surface reveals about itself. "At" is more cursory, a superficial and fleeting glance. But how to look on a surface obscured by such a blemish?

Then it occurs to me that the blemish is not covering the surface, but must be part of the surface itself, erupting, as a disturbance on the surface of one's skin, yet still connected to that skin. Will the water carried by the Martian canals eventually cleanse and heal this blemish? Will it vanish as mysteriously as it has appeared?

Perhaps I have just created a Martian story with an actual truth inside it! My brain races as I strain my eye to see more.

It is near dawn, but still dark enough. I continue looking at the blemish on the planet, now the sole focus of my attention, until the planet turns its face away, as it always does, moving just beyond my field of view.

"Harry," I call out and he is there, materializing beside me on the viewing platform. And then, just as suddenly, you are shouting from below: "Stop!"

I think you are having one of your nightmares, but I'm too far away to gently shake you awake, as I've done many times before.

"Get down from there!" you thunder.

I climb hurriedly down from the viewing platform in the near-dark, missing a step and tumbling to the floor, but you are too caught up in your rage to notice. I grab at my ankle, now throbbing in pain.

"What's the matter, sir?" Harry inquires from his perch.

"Get out! Now!"

You are known to have a temper when matters do not go your way. I have observed your railing against the household staff over seemingly minor infractions like a dusty tabletop or soup that is too thin. You became extremely upset of late, and rightly so, when someone left the trap door to the downstairs passage open at night and Mr. V.M. fell into it while coming from the darkroom. But this exaggerated rage is unjustified; Harry was doing nothing wrong, and I was only observing the planet, as we are supposed to do here.

"We must keep looking," you always remind us.

But the looking is over; we have been banished from the dome.

Harry helps me to my feet. With his support, I am able to limp toward the door of our Mansion.

You lock yourself inside the dome at night and in your room during the day for the next day and a half, and then refuse to speak to me for another three days. When you finally approach me in the library and ask me to take a letter, you seem sad, even subdued, and absolutely stunned to see me using crutches.

"What happened?" you ask.

"I sprained my ankle."

You seem not to remember what happened just a few nights earlier.

"Is there something wrong?" I query, but you only shake your head energetically, as if trying to clear some unpleasantness lodged within.

"That will be all," you tell me, although you have not dictated the letter you'd asked me to take. "You can leave me now."

"What about that letter, sir?" I ask.

"I know how to write a letter," you say, a little insolently.

-4-

Early the next morning Aunt Lulu's temper flared up again, and she shouted from her room.

"Not this time. You'll not send me away. I won't hear of it!"

When Letha and Vernon rushed into her room, she stared at them without recognition. Both her cheeks were bloody where she'd scratched long gashes with her fingernails. The blood under her fingernails had caked and dried into solid chunks.

"Leave me alone!" She refused to let either one of them clean her nails or apply salve to her torn cheeks. She lifted a small hand mirror from her bedside table, held it close and studied her wounded face intently.

Alarmed, Letha tried to take the mirror from Lulu's hand, but the old woman grasped its handle ferociously and would not relinquish it.

"I must keep looking," she announced.

The doctor who'd been called to examine Aunt Lulu advised restraints, but neither Letha nor Vernon could bear to tie the poor woman down. They committed themselves instead to watching her around the clock, calming her when necessary with bromides in her tea.

Lulu slept fitfully all day, then woke up early in the evening, feverish. She stood unsteadily and walked down the long hallway and out the door.

Letha, who'd been dozing, heard the door blown shut by the wind. She raced out the door and up the stairs, where she found Lulu perched on the roof, sorting through the stars, wearing just her nightgown and no slippers, on a clear, crisp autumn night.

Letha reached Lulu and tugged gently on her arm.

"I thought you'd come around once the stars came out," Lulu smiled.

"Let's go inside now," said Letha. She escorted Aunt Lulu back down the stairs and inside to her bedroom.

"Watch your step," Lulu cautioned her companion. "I fell down that time, couldn't get back up."

"When was that, Aunt Lulu?"

"That night you got so angry with me. You remember, don't you?"

"Sit down. Let's wipe those dirty feet before we get you back to bed."

Letha had just washed, ironed and put fresh sheets on Lulu's bed and she didn't want to do laundry again so soon.

"Watch out," Lulu shouted, "that ankle's the one got sprained. Call the doctor."

"What's wrong?" Vernon appeared in his pajamas, his hair a mess.

"Thank goodness you're here," said Lulu, who allowed him to clean the bottoms of her feet and ease her back into bed. "You remember, don't you?"

"What's that, Aunt Lulu?" Vernon sat on the side of her bed and held her hand. Her skin was hot to the touch.

Letha pulled a thick blanket up to the old woman's chest, but Lulu pushed the cover aside and closed her eyes.

"The time I lost one of my feet," she winced at the memory.

"You didn't lose it," Letha reminded her. "You just hurt it."

"Hurt's the same as loss," Lulu whispered.

"Go to sleep now," Vernon told her wearily, but Lulu's eyes popped open, alarmed.

"We lost all the melons that summer because nobody tended the garden and they withered up and died," she told him. "You were still in an uncertain mood and Harry had run off, after the calving."

Venus bellows incessantly over a period of several days, and only Harry can calm her. Whenever he strokes her head and runs his palm down her back and across her swollen sides, she eventually closes her eyes and grows quiet. He's been sleeping next to her in the barn, leaving only when his services are needed in the dome. He reeks strongly of wet hay mixed with animal scent and his own perspiration, but I've come to welcome his distinct odor. The other men who work under the dome have the delicate scent of lavender water, their fragrant, civilized efforts interrupted the moment Harry enters, emitting his pungent earthiness.

At night it is up and down for Harry, who must hurry between the dome up high and the barn built on a level field about fifty yards below the mesa. He is often out of breath, but he relishes the challenge, I gather, of attending to both the human and animal residents of this place, each with distinctly demanding needs.

Dr. P had endured quite enough of Harry's odor, however, and proposed a new hire, a stable man, so that Harry could once again dedicate himself to the dome. Harry wouldn't hear of it, saying he'd promptly gather his things and be off, so of course Dr. P had to back down. Although there are stable men aplenty in these parts, a reliable dome porter is hard to come by.

When we are observing and Harry is needed to adjust the dome, I am sometimes the one sent to fetch him from the barn. Even when it's pitch black, I know my way along the narrow path that Harry has cleared.

Someone has just kissed me tenderly on the lips.

I'm lying on a bed of soft hay.

"Ma'am, ma'am, please open your eyes, ma'am," Harry pleads.

Venus offers a sympathetic low from her resting place inside the barn.

I have tripped and have fallen on my bad foot, but Harry heard me gasp and groan and has run to rescue me. He's propped me up on a pillow of hay just outside the barn, and sits by my side, holding my hand as the stars spread out above us in a splendidly unfettered display.

Just then we hear the straining, groaning sound of wood on metal, as the roof of the dome begins to rotate. Harry chuckles.

"Dr. P must be moving the roof all by himself," he says.

"You should hurry to help him," I murmur.

But Harry refuses to leave my side.

"I'm all right," I assure him. "It's Dr. P who needs you now."

"Listen," Harry says. "The roof is moving without me all the same, so I'm not needed there, now am I?

"But he'll be furious," I remind him. "You know how he likes for situations to be taken care of at once."

"Yes, of course," Harry says matter-of-factly, "that's why I'm taking care of you right now."

No matter my beauty, my fashion, my two-step or my typing speed, I cannot compete with the heavens for your favor, it seems. But tonight, with all the stars and planets in the sky to be seen and described, important scientists to attend, and a distressed cow to be comforted, Harry has determined my worthiness to be above them all.

His kiss is surprisingly gentle, distinct from yours. In the throes of romance, you often push your lips hard against mine, when I'd prefer a lighter touch.

We are not hiding, as when you visit me in my room. Both Harry and I have just cause to be here, yet no one thinks to look for us. All the heavens spread above us are witness to our intimacy and yet our privacy is assured, our pleasure undisturbed.

By morning I'm able to stand, with Harry's help, and limp back to the Mansion. We receive curious looks from some of the servants.

You are most likely sleeping and do not know – unless someone gossips – about the night I've just spent with Harry.

I t's nearly dawn and Charles has been sweating in his vintage outfit since early the previous evening. He rolls down the window of the Observatory van and feels some relief at last. A light but steady rain is falling.

The city of Flagstaff calmly spreads its orderly streets and buildings up ahead. Hooded streetlights, in civic deference to the dark sky needs of the Observatory up the hill, bounce their soft glow onto the wet pavement.

Charles knows he looks like an idiot and that the emergency room staff will most likely share a laugh at his expense. He's known around these parts as the goofy scientist who likes to play dress-up, especially when lecturing school groups who come to tour the Observatory.

"Hang on," he tells his passenger as they hit a speed bump that nearly bounces him out of the driver's seat. "We're almost there."

The obstinate woman who'd fallen in the dome has finally agreed to go to the hospital, but not without a lot of cajoling on his part. The last thing cash-strapped Lowell Observatory needs is a lawsuit charging negligence, and the last thing he needs, as a new employee, is his name listed as primary culprit.

He hadn't done anything wrong, he keeps telling himself. She'd bullied him into the situation, and he'd only responded when he'd heard her say, "I saw them." He'd been obligated to climb up to verify her observation. She was a layperson; he was the professional. He couldn't have her going around telling everyone she'd seen the canals on Mars – not on his watch – although he couldn't help wondering, even now, exactly *what* she had seen just before she fell.

He pulls up in front of a rain-glazed entryway blazing inside and out with neon. "Emergency," a sign screams in red.

"You couldn't possibly have seen anything on Mars," Charles explains to her again as he halts the van outside the well-lit entrance. "The planet had already set."

This time there's no retort, no response at all.

He looks over to see the girl collapsed in her seat, her eyes closed, her mouth open, and her wet head dangling precariously out the open window. Whatever she'd seen, she's keeping it secret. Without even trying, she's managed to complicate his life, again: He'll have to pick her up and carry her inside.

I wake up in a narrow bed made up with crisp white sheets, the one covering me tucked in much too tightly. Slowly I work my arms out from under the covers and with some effort am able to push them off me. I've been stripped of my jeans and bloody t-shirt, and dressed in a hideous white gown. But that's not the worst part: I've become ancient while I slept.

I touch myself and feel what seems to be someone else's flaccid body. My skin is loose; my hands are wrinkled and spotted. My hair has grown long and frayed: I hold a loose strand in front of my face and see that it has turned from shiny brown into a lusterless gray. No wonder I've been sent away.

I labor to maneuver myself into a sitting position. Every joint in my body protests. Sliding myself toward the edge of the bed, I lower one foot, then the other, to the floor far below. When I put weight on the left one, trying to stand, the pain in my ankle makes me yelp, but I convince myself to keep moving. I have to get back home.

I find my car parked at the base of Mars Hill, just outside the stone columns. It's just past sunset and the rain has stopped. I can still get there in time for the opposition.

Turning the ignition key, I hear not the putt-putt of the engine coming to life but rather a soft stutter and then silence. This is not what's supposed to happen. I have to get to the top of the mesa; I have to see Mars.

I pop the back hood and lean in to take a look underneath. I am not mechanically inclined, but this has happened before after a steady rain, and I've learned how to fix it. I grab a soiled rag I keep in the trunk just for this purpose. People who don't know Volkswagens are always surprised that the trunk is in front and the engine is in back.

"Now I seen it all," I hear a throaty voice behind me. "A girl mechanic, working on a bass-ackwards car."

I decide to ignore the voice. Carefully I pull out each connection on the distributor, wipe it dry, then re-connect it.

"You look just like the real thang," the voice continues, "like you know what you're doing in there."

"I know enough." I say, slamming the hood down and walking around him to climb in the driver's seat.

Shit. It still won't start. He laughs.

"I don't know what you think's so goddamn funny," I snarl in his direction. "I'm late for an appointment."

"Aw, now," he croons. "You jus' tell me where you're goin' and I'll git you there."

And before I know it, I have both my arms around the leathery waist of a perfect stranger and he's guiding his wide Harley – with me perched on the back – through the dense and noisy atmosphere up the twisted road toward Mars Hill. He takes each sweeping turn low, nearly laying the motorcycle on its side. I lurch with him side-to-side, terrified but thrilled, the vibration of the machine constant and pleasing between my widespread legs. The sensation builds as the unsettled atmosphere grabs us and carries us forward, inward, upward, the momentum building until finally I'm released like a stone from a slingshot flung into the far reaches of space: a deep and perfect orgasm.

"Name's Harry," he shouts over the noise of the motorcycle and the wind. "Pleased to meet ya."

We've arrived on the silent, tranquil summit. Somewhere overhead, a red pinpoint of light is poised to display itself.

I jump off the bike and pass everyone in sight as I hurry up the hill, with Harry right behind me. But no matter how fast my trot, Dr. P is still locking the door to the dome by the time I arrive.

He turns sadly and tells me: "I'm sorry, ma'am, but the view has deteriorated."

Silently, Harry has followed me up the stairs leading to the dome.

"You show the little lady what she come to see," he growls into Dr. P's face.

"There's nothing worth seeing," Dr. P explains with a tired shrug.

"Look, Mr. Fancy Fellow," Harry moves closer and looks him in the eye. "I ain't gonna ask you again."

"Okay, look, then." Dr. P sighs and unlocks the door. He nods toward me and I rush inside, climb the viewing platform and step toward the telescope. I press my eye against it and wait for the atmosphere to clear, but before the view materializes, I feel my head spinning. I'm stepping sideways, trying but failing to counteract my growing dizziness, plunging toward a dark void.

This time, I wonder, who will catch me when I fall?

A frowning nurse in a winged white cap and crisp white dress steps quietly in front of me and steadies herself to break my fall as I'm preparing to hobble out of the hospital to freedom.

"Ma'am, you need to lie down and rest." She turns me around and steers me toward an empty bed topped by chaotic sheets, as if someone had recently struggled to escape from them.

"The doctor will be with you shortly." The nurse helps me back into bed and arranges the sheets tightly around me like a baby wrapped in swaddling clothes. There will be no escaping, she seems to be telling me with each sharp tug of the sheet.

"Now you stay put," she says as she walks away.

She's lying. The doctor will never be with me. He's the one who's sent me away. Harry's waiting, but he will not wait forever – unless you think of a clever way to keep him solidly grounded on Mars Hill.

-6-

There is only one reason you'd booked the passage from England yourself, instead of instructing me to take care of it, and that is because you'd decided the matter must be kept secret from me. Once she reached America, however, you left it to me to get her from New York to Flagstaff on the train.

You were still barely speaking to me, but you'd written her name on a piece of paper, with brief instructions about how to contact her in New York once I had reserved her seat on the westbound Express.

Olivia March, your note said.

You are bringing another Edna here to live! The unwelcome news stings like an angry hornet.

"And how did you meet Miss March?" I ask you sourly, when I bring the letter for your signature to the library where you are working.

"Oh, I've never met her myself." You sign the letter and dismiss me with a wave of your hand. "She's for Harry."

I'm in my room when Harry shows up outside my window.

"Venus has had her calf," he announces with a weary grin. "I thought you'd like to come and see it."

"I'm really quite busy," I tell him, but he will not take "no" for an answer and, I must admit, I've grown quite fond of our pretty Observatory cow.

I stand and make my slow way outdoors. Harry is already halfway to the barn.

"You must be looking forward to Miss March's arrival," I call out to him, stopping him in his tracks.

He says he didn't know she was coming.

Within days, Harry has thrown a fit and run off again, and I am dispatched to find him and cajole him into coming back to Mars Hill.

"He's like a spirited horse," Dr. P writes to me from Boston, where he has gone to collect yet another honor, his L.L.D. "I don't think we can tame him, but perhaps over time we can encourage him to behave himself more reasonably."

Dr. P has once again approved a small raise for Harry, if this will convince him to return.

I find Harry in a place no lady should find herself, but I'd been given instructions from my boss, so I step cautiously inside the little saloon next door to the Bank Hotel. Sure enough, there he sits, staring into a glass of whiskey. I take a seat next to him. He does not notice me until the bartender comes over to ask what I am drinking. I wave him away; I want nothing of this sordid place, except to be finished with my business here.

Harry finally looks up. "Miss Lulu," he says. "You've come to keep me company."

"I've come to take you back up the hill."

He shakes his head sadly.

"I shall have to marry her," he tells me, his eyes full of regret.

He motions for the bartender to refill his glass, but I cover it with my hand to stop him.

"We are going home now," I tell him firmly. "I've been authorized to raise your salary, and Dr. P says to tell you he is going to have the brothers build a little house for you and your bride. Now, will you come with me?"

He rises from the stool, taking a prolonged moment to steady himself before taking my arm.

"Step carefully now," Harry advises as we advance slowly under the starlit skies toward the horse and carriage waiting to carry us up the hill. He thinks he is a proper gentleman guiding and supporting me as we walk. But the truth is, I'm a lady working far too hard to keep a drunken man on his feet and moving forward – and am most definitely not, as I fear some patrons of this place will assume, a self-righteous, temperance-styled wife come to collect my sinfully inebriated husband.

I have no husband to collect.

- 7 -

Letha doesn't know what to do, and she's almost ready to panic. Should she send for Vernon, or just wait and see if Aunt Lulu's current spell passes?

The old woman had awakened Letha early with her moaning and wouldn't stop, even after being served hot tea with honey, and oatmeal sprinkled with cinnamon and brown sugar.

"What's wrong? Should I call Mr. Dawson, or the doctor?"

"Call the doctor," Aunt Lulu said. "Tell him I need him. He had no business dying so suddenly."

"You must be talking about Dr. P."

Letha and Vernon had decided, in private conversations about their new live-in relative, that "Dr. P" must be the late astronomer she'd worked for, Percival Lowell. Vernon had discovered by visiting the Boston Public Library that Lowell's Observatory was located near Flagstaff, Arizona, on a mesa he'd named Mars Hill.

"What happened to Dr. P?" Letha asked Aunt Lulu.

"He'll be here soon," Lulu declared. "He knows I'm waiting."

"I thought he was dead."

Lulu began sobbing.

"You loved him, didn't you?"

Lulu nodded through her tears.

"But he married someone else?"

Lulu nodded more vigorously and wept even harder. "He couldn't marry me," she explained between sobs, "even though…" She left the potent sentence dangling, overcome by heaving, coughing and more sobbing.

The history was slowly falling into place.

"Do you remember when a baby boy was born?" Letha cautiously asked. "His name was Vernon. You called him your nephew?"

"That was the first time I was sent away," Lulu said. She began wailing again and this time could not be calmed.

I see myself sitting at my writing desk; then I am no longer there. It can be that sudden – discovering you have departed, that you have arrived in some place you've never envisioned. No time to pack your trunk and outfit yourself for travel, no time even to complete the sentence you were busy writing. A fountain pen rolls from the desk and clatters to the floor, and no one stoops to pick it up. The ink so recently applied to the paper's surface is still wet, with no one poised to blot it into permanent respectability.

The jonquils in the alabaster vase will not be watered today or tomorrow, and the day after that they will no doubt wither and die. Dust will gather on the windowsill and the shiny looking glass hung above the bureau will grow dull over time.

The person who stumbles upon this desolate scene will leaf casually through the tortured pages of my abandoned life, trying to piece together facts that have been left visible because there was no time to tuck the book containing them into its proper hiding place beneath my mattress.

But I have taken unusual care in fashioning my private thoughts: My words spread in patterns on the pages of my book like the constellations across the night sky – an archer, a queen on her throne, the fish, the water bearer, the twins, the bears big and small – celestial scenes that are clearly visible to those able to see in the arrangement of stars something more.

But disorder, as we all know, is the absolute way of our unwieldy universe, and its irresolute state shall be my salvation: My carefully arranged words will appear to most as a mere scattering of stars.

C an't see the stars," Aunt Lulu swayed on her wobbly feet, fussing and mumbling.

In a sudden fit of anger, she'd ripped the top sheet off her bed and had unfurled it out the window, where it caught the wind and flapped for a short while like a white dove before she lost her grip. It fell pitifully to the ground.

I've lost a perfectly good bed sheet, Letha lamented to herself, hurrying to get to the old woman before she took a tumble out the window.

"Can't see the stars," Lulu kept mumbling as Letha helped her back into bed.

"Oh," Letha suddenly remembered. "Aunt Lulu, you can see the stars any time you want, like this," and she pressed lightly on the old woman's closed eyelids.

Lulu quietened and held herself absolutely still.

"Do you see them now?" Letha asked her.

Aunt Lulu was unconscious.

The unsettled haze descends like a quilt tucked over time's questionable progression, its myriad patterns a shifting view of all I've seen and imagined. I close my eyes and hold my breath as each troubling scene makes its way through pores and orifices, pushing past the sores I've scratched raw, settling in my mind, obscuring all the elusive views I struggle to clarify.

Even one memory would be of value, a rare and stunning jewel on which I could hang other facts and notions, connecting the logic between each one, perhaps eventually assembling a route of truth along which my uncertain thoughts could travel. A canal like a gold necklace strung with sparkling details I've managed to recover, places for my mind to rest, like oases in the desert. Thank you for the necklace. It's exquisite.

Do not look at it, look on it, the glassmaker told me. Instead, I look through it, beyond it. Finally I take a lingering look at what's obscuring it, examining the disturbance itself. *Oh.*

You were wrong. We should have not waited for the sky to clear, for the air to calm, for the truth to arrive. We should have faced the turbulence head-on, leaning into the wind, taking careful steps forward, looking in all directions for useful information.

"What do you see now, Aunt Lulu?" Letha asked the properly prepared corpse resting in the modest metal casket Vernon had purchased from Waterman's funeral home.

Aunt Lulu's eyes were closed and there was a faint smile on her painted lips. She was wearing the lace collar she'd always favored, with a pretty sky blue dress Letha had rushed to purchase at Filene's for this occasion. The astronomer's brother who had deposited her with Letha and Vernon a few months earlier had sent an extravagant spray of yellow roses, along with his neatly penned condolences.

"She has left this Earth and entered the universe," he wrote. "I should not be surprised to find her strolling alongside a Martian canal, on his arm."

There is a way to get from there to here, but it is not a published route. We don't have to take the train. We only have to open our eyes at the right time, locate the proper place in the sky, and settle ourselves down for a sustained and honest look.

The most amazing sights are seen and the most compelling stories told as night inches toward daybreak, when the air is calmest, the seeing best, and the brain has had an uninterrupted period of night sky darkness to settle itself. Confusion coalesces into clarity. Unspoken mysteries lead to distinct possibilities. Longing leads to tender caressing and murmurs of love, and to eternal bliss.

We have been instantly transported. What we see there cannot be described. And I still cannot tell you – as my hand rests on your arm and we step effortlessly across a vast red desert – all of my secrets.

Unmapped Territories

- 1 -

10 June 1908 (your wedding day)

Not Harry. You. It was always you. Always and forever you.

At last I've achieved the clarity that has eluded me for so long. I want to whisper the truth into your ear as you lie napping beside me on the yellow counterpane covering my bed. I want to keep repeating it until you wake up and promise to believe me with all your heart and soul.

"We can stay here forever," I want you to promise me. I want to see the sincerity of your words in your deep-set blue eyes.

But I fear the time for redemption has passed.

You have moved on, last week announcing your engagement. Today you are placing the wedding ring on her hand, not mine. She will come here to live after you return from your wedding in New York and honeymoon in Europe. The next time I see you, I shall work diligently to avoid thinking improper thoughts about you, a married man, and will find scant comfort in my success.

Edna, the splinter still lodged in my finger, cries out in pain. She's become deeply embedded over the years and quite swollen with infection. This time I must attend to her, using a thin needle from my sewing basket to attack her and dig her out. Afterwards, I cleanse my throbbing finger with iodine and wrap it in a sterile bandage.

There is nothing left inside me to respond: no more anguished weeping into my pillow at night, or railing against the unfairness of it all, or wondering what I might have done differently to keep you by my side. This morning when I stand and look in my mirror, I see no one behind me. As I pin up my unkempt hair and apply color to my pale lips and cheeks, I realize I am no longer reflecting you; I have discovered a freedom beyond the pain.

I will continue to type your letters and manuscripts and assist your scientific endeavors in any way I can, but it is no longer required that I mirror your every belief, agree with your every observation, support your every interpretation of what you have seen. Our connection has been undone. I am free to see for myself, to decide what I have seen, and to say what I please about Mars, canals or no. I am even free to look elsewhere in the universe for inspiration and edification.

I am no longer a neophyte.

VENUS ON MARS HILL

-2-

The momentous change in my life had come in two blinks of an eye.

Late last night, just as I'd fallen and banged my head, or maybe just before, when I'd looked though the historic telescope, I'd blinked once and opened my eyes to see the thing I'd been told was impossible to see: Mars, up close, the very moment before it disappeared. That one fleeting glance of the red planet had instantly erased years of uninspired image processing for the nation's finest rocket scientists. That glance had replaced my up-to-date cosmic knowledge with unfounded notions that I'd traveled backwards in time, that I'd become Great Aunt Lulu, and that I'd seen what she'd seen through the big telescope. I was almost convinced that the strange little man by my side was her Dr. P and that the two of us were stepping across the Martian landscape in our Victorian finery.

Then I'd blinked again.

This time when I open my eyes I find myself lying in a hospital bed. I won't be heading back to Pasadena any time soon, the remainder of my life now inexplicably altered – just the kind of change I'd yearned for as I'd approached Flagstaff, only I hadn't imagined there would be so much pair involved.

At least there are good drugs in this life.

"Take this," the nurse says, handing me one paper cup with a thick white pill inside and another cup half-filled with water.

It's amazing how quickly the medication works, dulling the pain and loosening the troublesome thoughts trapped inside my aching head. Within minutes the pill smoothes the contours of my brain, then works its warm way through the rest of my body until all my concerns fall away And all I have to do is ask and they'll bring me another lovely pill.

"No concussion," the emergency room doctor announces later that day when he releases me. But my severely sprained left ankle will keep me from driving a manual transmission for three to five days. I have no choice. Perched on the crutches I've just been given, I make the call from a pay phone just outside of Flagstaff General.

I insert the coins and wait for the long distance operator to connect me, rehearsing my triumphant speech while waiting through six rings for him to answer: "You'll never believe what happened when I looked at Mars..."

But I never get the chance to deliver my news.

"I hope you're phoning me from just down the hall," Dr. Dick growls as soon as he realizes it's me calling. No manners at all.

"Actually, I'm in Flagstaff. I've sprained my ankle and can't drive right now."

"Dammit, I warned you about this, and you didn't listen to a word I said. What's wrong with you?"

Now that's a question for the ages. But before he gives me time to respond, or even contemplate a clever comeback, Dr. Dick fires me.

"We have work to do here," he announces sarcastically, "*important* work – not that you care one bit about it. You and your self-serving, free-spirit, hippiefied-far-out road trip."

"But I –"

"Enjoy your vacation!" He shouts so loud I have to hold the phone away from my ear. "You take all the time you need to find yourself and then stay there as long as you want. In fact, don't ever show up here again. This is the end of the road for you at JPL."

Goodbye, I say to myself when I hear him slam down the phone on his end.

I quietly replace the receiver.

But as I've learned from the Book of Great Aunt Lulu, "goodbye" is only the beginning. I'm feeling quite thrilled by my sudden emancipation as I kick open the phone booth door with my good foot and notice for the first time that the sky here in Flagstaff – unlike the one above smog-ridden Pasadena – is radiantly blue and uncommonly clear.

This must be how Great Aunt Lulu felt when she stepped off the train at the Flagstaff station for the first time. What she'd written on the first page of her journal makes perfect sense to me now: A departure is also an arrival for what comes next. When one thing terminates, another thing begins. Goodbye is just another way to say hello.

I exit the phone booth, half-expecting to see Harry – the one I'd dreamed up – perched on his Harley, waiting to see if I'm going with him. He told me last night he'd wait for me.

You ain't got nothin' else to do, he'll reason.

Where to? I'll ask.

He'll grin and shrug his shoulders.

Down the road a ways, which means he doesn't have a clue. I need at least a clue before committing myself to any more unnecessary roadside diversions.

But Harry isn't there. Neither is Dr. P.

It's time to get some clarity on the situation, I lecture myself, struggling to think beyond the pain pills. I should be able to figure out my next step, at the very least – wh ch normally would be toward my car, a convenient escape that has always been there for me. Until now.

My Karmann Ghia, as best I can remember, is still parked on top of Mars Hill, and I have no way to get there. I use another dime to place a call to someone whose actual na ne I do not know.

"He was there last night, wearing an old-fashioned suit…"

The woman who answered the phone laughs politely. "I know exactly who you're looking for," she tells me.

The man who'd been masquerading as Dr. P says he can pull a few strings and get me a place to stay at the Observatory while I recover. I agree to take him up on his offer. I'm running out of money and without any more paychecks to count or, there's no hope of replenishing my bank account in Pasadena any time soon.

"It's the least we can do," he reasons.

Yeah, especially since it was his fault for pushing me off the viewing platform last night, but I decide not to remind him of the details.

When he comes to pick me up in the Observatory van, we don't discuss last n ght at all, or my accident, or what I'd seen through the telescope, or anything that happened afterwards. I'm full of pain pills and he's full of shit, I decide, so the less said the bette .

I check him out now from behind my sunglasses, in the crisp, unforgiving daylight. He looks like a worn-down matinee idol who's suffered through too many retakes: perfect hair, sideburns and moustache, but faded gray eyes and a pale comp exion weathered by the years he's lived without the comforts true stardom would have afforded him.

"Your eyes were bluer last night," I tell him.

"Tinted contacts," he replies. The trumped-up accent he'd used last night has vanished.

"And last night you were bitchier," he reminds me with a wry smile.

"Sorry."

I can't quite get a mental grip on what happened last night – seems like a lifetime ago – and I can't think of a clever retort for this strange little man, so I keep gawking at him instead. He looks familiar, but I realize he's just a type I've seen a lot around JPL. He's dressed in the standard outfit so pervasive there, a white short-sleeved shirt punctuated by a vinyl pocket protector. He's added a dark, narrow tie scattered with stars, a scientist's feeble attempt at fashion.

"Who are you?" I finally ask.

His name is Charles, he tells me.

"You're not from Boston, are you?"

"Gilman, Illinois," he says, "by way of Pasadena."

"You used to work at JPL?"

"Yes, indeed."

"So did I."

Reality is setting in much too quickly, so I swallow another pill, forcing it down my dry throat without water. The pill kicks in as we drive past the sedate stone columns, allowing me to drift quietly this time from one soft curve to the next as we circle and climb to the top of the mesa. As the twisted road comes to an end, we pull right up in front of a stately stone structure topped by a silver dome.

"The Slipher Building was constructed to align perfectly with the quadrants of the compass," Charles says, describing my new home as he helps me exit the van and balance on my crutches. "And at night the dome reflects Polaris, directly overhead."

I live here, I think in wonder as I watch the afternoon sun bounce its rays off the shiny dome.

Just a few hundred feet away stands the white flat-roofed "dome" housing the big telescope, and beside it, a much smaller structure with an actual miniature dome: "The founder's mausoleum," Charles informs me.

In the opposite direction lies a low, modern brick building – the Planetary Research Center where Charles works his day job. There's no Baronial Mansion anywhere, no barn, no Harry or Venus the cow. Last night has become a distant and unorganized memory, none of it real.

"Some who visit the Slipher Building claim they feel the Earth's magnetic field when standing just under the Saturn lamp inside," Charles adds, his spiel pouring forth unchecked, his tour-guide self in full flower.

I take a careful step forward, wondering it that's what caused last night's unusual events and my ongoing disorientation.

The ability to carry on any useful conversation still eludes me.

"Hmmm," I manage to reply.

The upstairs guest quarters are difficult to get to. I can't climb the stairs with my crutches, so I turn around and sit down on the bottom step, then ease my butt backwards up one stair at a time, taking care not to bang my sprained ankle along the way. Charles follows, carrying my suitcase and purse. At the top of the stairs he steps around me to unlock a door, and helps me stand and hobble inside.

My struggle is well worth the effort: This apartment is grandly furnished with fat brown leather chairs and a sofa, a generous stone fireplace, a tall bed with a brass frame, thick pillows – lots of them – and an unbelievably soft down mattress. There are Mars references everywhere, including three books on the subject written by the founder himself.

"This apartment was designed for visiting dignitaries," Charles explains, "in particular, for his brother who was writing a book about him."

I'd noticed already that the founder's name is rarely spoken; "he" is understood to be Percival Lowell, a name apparently too revered to be said aloud. In her journal Lulu had always referred to him as "Dr. P."

"But his brother," said Charles, "never so much as came near this place."

Well, "his" brother's loss is my gain.

After Charles leaves, I nap for a while on the wide leather sofa. Then I get up and hobble into the kitchen where I heat water in the antique teakettle on the old gas stove and make myself a pitch-perfect cup of tea. I settle myself in the wicker rocking chair on the upstairs porch, prop my sprained ankle on a banister and watch hawks circling above the mountains. The blue sky is just beginning to turn golden as late afternoon progresses toward evening.

This is the exact view Great Aunt Lulu described in her journal. That means her room in the now-demolished Baronial Mansion must have had windows facing in the same direction. I'm beginning to get my bearings and want badly to jump up and begin exploring Mars Hill. But my ankle is all wrapped, and I've been given strict instructions not to stress it until it heals.

I have three to five days to do nothing but sit still, pop another pain pill and finish reading the Book of Great Aunt Lulu – which is beginning to make more sense to me on Demoral.

~ 3 ~

J ust past dawn. One tiny warbler chirps its daybreak greeting outside my window. I am sitting at my writing desk, at risk of ruining not only what appears to be the beginning of a perfectly good day, but possibly the remainder of my time here on Mars Hill.

The recent turbulence in my life has led me to privately reconsider my views on the universe, and this morning I am preparing to commit my thoughts to paper. I have grown weary of their pent-up activity inside my brain and have decided to let them run freely across the pages of my journal instead.

I realize I am turning against you – the cherished one who has provided me with everything exquisite in my life. But you have already turned away from me: You and your bride lie side by side behind the closed door of your sleeping room. She has perfect white skin, ebony hair that shines, and a tiny waist. Each evening she wears to dinner the extravagant diamond ring and wedding band you have given her; they sparkle whenever she lifts a fork in her left hand to anchor her meat while carving it. Her demeanor rarely varies; she seems always unhappy to be in my presence, and you seem quietly aware of her sour mood.

She will not go to the dome to observe the heavens. She says she'd prefer a good night's sleep, kissing you farewell with uncharacteristic drama each evening whenever she knows I am watching, as if the two of you are parting for a very long time.

And yet I am the one left alone. My heavenly observations have been diminished, our times together have grown awkward, and I no longer feel welcome under the dome. I stay awake all night sometimes wondering what celestial displays I am forfeiting because of your marriage.

Your handsome photographic portrait stationed on my desk watches me with one raised eyebrow, a tiny upturn of your lips expressing incredulity over my unvoiced sentiments and the subversive actions about to take place. Defiantly and before you can say a word to stop me, I pick up my pen and fill it with ink, but it pauses midway to the page of my open journal and will travel no further. I put the pen down and turn your portrait away. I again pick up the pen, and at last it touches the paper. You shall not see the black cursive markings that silently shout the heretical words as they are formed on the page.

Outside my window, your wife, wrapped in her lavish mink stole and wearing your big galoshes underneath her skirts, steps carefully through the garden, its neat rows of seedlings still glistening with morning dew. She scolds a naughty blue jay pecking there until he flies away.

I see that only two places are set for breakfast on the veranda. You must still be sleeping after a night of solitary wonder under the dome. I shall stand now and close my journal, lift one side of my mattress and slide the book underneath. I shall smooth my skirt and steel myself as I walk outside to join her at the sunlit table, where determined pleasantries will be exchanged over tart grapefruit and streaming bowls of oatmeal.

I have rehearsed my part until it's perfect: "Good morning, Mrs. P…"

Just after Lulu died, while changing the sheets on the twin bed in the room where she'd stayed, Letha found the little leather book tucked underneath the mattress. She decided not to mention it to Vernon, hiding it instead in her lingerie drawer, a place she knew he'd never go. Letha had never kept secrets from her husband and wondered why she was doing it now. It was as if she could see inside the book she had not yet opened, where there were pages prepared specifically for her, containing words so potent she would need to savor them privately. Once she'd peeked inside, she was not disappointed.

"Goodbye," Lulu had written on the first page.

The book was not written in order; its end was at the beginning and its pages were filled with crisscrossed words and sentences that sometimes turned corners and kept going. Letha committed herself to reading it this way also, each time opening the book to a random page, turning the book this way or that, reading a sentence or two before returning it to the drawer, underneath her neatly folded slips, brassieres and underpants.

Whenever Vernon left the house, she hurried to retrieve the book, her growing guilty pleasure. She'd adjust her thick eyeglasses and, squinting, read out loud to herself tiny passages at a time. She even memorized some of the words she read, murmuring them reverently to herself during the day and dreaming of them by night.

We are in disagreement over the value of clarity.

You want to see a perfect planet, one free of blemishes, so that you can clearly observe and interpret the story of the canals and the beings who have constructed them.

But I think there is less truth in perfection and rather more value in what conditions may stand in its way. I think the blemish itself may have a story to tell, perhaps a tragic one of pestilence and disease, or perhaps a joyous one of rain falling, plants growing and bearing fruit to feed a hungry population.

"I do not know this story yet, but I am determined to learn it for myself," Letha murmured aloud.

"What did you say?" Vernon would sometimes inquire when he'd discover Letha whispering to herself while cooking dinner or washing up afterwards. She'd shake her head and stop herself from speaking the words aloud, while they continued their unregulated dance through her mind.

Unsettled autumn turned into dismal winter and then into a gloriously awakened New England spring as Letha continued to study Aunt Lulu's journal, parsing the odd language within.

Aunt Lulu's writing was a crazed and chaotic journey. Its goal was not to get from one place to another, as from the first word of a sentence to the period ending it, or from an opening comment to a neatly logical conclusion; its pleasure was not found in grasping the meaning of an entirety, but in recognizing and reflecting upon the bliss within each tuned and blended part along a free-flowing route.

The oddly placed farewell, Letha realized, made sense. What came after the first word on the first page followed logically, though not absolutely. Everything could change, even the smallest change could change anything else, and "goodbye" could come at any time.

Letha saw in her mind's eye – the private eyesight that she increasingly relied upon – that this word and all it represented would eventually position itself squarely between Vernon and her. Although she did not yet know when, or how.

-*4*-

Charles has planned for himself a busy afternoon in the basement of the silver-domed Slipher Building, where cool dark rooms lined with sturdy shelving are packed floor to ceiling with the rich history of this place. He hardly notices the intermittent rumbling overhead, most likely a passing thunderstorm. Surely the sky will clear in time for tonight's viewing: Mars, slightly more distant but still spectacular.

He hasn't slept since the opposition began, and sincerely hopes the girl who'd kept him awake – who'd caused all the turmoil, and sent him down here to delve deep into historic log books stored in the dusty archives – would stay put tonight, subdued and sleeping soundly, thanks to the potent pain prescription she'd been given by the emergency room doctor.

"Did you know my great aunt used to work here?" she'd asked him this morning when he'd taken her a cup of coffee.

Her uncombed hair was a mess. Her blue eyes were dull and her speech a little slurred.

The pain pills were doing their job, he noted with satisfaction. She seemed positively mellow compared to the rude and demanding girl who'd exhibited such uncalled-for behavior under the dome.

She was still in bed, propped up on thick pillows, her sprained ankle elevated and parked on its own tower of pillows. On her lap was a worn book with yellowed pages she claimed was the journal her great aunt had written about her adventures here at the Observatory.

"Her name was Lulu. She was his secretary."

As the Observatory's unofficial historian, there was not much Charles didn't know about this place, but he hadn't heard of this employee. By day's end, however, he'd verified that the girl's Great Aunt Lulu, a Miss Wrexie Louise Leonard, was real. She was not only the founder's secretary, but a dedicated observer of the heavens, as well. Over the afternoon he found her initials "WLL" appearing frequently in the observing logs, often alongside the founder's, and her detailed drawings of Mars, Venus and Saturn rivaled any the founder had done himself.

Charles realized he'd never until now considered the fact that a woman might have spent nights under the dome during the Observatory's nascent years. A woman observing the stars and planets before the turn of the century. A woman, it seemed, who'd been far ahead of her time.

He wasn't allowed to remove the historic logbooks from their cool storage area in the basement. Their pages were brittle and the unique astronomical history recorded on them could be easily damaged. He couldn't bring the girl staying in the apartment upstairs down to the basement until her sprained ankle healed enough for her to negotiate the stairs. He'd have to find some other way to show her what he'd discovered.

When the Baronial Mansion was razed, some personal artifacts had been packed and stored in the basement of the Slipher Building. Soon after Charles had come to work, he'd found in an old trunk the vintage suit he liked to wear on special occasions. Alongside it was an exquisite white dress with a long full skirt and tight fitted bodice, a wide matching hat with netting and feathers, and tiny white lace-up shoes. He'd always assumed the female outfit had belonged to the much-maligned Mrs. Lowell. Until now.

Here, in a yellowed photo album in the basement archives, sits a woman wearing this ensemble. She's posed somewhat provocatively in the viewing chair under the dome. One of her wide-open eyes is positioned at the telescope's eyepiece, and she's smiling, prepared to be properly awed by the heavenly sights displayed above her. But she's also looking forward, perhaps at the photographer. She's frozen in time as she waits for him and his camera to complete their task, to capture her likeness for an eternity.

This woman is not Mrs. Lowell. Charles could tell by comparing this photo to other photos properly labeled. Mrs. Lowell never smiled.

"Meet me under the dome in an hour," you instruct me one afternoon after you've finished signing the letters I've typed. "The door will be locked. You must knock twice, wait and then knock twice again, and I shall let you in. Tell no one of our appointment.

Wear your wedding dress."

My white ensemble is the one you laughingly call my "wedding dress." You used to become amorous whenever I'd wear it. After your marriage, I'd had it laundered, pressed and properly scented; then I'd wrapped it in soft paper and hidden it away in my closet.

Now, as I button up the dress, lace the matching shoes, set the hat perfectly on my head and step quietly and carefully toward the door of the dome, I feel as if I've traveled backward in time. Sadly, this is an illusion I shall not be able to maintain. The present will come calling soon enough and once more I shall become the spurned woman who devoted herself to you and your work, with precious little to show for all her efforts. I lift my chin, set my smile in place and knock according to your directions. You open the door and usher me inside.

"Sit down," you say, gesturing toward the viewing chair just beneath the telescope. Then you quickly move to lock the door behind me.

I take my seat and fold my white-gloved hands in my lap, waiting while you set up your new Kodak camera, the one I'd ordered from New York, on its spindly three-legged perch. Soon after it had arrived, I'd asked you to photograph me, as I wanted you to have me sitting on your desk as you are always perched on mine. I'd almost forgotten my request, but you had not.

You approach and take great care to pose me properly.

"Will you lift your skirt a bit so I can see your stockings? May I loosen your jacket to see just a peek of the lovely lingerie blouse you're wearing underneath? Let's see a pose in which you lean back slightly, as if you're overcome by the heavenly sights you're seeing."

Finally, with my arms placed just so, my head tilted up toward the great telescope, my right eye positioned just below the eyepiece as if I'm about to look but haven't yet, you approve the pose. It's an odd posture, but one, you assure me, that looks very fetching.

"Now hold completely still," you instruct me from behind the camera.

I take a deep breath, hold it, and listen for the noise of the camera as it performs its elaborate task. Then I allow myself to breathe.

You are by my side preparing, I think, to pose me another way.

Instead, you offer a hand to help me stand, then sit in the viewing chair yourself and pull me sideways onto your lap, surrounding me with both arms. Your sweet warm breath caresses the back of my neck.

"Let's create another lovely pose, the both of us. This one will be for the Martians," you tell me, just before your lips touch mine. We fall silent; no more photographic portraits will be made.

A temple we have long considered sacred, in one afternoon made profane.

Like an unrequited and slightly annoying suitor, Charles brings me something new each time he visits. This afternoon it's a turkey sandwich and soda to share, and a long cardboard box. He sets the box on the dining room table, opens its flaps and unfolds layer after layer of delicate tissue paper, finally pulling from its depths a long, old-fashioned dress with a severely fitted waistline. It's white, yellowed only slightly with age. From a second nest of tissue paper, he pulls a wide-brimmed white hat generously trimmed with ostrich feathers, lace and netting. And from yet another nest, a pair of satiny white lace-up shoes.

"Looks like a wedding outfit," I guess.

"Nope," he replies. "This outfit belonged to your Great Aunt Lulu. She never married."

"But she had the dress."

In a flash of fluffy white fabric, I come to know my Great Aunt Lulu, and perhaps a few of her secrets.

An elegant frock with fond memories tucked inside each pleat of the skirt, and sweet innocence sewn into each dart of the bodice, now soiled with undeniable knowledge of the improper woman I have become.

I fold the dress and pack it carefully, then put it away. The hat and the shoes follow it into hiding. I shall not wear this ensemble again — not even if you ask very nicely.

Her Dr. P had married, and so had Harry.

Lulu, who had perhaps anticipated each might be her future husband – and most likely had imagined herself wearing her beautiful white ensemble during the wedding ceremony – had become instead the odd woman out, forced daily to endure the presence of the other men's wives without understanding why they'd been chosen for matrimony instead of her.

Another night of solitary agony as you lie with your wife. Another splendid morning on Mars Hill, all of us pretending to behave nicely over our soft-boiled eggs and coffee, chatting determinedly as if nothing has changed.

Later, back in my room, another heresy about to pour unchecked from the venomous pen in my hand that will not stop its writing.

I think I shall not be a planetologist after all. The designation you have chosen for yourself seems too limiting. I am fast turning my attention toward the distant stars, and my interest to learning what lies beyond our own planetary neighborhood. The Martians who live next door, I'm sure, will carry on their lives well enough without my constant attention. They will still have all of yours.

I have come to believe that we live in an energetic universe. As humans, in particular the busy ones, rarely sit still for any extended period of time, and often travel from one place to another to get on with their lives, so must our celestial acquaintances turn and fidget constantly as they proceed with their own journeys through the universe.

I think any observation of the heavens above must be less like a single photograph and more akin to the cinema, the new entertainment that has so captured the public's imagination and enthusiasm. The cinema does not present stillness, but rather life in motion, people going about their business of working, traveling, falling in love, fighting, kissing, always moving from one moment in their lives to the next, and to the next one after that. So, I think, it must be for the heavens, and I must ask:

Why, if everything in the universe is in motion, must the air around us be still? Why must we wait for a calm atmosphere to insure a moment of good seeing?

Sitting absolutely still, as when posing for a photographic portrait, seems unnatural, and the resulting impression – a frozen moment – far too limited a view. It's almost as if sitting still stifles one's very existence. Upon that realization, the undeniable urge is to move and keep moving. But it's the moving that disturbs the seeing. So whatever is real cannot be seen for what it clearly is, and what is clearly seen cannot be real.

Dare I say this? Your scale of seeing needs to be inverted. When seeing is at its worst, there may truly be something worth seeing.

The Universe is Expanding

- 1 -

*S*hit, shit, shit. A chunk of Great Aunt Lulu's journal is missing.

Just as I'm settling in here, just as she's starting to expound on the whole universe, I discover some pages have been removed, cut out neatly, as if with a sharp knife. In the entry she'd written just before the gap, she'd announced that she was going to Europe, but she wrote nothing about her trip after returning to her job. Just two words, ten weeks and many missing pages later: "I'm back." No hint of what she'd been up to while she'd been away. No account of the ocean crossing, either way, and no mention of exotic destinations, traveling partners, chance encounters - experiences often associated with travel that easily generate tales of one's adventures while away. But there *had* been adventures, I was sure. What might have been written on the missing pages haunts me as I hobble from the bed to the toilet, and from the sofa to my favorite rocking chair on the porch – the one with the fabulous view.

I've stumbled on my way to the lavatory in the middle of the night — my stomach was distressed, again. Someone must have left the trap door open. I plunge into the darkness, landing on my bad ankle, and I cannot get up. I feel the wetness between my legs and realize I'm bleeding, but it's not my monthly time. I'm feeling too weak and dizzy to call out for help; a whimper is all my voice can manage.

You no longer use the underground passage, you have confided to me; your wife is a light sleeper and a suspicious bedmate.

"Where are you going?" she asks each time you rise from your wedding bed.

"To the dome," you always answer. "You know I must keep looking."

But no one is looking for me in this dank and deserted place. I think I shall lie here until I die.

This is the distinction between us. You have always been able to negotiate the darkness effortlessly, to explain its significance with intelligence and wit, to enter and then gracefully emerge from its shadows. But I am stalled here, unable to progress in any direction, confused beyond belief, and wretched with secrets I want desperately to spill.

Your greatest discovery is not the Martian canals, nor the beings who constructed them, but rather your ability to bend and transform all the universe according to your unrelenting will. You have married and at the same time you remain a bachelor. I am your secretary and at the same time someone who will unfasten her lingerie blouse when you ask nicely.

Whenever you invite me to share the dome, I am discreet, never arriving or leaving at the same moment as you, never mentioning the activities in which we engage there – that have nothing to do with stargazing – behind the door that is always securely locked.

For some reason Lulu had written more and then had second thoughts, removing what she was not willing to reveal, leaving only references to its sensitive nature.

My mind races to fill in the blank pages but comes up blank as well. I blame this on my time at JPL and, in particular, on the prime rule of image processing. We had to work with what the cameras had recorded – as if they were in charge of the story. If they added transmission noise, we could remove it. If they distorted the image, we could straighten and realign it. We could push and pull the contrast to extremes. But we could not add anything they had not seen and recorded with their own glassy eyes.

"Adding information is not permitted," Dr. Dick would remind me over and over.

But Dr. Dick isn't here. It's just me with Demerol-induced blurriness permeating my brain as I struggle to comprehend the maddeningly incomplete Book of Great Aunt Lulu, which seems to be saying to me:

You have to add more information. You have to read between the lines.

In the darkness I hear a flapping sound, the bloody bed sheets being changed, crisp clean ones unfurled in the air before they are carefully folded around me.

When I open my eyes, Mr. V.M. and his wife hover above me.

"The doctor's been called," Mr. V.M. tells me, while his wife wipes my forehead with a cool damp cloth. "You must stay perfectly still now."

But the sheets in which I've been newly swaddled have come loose already; they are blown into the night sky. Mrs. V.M. hurries to retrieve them. Without the sheets to cover and contain me, I find myself floating upward to join the turbulent currents circling the mesa.

The sound of the unsettled air merges with a screaming siren, its uneven pitch coming to an abrupt stop nearby.

"The universe is expanding," I whisper into the chaotic air around me.

"We will speak of this to no one," Mr. V.M. whispers urgently as he and the doctor carry me to the ambulance that has been summoned to carry me away from here.

"You'll be taking a grand holiday," Mrs. V.M. tells me with a comforting pat on my arm.

But I have not planned a holiday. I have no passage booked, no time off from my job here, no hotel reserved in London, Paris, or Vienna. No joyous anticipation in my soul. Instead, I have a growing fear that someone else has taken charge of my life – based on a fact I cannot deny:

Our secret liaison has shed its innocence.

I'd have to violate the prime rule.

A proper lady of Great Aunt Lulu's era was not always allowed to tell the truth. need to recover the words she'd removed from this journal in order to locate the elusive truth that had to be dressed up in an elaborate Victorian ensemble, hiding more and revealing less. A flash of crimson stocking showing from underneath a soiled white wedding gown – and the shame of a blood-stained bed sheet – are all I need to assemble the rest of the unwritten story:

We have reversed our situations. You are still at work on Mars Hill, while I am here, back in Boston, wrapped in clean white sheets that are changed each morning. I'm cared for day and night by solemn women in soft gray uniforms who look and move like doves.

I must remain perfectly still. I am not supposed to sit up or walk, and I must turn myself with extreme care, for fear that my movements might dislodge the tiny fragile creature inside me, who must be born, it has been decided, even if the child will never know me as his mother.

Mrs. V.M., who writes to me daily, has convinced me that the baby will be well-cared for by the Grey Nuns of Ottawa, who have moved to a town nearby to operate the orphanage there. She has already made the arrangements. I shall never be allowed to visit you there, but I shall think of you constantly, as I always think of faraway creatures of whom I've grown fond. You shall be my tiny secret Martian.

"Can someone bring me notepaper," I ask, "and a fountain pen?"

The quiet woman shrouded in grey robe and hood, her bodice ornamented with a single silver crucifix, tiptoes in to deliver the items I've requested. She fluffs my pillows and smoothes the colorless quilt covering my narrow bed before departing as silently as she'd arrived.

I use the bottom of the cup I drink water from to draw perfect circles, then I fall asleep, dreaming of how I shall fill them: crisscrossed features on the surface of a distant planet, or the patterns on a newborn infant's wrinkled face? Fanciful scenes I shall construct to comfort myself while I am away from the mesa.

When I return, Mrs. V.M. cautions, I shall never speak of the child. His existence shall never be known. I am not sure, however, that the entire universe can keep such a precious secret forever.

There was only one reason a single woman of Great Aunt Lulu's era would go away for an extended period of time and come back to reveal nothing about her absence.

In my mind, only one question remained. A question I shouldn't even allow myself to contemplate, but one nearly impossible to dismiss:

Harry or Dr. P?

-2-

Spring 1945

L etha had been keeping her condition a secret from her husband and was determined to preserve the charade as long as she possibly could. She feared he'd be upset about their having a baby, especially now while we were at war with both Japan and Germany. But when she was five months along and none of her skirts would button at the waist, she feared even more that Vernon would leave her because she was getting fat.

"I'm expecting," Letha finally announced one evening as they were locking up the optical shop.

Vernon didn't say a word all the way home, nor did he speak during dinner – a silent Deep-South-styled affair with salted pork chops, buttered corn on the cob, green beans seasoned with fatback, and fresh sliced tomatoes – made difficult to digest because of the news Letha had served up alongside it.

"It seems we've both been keeping secrets," he finally spoke at the end of their meal, wiping his mouth with a napkin, folding it and placing it under the rim of his dinner plate. "I've been drafted."

"I've been so worried," said Letha, curled in Vernon's arms as they sat together on the sofa, "that you wouldn't want a baby."

"And I was worried about having to leave you," he confessed.

"Maybe this will help." She put his hand on hers, and then both their hands on her abdomen where the new little creature had been planted. "You're going to be a father now. Surely they'll exempt you from serving."

"War or no, I never want to be far away from you." He encircled her with his arms. "I'll go down to the Selective Service Center in the morning, straighten this all out."

No more secrets, they promised each other.

Letha relaxed and felt the baby growing inside her, its first flutters like a fragile butterfly, then its movements stronger as the last few months passed before the hurried trip in a taxi to Massachusetts General. She endured the agonizing hours spent in labor, listening to the hushed tones of the delivery room doctor and nurses unsure what the outcome would be when the baby got stuck midway through the birth canal.

Letha had lost blood, nearly more than she could afford to lose. She felt herself losing consciousness as well. She fought to stay awake until she knew her baby was safely delivered, and that the child was a girl, and that the infant's tiny blue eyes darting in all directions looked exactly like Vernon's.

The new little creature screamed her first greeting into the world, just as Letha passed out.

- 3 -

I'm going to need some clean underwear," Letha told Vernon the night before she and the baby were to be released from the hospital.

Letha was still weak and would need more bed rest at home. But the baby was healthy and seemed ready to get on with her life.

Vernon wanted them both home with him. Their flat seemed big and empty without them. He could take on the household duties, giving Letha time to rest and recover. He'd go home tonight, do the dishes that he'd left soaking, change the bed sheets, and clean the house until it sparkled.

But when he opened Letha's lingerie drawer and sifted through the cool silky undergarments, he was surprised to find something solid nestled among them. He unwrapped a small leather-bound volume filled with unusual handwriting that flowed in all directions.

Vernon stayed up all night long, not straightening up the house, but devouring the words written inside the journal.

The next day when he arrived at the hospital, he told his wife matter-of-factly: "We're going to name her Venus."

And Letha had not disagreed.

The early days of fatherhood were chaotic for Vernon. Since he'd brought Letha and baby Venus home, he'd had little time to spend rejoicing in the birth of a healthy baby and the expected full recovery of his wife. He'd had even less time to wonder why Letha had kept the journal a secret from him. He had placed it back in her underwear drawer without mentioning that he'd found it.

While Letha rocked baby Venus to sleep, Vernon sat in the living room at night, listening to the radio's reports of hopeful progress in the war against Germany and Japan. But he could not stop thinking about what he'd read in the journal, and especially about the pages he'd found missing – removed cleanly, as with a sharp-edged knife. He wondered why they'd been cut out, and by whom. Although he did not know it yet, the absence of the pages would provide an unwritten itinerary for the journey that would eventually carry him away from his beloved wife and precious infant daughter, toward the missing pages of his own existence.

Letha slept fitfully but ate well, growing stronger each day until she could resume most of the household chores, encouraging Vernon to re-open his optical shop. She did not tell him her eyesight had changed again. When she held tiny baby Venus in her arms to rock or feed her, she could not see her daughter's face; the infant's features had been replaced by an unfocused pink patch of nothingness. The more she tried, the less she could see, and her eyeglasses were of no help at all. Her vision was failing rapidly.

"I nearly died having you," my mom liked to say, as if to remind me of all she'd sacrificed on my behalf. The legend of my difficult birth, apparently, was just the beginning.

Within a few months of the day she'd brought me home, my dad was gone and so was her eyesight: She'd become totally blind.

My mom picked up the telephone, felt her way to the "zero" on the dial and asked the operator to help her place a long distance call to New Orleans. Before the week was up, Uncle Ollie had come to visit and to help out until she felt strong enough to take care of us both.

When Ollie arrived, Letha was lethargic and nearly unresponsive, and I was screaming my head off.

"You're gonna get better," he said. He carried Venus in his big hands to Letha so she could nurse the baby in bed. Then he sat at her bedside trying to encourage her. "It's just gonna take some time."

She shook her head as if she did not believe him. She pointed to the chest of drawers, the second drawer from the top, gesturing as if she urgently needed him to get something from it. He walked over and opened the drawer. All he saw was her underwear. But she insisted he probe deeper, underneath the silky garments.

He found and lifted the small handwritten journal, and carried it over to Letha's bed.

She couldn't see, and Ollie couldn't read much at all, but over the next few weeks Letha taught him how to sound out one word at a time. He read short passages aloud to her, and together they marveled at the journal's contents. When they got to the missing pages, they began telling each other stories, imagining what might have been written there. Sometimes they stayed awake all night entertaining each other with their inventions.

Once Letha got stronger and her vision improved, she sent Ollie back home on the Trailways bus. Packed inside his duffle bag was the journal he now could read all by himself. He knew it was not his to keep forever; he'd promised his sister he'd pass it on when the proper time came.

Letha had given him the journal because, by now, she'd absorbed all of its lessons and knew it would be of no further help to her. It was the only thing she had of value, and the only way to repay her big brother for everything he'd done to help her through this roughest of times. Ollie would find inspiration in the book, just as she had. He would set his sights on useful goals and summon the courage to attain them.

After Ollie left, Letha waited for Vernon to get home. And waited and waited. She waited while Venus thrived and grew, standing unsteadily on her feet, gurgling expressions that came close to sounding like words, finally offering sentences and an occasional smile that had to be coaxed forth each time.

She will start asking about her father any day now, Letha fretted. So she resourcefully began creating sentences in her head that she would offer Venus when the inevitable questions poured forth. Some were based on the stories she and Ollie had told each other. What you don't know, you can always make up, she'd learned.

Reasons for Leaving

− 1 −

Vernon did not remember making a decision to leave home. Some previously unknown part of him emerged from deep within to make the decision without his being aware of it.

One morning he'd shaved, dressed in his brown tweed business suit, and then kissed a drowsy Letha and sleeping baby Venus goodbye. He next remembered standing under the big eyeglasses in front of his shop in Kenmore Square, pulling his keychain from his pocket, preparing to insert the key into the lock on the door. But he didn't. Instead he put the keychain back in his pocket and took the underground trolley to South Station, where he waited to board the next train westward.

The journey was instantaneous. He got off the train, thinking he must have changed his mind about traveling and was still in Boston. He figured he'd walk back to Kenmore Square, open the shop and apologize to customers for being late. When he looked around, though, he saw not Boston but rather a frontier town with low stone buildings and a lazy Main Street with sparse traffic where local shopkeepers were opening their businesses to sell clothing, repair shoes, print a small town newspaper, cook and serve breakfast to those just beginning to populate the wide sunlit sidewalks. Spread over it all was an expansive blue sky to die for.

Vernon merged effortlessly with the townspeople. He checked in his jacket pocket for money to order some ham and eggs, but instead of dollar bills he found a frayed folded piece of paper he didn't remember having put there. He pulled it out and unfolded it to see a vaguely familiar image: branched lines contained within a nearly perfect circle. It was the drawing he'd made to show Letha what the inside of her eyes looked like the first time they'd met. He remembered having her look at it while she tried on eyeglasses.

"You must keep looking," he'd told her, placing yet another pair of eyeglasses on the bridge of her nose. "Now tell me, is your vision better or worse?"

"Keep looking." He'd read these same words more recently in Aunt Lulu's journal, as delivered authoritatively by her boss, Dr. P, under the dome with the telescope.

That's why I'm here, Vernon realized, abruptly turning around and strolling briskly toward the west end of Main Street. It took him nearly an hour and a half to climb the winding road to the top of the hill on the west side of town where he'd seen the shining white structure he knew he must visit before heading back to Boston.

He'd come to a place offering the thing he had so desperately been seeking: the secret of good seeing. He'd read about this in his Aunt Lulu's journal. He would discover the secret for himself, then take it back to his beloved wife before she even noticed he was gone. If successful, he'd be home in time for dinner. Afterwards, in the living room, he'd whisper the secret into Letha's ear as she rocked baby Venus to sleep. Letha would look up at him, tears of joy in her instantly repaired eyes, seeing him for the first time perfectly, without squinting, without pain.

"You are so handsome," she'd tell him, and he'd almost smile.

-*2*-

E arly this morning in his office within the Planetary Research Center – a distinctly modern structure compared to the other buildings on Mars Hill – Charles studies the newest images of Mars received in the overnight mail from the other observatories of the International Planetary Patrol. They'd been processed as 70mm negative filmstrips. The astronomers here would use a filmstrip projector to examine each image, only a few inches wide, in order to judge which ones should be enlarged and printed as detailed 8x10s for further study on the more sophisticated planet plate projector.

But Charles can't wait. Percival Lowell had used a magnifying glass to look at early planetary negatives, so Charles grabs the modern equivalent: a photographer's loupe. He hurries to place the negatives on the light table where, sure enough, he sees the Martian blemish on the photos taken at observatories in Chile, South Africa and Australia. The same blemish as in Flagstaff: a small dark fluff visible for two days and then gone.

There seems to be eventual agreement among all the astronomers who study the new images. They all see what they call "transient phenomena," temporary changes on the planet's surface, not uncommon. No one reasons that these areas may in fact be dust storms forming, or that a small dust storm may be the prelude to a much larger one, and Charles has not suggested otherwise. It is not his job to tell the astronomers what they've seen. Instead, he works privately on the paper he's presently refining, in which he has written his bold pronouncement:

The seasonal tilt of the Martian axis and its related temperature change increase the occurrence of dust storms, particularly south of the planet's equator. Conditions are ripe for a massive dust storm to develop within the next few months.

Carefully, with a grease pencil, he marks on the filmstrip sleeve which images are appropriate for printing, requesting extra copies of each that he'll release with his written prediction. He needs to get his paper into the proper hands, someone who'd not only agree with him, but would act on the knowledge – and soon. If the storm forms according to his prediction, it may seriously interfere with the Mariner spacecraft now approaching the red planet.

All along Charles had thought this was a solo act, but he realizes now he needs someone in a supporting role. All his contacts at JPL are hopelessly out of date – and he'd not left on the best of terms. "Flighty," they'd called him. Unfocused enthusiasm when grounded thinking is required.

He thinks briefly of the girl convalescing just across the courtyard in the Slipher apartment, whose name, he's learned, is Venus Dawson. If only she hadn't gotten herself fired from JPL, she might be able to help him. Maybe she still could.

"Did you know I was named after Venus the cow?" she'd challenged him this morning when he'd brought her a mug of coffee and a doughnut with candy sprinkles. She'd picked the sprinkles off, one by one, before tasting the doughnut.

"Now I do," he'd replied.

"Will you show me the barn where she used to live?"

"Sorry, no can do," said Charles. "It was torn down sometime in the forties and another residence built in its place. I think the caretaker used to live in it."

"What was the caretaker's name?"

The girl showed an uncommon interest in events long past and in buildings long demolished. He'd have to find some way to entice her back to the present.

After he'd descended the stairs into the basement archives, he climbed back up, breathless with the name he would present to his curious guest. Now he knew exactly why the past still held sway in her life. Moreover, he knew what she was doing here.

"The caretaker's name," he told her, "was Vernon Dawson."

The thin blue-eyed man in a worn tweed jacket had shown up, looking for work, nearly twenty-seven years ago.

"What kind of work do you do?" the director had asked him.

"I'm not fussy," he'd replied. "I'll do whatever needs to be done."

V.M. Slipher, who'd become director upon the founder's death, had encountered similar visitors during his forty-year tenure on Mars Hill. They always appeared suddenly, asking for little, but needing desperately to stay, as if some invisible beacon had called to them from afar and they'd come, drawn to the safety and the mystery of its powerful beam.

"I have a building that needs to be cleaned out," Slipher said. "I'm not sure what to do with it, but it's just sitting there now, and surely could be put to some use."

The two men walked across the Observatory grounds and up a slight incline to a low, igloo-shaped structure cloaked on all sides by thick stands of pine trees.

"Just before he died, our founder built his second dome partially underground," Slipher explained, descending a few steps before unlocking a weathered wooden door. "He was convinced the air below ground was calmer than the air above it."

They entered a domed room where a tilted metal tower with a broad circular base loomed center-stage.

"Unfortunately, he was wrong. The turbulence below ground is even worse, and we've never been able to use this telescope effectively."

"How big is the reflector?" the visitor asked, pointing to the wide mirror anchoring the instrument.

"When it came, it was forty inches." Slipher was pleased to find out this man knew his way around a telescope, or could at least recognize one. "But now it's housed as a forty-two-inch."

"Perhaps I can work with it when I'm done cleaning up here. I know a little about optics."

Back in the director's office, the two men came to an agreement and shook hands to seal it. Slipher pulled a thick leather book from a table near the door.

"This is our tradition," he explained. "Everyone who comes here signs the guest book."

Vernon Dawson, wrote the newest employee on a vacant line. In the space labeled "Hometown" he paused before penning: *Cosmos.*

"I see." The director stared at the last word his new employee had written – it was the same word the founder had often used to describe his own location in the universe. Slipher looked into the man's deep-set blue eyes and realized that the expanding universe he'd charted during long cold nights under the dome had come full circle here on Mars Hill.

The man who did not exist had come home.

- 3 -

No more pills. I flush them down the toilet. As warmly and crazily seductive as they are, I'm in greater need of all the mental clarity I can muster.

I'm out of bed, hobbling around, ignoring the pain, trying doors to rooms I haven't yet explored, and finding most of them locked. One opens, surprisingly, and I limp through it, coming face to face with Saturn and its glowing rings.

I'm on the upper level of the rotunda, still illuminated by the Saturn chandelier even though it's after midnight. Built-in bookshelves curve with the circular walls. The books lining the shelves are old, emitting a distinct moldy odor. Every edition of the *Annals of Lowell Observatory* is here, plus assorted scientific volumes and probably every book ever published about Mars and the other planets. The visitor logbooks are arranged by year. I find the date I was born, ease myself onto the top step of the spiral staircase and start reading forward from there.

Finally, around 2 a.m., I find the name I've been searching for.

Vernon Dawson had excellent handwriting – the capital V looped at the top with a distinct bottom point, the D also with an upper loop and crisp bottom point.

Next to the name, another carefully penned word, his hometown: *Cosmos*. Not Boston. Not any other place that could be visited. Not anywhere he could be found.

I run one finger across the carefully inked letters, trying to learn more about the man who'd written them, but they offer no further knowledge. I feel no connection to these words, nor to the person who'd penned his name so neatly, my supposed father.

Vernon had awakened in the calm just before dawn on the cot in his newly constructed home.

"Everyone who works here must have a place to live," Slipher had explained. "It's our tradition."

The wood-shingled cottage, modest in scale and barely furnished, stood near to where a barn used to be. There were no animals here now, only scientists and occasional visitors from the town below. But there still were references to the beloved Observatory cow named Venus, after whom Vernon had named his baby daughter.

Vernon realized he'd been away from his Boston home for over a year now. He missed his family, but persevered in his quest. He could not go home empty-handed to Letha and Venus who, by now, must be toddling around their Back Bay flat.

Each morning he sat on his cot, put his head in his hands and lamented his failure thus far to discover the secret of good seeing. Each morning he'd talk himself into standing up, shaving and dressing. Then, prepared for his day, he'd exit the cottage, leaving the door slightly ajar to encourage fresh air to enter. Summer days in Flagstaff could be relentlessly hot and often humid as well, unless a thunderstorm came along to freshen the air.

No one wanted to use the oddly sunken telescope Vernon had seen when he first arrived on Mars Hill, "a dog," one of the astronomers called it, so Vernon had easily claimed it as his own. Now, as he did each morning, he hurried along the untraveled pathway leading to the unpopular instrument, the familiar anticipation building inside him.

As maintenance man, Vernon had free run of the grounds and keys to all the buildings, which he kept on a key ring attached to his belt. Now he pulled one key apart from the others, unlocked a door and descended into a little round room. Quickly, before the sun rose to outshine everything else in the sky, he turned the mirrored telescope toward the planet whose position he now knew without calculating.

The air currents outside the sunken dome cast their typical soft filter over the reddish object, offering smudged shapes rather than crisp lines on its surface, but Vernon took it all in, pleased to look for meaning in the turbulence. His Aunt Lulu had written in her journal that looking over time offers a view that is constantly changing; the change itself provides the truth we're looking for. But how could good seeing come out of this lack of clarity? How could clear-headed understanding solve a problem whose solution is always visibly blurred? This is where his thinking always stalled, and he could get no further.

His boss, V.M. Slipher, had figured out long ago, by using a spectrograph, that celestial change can be charted according to the color of the light emitted by distant objects shifting as they continue along their routes: bluer if approaching, redder if receding. Years later, a brilliant interpretation based on Slipher's data, by another astronomer named Hubble, made the bold but convincing case finally accepted by the scientific community and the public: The whole universe was in motion, expanding, in fact. Distant galaxies were rushing away from us, even as others, like nearby Andromeda, were speeding closer. Trying to see one object in one still instant – an elusive goal the man buried in the splendid mausoleum over near the dome had spent the final years of his life pursuing – is meaningless. Aunt Lulu, Vernon reasoned, must have gotten some of her strange notions from Slipher.

"You've worked here for a long time, haven't you?" Vernon finally got the courage to ask his boss one afternoon when he went to the director's office to collect his weekly pay. "You must have known Miss Lulu."

"Is that why you've come here?" Slipher inquired.

"I'm not sure," Vernon answered truthfully.

"She was a lady ahead of her time," the director said, as if suddenly remembering someone long forgotten. "A little eccentric, to be sure. She always said we had to keep looking, even when there was nothing to see."

"Looking at what?" Vernon wondered out loud.

"Precisely," Slipher chortled. "Looking when there's nothing to see is a good man's waste of time."

Red-cheeked with shame, Vernon fled the director's office; he'd just been told he was not a good man.

A good man, he knew, would not be here, tinkering with tools and telescopes, stubbornly pursuing a vision that made no sense.

A good man would be at home, earning a decent living, taking care of his wife, learning how to make his daughter laugh out loud.

A nother day, another visit.

This morning Charles brings me a thermos of coffee, a raspberry Danish and a stack of worn folders. I don't really like raspberries, I don't need the extra calories in the Danish now that I'm practically immobile, and the stack of folders reminds me of all the work orders I used to get at JPL.

But I decide not to complain, and thank him instead. The painkillers, I realize, must have encouraged a softer side of me that continues even though I'm off them now. Which is just as well, since I'm so dependent upon the kindness of strangers. And they don't get much stranger than Charles.

Today he's wearing a white sports coat over his white shirt, and navy blue trousers that are too short, revealing his white socks and white loafers. Let there be no confusion here: He's still auditioning for the hero's role.

"You might want to look through these while you recuperate," he says, placing the folders on the kitchen table. "Please handle them with care. They're from our personnel files."

Within an hour I'd learned the truth about the employee named Vernon Dawson: He'd worked here for nine years as a janitor and handyman before disappearing from Mars Hill as suddenly, it seemed, as he'd vanished from Kenmore Square.

The person who'd signed all the personnel papers was director of the Observatory: V.M. Slipher. The same Mr. V.M. that Aunt Lulu had written about in her journal, the person for whom this building was named and, according to Charles, the mostly unheralded astronomer who'd found the initial evidence that the universe was expanding. Slipher had hired my dad a few months after I was born and had assigned him various inglorious duties, including one working as caretaker of a sunken dome I hadn't realized existed until now.

The final document in the files was Vernon Dawson's separation notice. On it Slipher had written on the line after "Reason for Leaving": *unknown*.

"Where'd he go?" I demand, so angry that I'd hobbled down the steps from my apartment and over to the modern brick building.

The receptionist seated just inside looks up quizzically. "Just who is it you're looking for, Ma'am?"

In a small windowless room at the end of a long hallway, Charles sits at a messy metal desk surrounded by tables strewn with cardboard boxes and film canisters. Large photos of Mars, Saturn and Jupiter are tacked haphazardly to all four walls of the cluttered room. This place offers none of the regulated spic-and-span sparseness so prevalent at JPL.

I toss the stack of files onto his desk.

He looks up, surprised. "You can walk."

I'd been in too much of a hurry to use my crutches, and didn't realize until now that my ankle had healed enough for me to put my weight on it.

"Yeah, I guess so."

"If you're looking for your father," he says, reading my mind, "I don't know what happened to him. No one does."

"Can you show me the cottage where he lived?" I ask, knowing the answer before he says it.

"Sorry, it's been torn down."

Didn't anything last around here?

"What about the sunken telescope, then?"

"It's still standing, but you'll have to walk all the way to Pluto," he tells me with a silly grin.

The "Pluto Walk" is an inclined route whose colorful signage and scaled-down mileage markers demonstrate the relative distances between one planet and the next.

"I'll spare you the spiel I usually deliver along the way," he tells me, sensing my impatience as we pass the asteroids on our way to Jupiter.

"That's nice of you," I reply, wincing, trying to keep pace with sure-footed Charles.

He stops to let me catch up at Pluto, the most distant planet situated at the end of the walkway. He points with pride to a round stone building just beyond it, topped with the flat white roof so typical here.

"The Pluto dome houses the telescope used to discover Pluto," Charles explains. "You wanna take a look inside?"

"Nope."

"Suit yourself."

"Where's the sunken one?"

Charles gestures off to the left, then heads toward a low, curved silver structure nearly hidden by a thick stand of pine trees.

"This place isn't even on the tour," he grouses as we approach.

Up close, the sunken dome looks like a displaced igloo built with shiny aluminum foil instead of ice. Since there are no vertical supports, its foundation must lie underground. Shovels, rakes and a wheelbarrow are propped against its gracefully curved sides.

"We use it as our landscaping headquarters now."

Three steps down take us inside to a big, round, nearly empty room ripe with the earthen scent of freshly turned soil – the smell I associate with gardens and, more recently, graveyards.

"Step carefully," Charles advises me, pointing to a low metal platform built into the center of the floor.

"That's where the telescope was mounted," he tells me.

"What happened to the telescope?"

"It's out in the courtyard. You've passed it several times already."

A massive telescope that must have cost a lot of money, reduced to garden décor? I have to know why.

"Bad luck, pure and simple," Charles explains. "Bad luck for everyone who touched it."

The glassmaker has been summoned once more to Mars Hill. I've just posted the letter in the afternoon mail. This time you have instructed him to build a looking glass that will literally reflect the heavens. You have made a bold decision about how to control the light traveling through the night sky. Your new telescope will bounce the light onto a perfectly polished mirror and from there to the lens, where the eye will encounter it.

Of the three requirements you have set for good seeing, the glassmaker has mastered one: the perfect instrument. And you offer another: the intelligent eye. The third, however – a clear and calm atmosphere – still eludes you.

"The light that shifts, the glare that drifts," you describe it despairingly.

You decide to house this reflector in a new dome that is being built partially underground. Ten feet are dug out of the earth in a large circle; tall arcs of curved wood crisscross above to create the frame. The enormous instrument, its mirror forty inches across, will be carefully installed in its wide sturdy base. You say you will not be bothered by unsettled air when you are underground.

Mr. V.M. is not convinced that the sunken dome will perform as you claim it will, and says privately that you might as well be digging a grave for yourself.

I step around the abandoned telescope mount and wander into an alcove where small gardening implements of every shape and style hang from racks mounted on one wall. Opposite, a worktable and shelves above it are lined with tiny figures made from what appear to be metal scraps. On each one's face, a shiny fragment has been glued. I step closer. Mirror shards. Hundreds of them with shiny faces, each one reflecting me.

"Far out, huh?" says Charles. "The current handyman makes them out of whatever he finds lying around here."

"I call them the Martians," another man's voice announces.

I turn to see that a slight but solidly built young man wearing workman's clothes and carrying garden shears has entered the sunken dome. He smiles at me with an eerie familiarity and I recognize him, even though I'm certain we've never met: He's the Harry of this place now.

"Where'd you get all the little mirrors?" I ask him.

"It used to be one big mirror..." the young man begins with a heavy sigh.

"Quite a tragic story..." Charles solemnly confirms.

Autumn 1956

Over the years Vernon had become comfortable, an unfavorable sign, he acknowledged. There was no edge, no instinctive drive toward discovery, and worst of all, no revelation that would take him back to his family – if they'd even have him now.

He'd become a tinkerer, finding one thing and then another to fiddle with – so much so that the director had once said that Vernon reminded him of the long-ago brothers who had engineered and built most of this place, the ones who'd had a sign on their shop downtown that announced they were "makers and menders of anything."

"We're going to spruce up the reflector," Slipher announced one day, "Maybe give it another chance to shine."

The director seemed sincerely saddened that their largest telescope was also the worst for viewing.

"See what you can do about polishing the mirror," he instructed Vernon.

By now Vernon knew the sunken reflector well. He'd adjusted the inclination of the axis of the telescope to the correct angle, to align it with the Earth's axis. He'd adjusted the drive clock, enabling the instrument to follow star motions more accurately. He'd fixed everything that could be fixed, and still no one wanted to use it.

While everyone else employed or visiting here gravitated either to the historic twenty-four inch telescope, or to the newer refractor in the Pluto dome, Vernon alone had come to appreciate the quirkiness of the one housed in the sunken dome. He steadfastly believed the massive instrument and its unusual placement underground held some truth intended specifically for him, a truth he'd just not yet been able to see.

He had carefully removed the old mirror coating and was now busy applying the new reflective surface when he heard the lighter-than-air sound of glass splintering. He watched helplessly as the mirror shattered into thousands of pieces.

Vernon raced from the sunken dome and fled down the hill, passing the silver-domed administration building, hoping his boss was not at that moment peering from his corner office window. He fled to the rear side of the abandoned Baronial Mansion, up onto the veranda. And before he knew it, he'd descended into the darkness. He closed the trap door above his head, climbed down the rustic staircase, and wedged himself behind it, weeping with anguish and regret. A once-good man as broken now as the ruined mirror he'd left in shards.

I'm high enough here, even without the pain-killers.

Mid-afternoon and I'm back in my upstairs apartment, splayed across the wide leather sofa, my sweaty skin stuck to it. I've opened all the windows and doors to encourage whatever breeze can be summoned, but it's not just the heat that's exhausted me – it's the ultra-thin air at this seven-thousand-foot elevation. My whole body aches. I'm wiped out after the "Pluto Walk" and its revelations. This is the most I've moved – or thought – in over a week.

Outside a stronger breeze picks up, and a cloud scooting across the sun momentarily dims the daylight. But that's just the beginning. Soon the wind begins to howl, forcing its way down the chimney and out through the fireplace into the living room, as if hell-bent on rearranging all its furnishings. The old glass windowpanes rattle in their wooden frames as an afternoon thunderstorm – the sudden kind that gathers steam quickly – unleashes itself. Torrents of rain follow, pushed nearly sideways by the wind, and I must jump up and hurry to close all the windows.

Suddenly I'm furious with the realization that this place delivers the opposite of the clarity it claims to offer. There is no calm clear air here: Mars Hill is a messy whirling vortex of time and space, an insistent atmospheric eddy whose predatory currents circle the mesa constantly, upsetting the souls and visions of all who climb to the summit.

Just like my lame-ass dad, I'm one in a long line of here-today-gone-tomorrow transients who have no idea why they've arrived on Mars Hill. Sooner or later we all show up, and sooner or later we all have to leave. But not before some amount of unraveling occurs.

Everyone who comes here, comes apart here.

-5-

*J*am far away in civilized New York, on my way back from Boston to Flagstaff, when the sudden announcement is delivered to my hotel, a terse and painful telegram from Mr. V.M.

You'd collapsed suddenly; a brain hemorrhage. No one saw it coming. You'd spent your final night on Earth observing Mars – small comfort to those remaining.

Within hours another telegram arrives, this one from your stern widow, ordering me not to return. My services are no longer needed; my trunks will be packed and shipped to me in Boston. I shall not be able to see Mars or Mars Hill again. I imagine she'd actually smiled as she composed this message, this time banishing me forever.

She has decided to keep you with her on Mars Hill. You will be interred in a grand mausoleum honoring your memory. She will spend the remainder of her days mourning your loss, polishing your reputation, and making certain the world remembers your uniquely visioned and reasoned contributions to it.

But I think you have already left the mesa, your spirit and intellect relocated to Mars, certainly your idea of heaven. I hope water flows there along the finely engineered canals you discovered, and that your Martian garden grows as bountifully as your earthly garden once did. Are the Martians as charming as you described them to me? Do they appreciate your sparkling wit, your quick turns on the dance floor, your unwavering dedication to discovering and telling their tragic yet inspiring story? Have you found capable Martian brothers to build you a little house in which you have settled down?

We Earthlings may never know what you saw through the telescope that final, fateful night of your life. You departed suddenly, your viewing log still open by your side, your writing instrument tucked securely in your hand as if you were preparing to enter evidence of what you had just observed. A heavenly revelation, perhaps, that shall remain unvoiced.

I must remember to ask you, when I have left this Earth, as well, and encounter you again, as I truly believe I shall, in the unrestrained lives we shall lead after our deaths: *What did you see that took you away from us?*

Now that I can walk again, I know I'll have to leave soon, but not before I take my own self-guided tour of Mars Hill.

This afternoon, slowly and carefully I descend two steep flights of stairs from my upstairs apartment into the cool dark basement of the Slipher Building, my first stop. There's a musty smell and a slightly claustrophobic feeling: The hallways are narrow, the ceilings low, and all the closed doors seem slightly undersized.

I open each one in turn and peek inside to find mainly tall cardboard boxes full of loose papers I don't have the time or patience to sift through. One room reveals more, however: a wide table stacked high with dog-eared photo albums – a visual history of the place I've only been able to read about so far!

I pull up a chair and make myself comfortable, select an album, and turn its wide brittle pages slowly and carefully, each one revealing more: The Baronial Mansion as a compact cottage, then as the rambling residence it came to be. Harry and his wife posing in Sunday-best on the wide veranda. A spotted cow grazing outside a rustic barn – Venus! Percival Lowell tending his garden. Percival Lowell posing with his mink-wrapped wife. Percival Lowell wearing a beret and looking through the big telescope. An unidentified but nicely outfitted Victorian lady sitting rigidly upright, one open eye positioned near the eyepiece of the same big telescope, wearing all white, smiling like a just-pronounced bride – Great Aunt Lulu!

You cannot send me away. I shall never leave my place in the viewing chair, never dress in another outfit, never take my eye away from the distant view that is exclusively mine for the moment. Did you think I was taking a walk on the mesa? Practicing my serve on the tennis court? Did you think I'd gone to nap in my room or into the library to type a letter? Then you are mistaken; I'm still here. You sat me in this chair, under this telescope. You told me to hold still. I shall do as you say; I shall keep looking as long as this likeness remains.

This photo – and what it says to me – is all the proof I need that Great Aunt Lulu had not left Mars Hill, like all the others. Some otherworldly part of her must linger here still. Some unsettled part of her soul still wearing her wedding ensemble, hovering inside the dome, one patient eye positioned at the eyepiece, determined to keep looking.

There was always more to be seen, she'd written, *always more begging my understanding.*

Her physical self may have been banished from the Observatory, but even this act had not put an end to her "observations."

I have no telescope here.

Last week I took a trolley over to the Harvard Observatory in my efforts to locate you. But without you on my arm, they would not let me in to take a look.

Do you have a telescope on Mars, and is it trained toward Earth? If so, I hope you will look for me – I'm back in Boston, in my Newbury Street place. I shall be standing in the front window at twilight, just as your new home, your red planet, emerges in the darkening sky, a tiny point of rosy light.

"A little light in the sky serves to balance the glare of sunlight reflected onto the planet's surface," you often said. "It brings out the details."

Do you see that I am wearing the lace collar you gave me?

As I climb from the basement, I hear the sonorous voice using a fake Boston accent tuned for dramatic effect:

"This, my friends, is where the Lowell story began…"

I follow the sound of Charles' voice and step through a door leading to the rotunda. He's clad in his vintage outfit, now topped by a red beret, and stands amid a barely contained group of middle-schoolers, gesturing to the shiny brass telescope perched on its tripod.

"This was Percival Lowell's first telescope. He sent A. E. Douglass and this instrument to the Arizona Territory in 1894 to seek out a suitable site for his new observatory."

A freckled-faced boy turns to accuse his teacher: "You told us the telescope here was really big."

Charles steps in to rescue her. "The big telescope is in the dome," he announces, gesturing toward the door. "This one has a six-inch lens. The big one has a twenty-four." He gets the boy's attention again by spreading both arms wide to indicate how increcibly massive the other telescope is.

"When can we see it?" a sweet-faced girl asks, her inquiry echoed by a chorus of "yeah-whens" from her less patient classmates.

"Soon," Charles promises. "But first, take a look at this." He steps to the next display. "This instrument, a comparator, was used to discover Pluto. When two photos of the same part of the sky are compared, any object moving across the stars – which remain staticnary – may be a new planet. Anybody want to take a look?"

"Who cares about lousy Pluto?" the same wise-ass boy complains.

I'd heard enough from the rude children. But as I leave the rotunda a crazed but inspired thought hits me: Charles just said his tour group would be heading to the come next. I need to see the telescope one more time. I have to find out if Lulu's still there, like she said she'd be. This may be my only chance.

He has invited me to visit the dome this afternoon and, of course, I can deny him nothing

I climb the stairs back to my apartment and emerge a few minutes later, stuffed into Great Aunt Lulu's white dress. Without a Victorian corset to minimize my waist, I'm unable to fasten all the tiny pearl buttons on the back of the bodice, so a gaping hole reveals my skin there. Moreover, the dress is much too long; Great Aunt Lulu must have been a tall lady. The shoes are too small, but the ridiculous hat fits, so I perch it on my head.   cross the short patch of lawn, climb the steps to the door of the dome, now propped open in anticipation of my arrival, and slip inside.

Maneuvering quietly and carefully behind the tour group, I raise my long skirt to avoid tripping. I look down and see my flip-flops crossing the old wooden floor; they're the only things that keep me grounded in the present.

"Some unusual methods have been employed to support the substantial weight of the roof," the man in the red beret tells the school group. He pushes a button on a conso e near the telescope and the wooden dome comes to life, creaking as it begins to move, buoyed by thirty or so large tires mounted at the juncture of the roof and wall.

"The Ford truck tires you see all around were improvised by a creative handyman sometime around 1956," he tells them. "As you can see, they work quite well."

Quickly, while the schoolchildren are all mesmerized by the rotating tires and groaning roof, I climb the viewing platform and place myself in the viewing chair, arching my neck and positioning my eye near the eyepiece of the big telescope, as if I'm about to take a look.

It's an odd posture, but one, you assure me, that looks very fetching.

"I'm here," I announce as the roof stops turning and the creaking stops. Everyone looks up.

"It's a ghost," one child squeals. A few others scream.

"I'm wearing my wedding dress, just as you asked."

"Who's that?" someone asks.

I introduce myself to them: "I am Lulu Leonard."

"Who's Woo-hoo Leonard?" the wise-ass boy with the big mouth inquires.

"Uh, she used to work here," says Charles, struggling to maintain control while trying his best to shoot me an evil eye.

But his glare veers way off-course, because by now I've convinced myself that I'm no longer Venus. I'm channeling pure Lulu. The next words pour forth all on their own.

"I was in love with you, Percival Lowell," I tell the man in the red beret.

"The whole world was in love with me – with *him*, I mean, Lowell," Charles counters nervously. "He was a brilliant, handsome and thoroughly charming fellow."

"I had your baby."

Now the school children giggle uncontrollably. Their teacher claps her hands together sharply. The room falls silent.

"Come with me, boys and girls," she leads her unruly students outdoors. The big-mouthed boy turns to blow me a kiss.

"I'm going to have to ask you to leave now," Charles tells me after the school group has departed.

"I was just about to go anyway."

"Good, then."

At last the truth is told. And just like that, you've banished me from the dome – again – for telling it.

OBSERVING RIGHTS

-7-

I am finally settling into my place on Newbury Street. Just yesterday a brand new writing desk was delivered. The desk is much like the one I left behind on Mars Hill, a small but sturdy piece, with Chippendale legs and a fold-down surface that reveals lovely drawers, nooks and crannies for storing all my writing materials that I've now managed to restock by visiting the stationery store a few blocks east.

This morning I have filled my fountain pen and have opened this little notebook. This time there is no hesitation; the ink from my pen flows freely across one page and onto the next, forming words of adoration, heartfelt expressions of the exquisite bond you and I still share as citizens of the universe.

Now that you are dead, your wife can no longer claim you as her own. You belong to history; I am part of your history, and you are part of mine.

And yet I am a proper lady and discretion still seems appropriate. As I write, I hide your initials and mine inside innocuous words. Our names are nestled together between the covers of this volume, wherein our private story shall remain undisturbed for an eternity. I call my new pages "An Afterglow," referencing the part of your brilliance that remains with me still.

My words are true but also respectful to us both. Our history is real but also inventive, because you are gone and I am left to sort it out as best I can.

AFTERGLOW

My last night on Mars Hill, I'm in the splendid apartment I'll vacate tomorrow. I'm standing in front of the full-length mirror mounted on the door of the enormous oak armoire, when I see a handsome gray-haired man with deep-set blue eyes standing behind me. I recognize him: The founder's portraits are everywhere. (Didn't Great Aunt Lulu describe seeing him in her mirror just like this?) But then, using that hopscotch logic that works so well in dreams, I realize instead that he's my long-lost father. He looks exactly the way my mom had always described him – tall, clear blue eyes, the barest hint of a smile.

I bombard him with questions: *What are you doing here? Why'd you leave? Where'd you go? Why didn't you ever come back home?*

It's like I'm a whiny little girl again.

The man in the mirror says nothing. Instead he pulls one pair of eyeglasses after another from his trouser pocket, offering each to me as if to say, *Try these on.*

I don't need glasses, I keep telling him, *but he is insistent.*

Finally I turn my back on the mirror, face him and look directly into his deep-set eyes. They're mine, the same eyes, the same shade of blue. I have discovered the missing link and the reason for my being drawn magnet-like to this dark place: The founder, my father, me – we all look the same!

I'd always suspected that my mom made up the story of my dad but never could figure out why she'd gone to such great lengths to deceive me. It's true that being an unmarried mother was taboo in oh-so-socially-conscious Boston. But maybe, I'd thought, she had just enjoyed inventing things, adding fancy to fact, savoring and sharing with me the curious results.

If my father did not exist, then who am I but the illegitimate child of my less-than-honest and wildly imaginative mom? Yet, if my father was real, then he could have been Lulu's baby, born out of wedlock and given up for adoption soon after. Perhaps he'd come here, as had I, to discover her secrets. In some universe or another both possibilities exist. Unfortunately, in the one where I currently reside, the truth will never be known.

The man in the mirror shifts his weight impatiently from one foot to the other. He's been trying to help me see clearly, but I've resisted his efforts. And now he's leaving.

"I shall never stop looking!" I call out.

But he's vanished again from this place. The blue-eyed man I've never laid eyes on but want so desperately to claim. The father from which I've managed to construct my off-the-cuff lineage, by looking in an old mirror.

-9-

Vernon woke up in the underground passage, stiff with discomfort from sleeping curled up behind the stairway. He realized he'd spent all night dreaming about his blue-eyed daughter Venus, nearly ten years old now. Had Letha even told the girl she'd had a father, once? Did Venus know his name? Did she ever ask where he was?

Vernon had never known his own father's name. Here everyone knew the truth, but no one acknowledged it. Vernon's own deep-set blue eyes mimicked those looking down from nearly every wall: photographs of the founder, who'd set up this place for "good seeing," the man whose own acute vision had enabled him to see the canals on Mars – canals Vernon had never been able to see with his own eyes. He'd failed every time he'd tried to focus blurred shapes and soft shadows into crisp networked lines. He hadn't been able to see the heavens according to his Aunt Lulu's instructions, either; the more he'd looked for meaning in the turbulent air, the less he'd been able to see.

Over the years he had searched the Observatory records for clues to his own history and had discovered that the founder and his wife never had children. She had been well past her childbearing years when they'd married. The name of his mother remained a mystery. The founder had a reputation among the women; he'd romanced them all. Any one of his lovers might have given birth to a boy named Vernon, then sent him off to an orphanage to be raised. Ironically, this orphanage was in Lowell, Massachusetts, a town named for the founder's family, from where Vernon had been rescued by "Aunt" Virginia, perhaps a trusted and tight-lipped family friend who'd managed to bring a mysterious and disjointed family of stargazers back together before she'd disappeared for good.

His more recently discovered aunt, Aunt Lulu, must have known about his true parentage, but had offered scant clues during the brief time he'd known her, most likely unreliable information due to her dementia, and she'd died without answering any of his direct inquiries on the subject. Vernon had searched here for more information about Lulu as well, but had not found any evidence that "Aunt Lulu" was actually his aunt. Why the woman had claimed kinship, he had yet to fathom.

The clarity he'd come here seeking had eluded him on all fronts: in the heavens above and in the historical records all around him. He was miserable with the enormity of his failures.

Vernon crawled outside and stood unsteadily. He shoved his hands into the pockets of his wrinkled jacket to straighten it and pulled out the drawing he still kept folded there. Networked lines inside a perfectly drawn circle – canals on Mars! The drawing of Letha's eyes and the surface of Mars had fused into one and the same. He'd had the answer with him all along, but only now could he follow the logic he held in his hand to its inevitable conclusion: *Good seeing is a reflection of the vision seen.*

Seeing and being seen are compatible events. If one is determined to see with clarity, then that same one must be willing to be seen with the same definition. If there is difficulty seeing, then there must also be difficulty in being seen. Both problems must be addressed and corrected in concert, or no good seeing will result.

Vernon fished inside his other pocket and was surprised to find there a shard of glass from the telescope mirror he'd broken. He lifted the shard and looked into it, expecting to see reflected there a miniature version of himself, his entire being and his life history on the surface of the shiny fragment. Instead he saw nothing, and at long last Vernon learned a startling truth about himself.

He could not see himself now on Mars Hill because he'd never actually been here. Letha, baby Venus, and he – never a family. His own drab life, first as a dispensing optician and then as handyman all an illusion, none of it real.

His actual parents had not left him behind after all; they'd taken him along with them on their fateful journey. He'd been on the train that had left the tracks, written up in the newspapers as an accident claiming the lives of all on board.

But they'd not been killed after all! They'd just relocated – to a distant planet in another universe where life went on much as it did on Earth, with the identities of its inhabitants shifted slightly toward the blue or the red, just enough to hide themselves from curious eyes peering though telescopes on Earth.

Slipher had been right all along: The universe itself is a giant version of the underground telescope, a massive mirror curving in upon itself, offering its infinite visions to the one who is willing to look and to be seen there. When Vernon shattered the mirror, he'd splintered his own universe.

He pocketed the mirror shard and walked away. Only on Earth had Vernon ceased to exist.

MANY WORLDS

-*10*-

L
etha had awakened in her afterlife, refreshed from a long and sound sleep in a comfortable bed covered with a soft yellow counterpane. She'd already made the bed, pulling the sheets tight and tucking them in, smoothing the counterpane. Now she was sitting in a wide rocking chair positioned in front of tall double windows.

At first she thought she was in her old room at the YWCA, then realized the view out the big windows was not the long green Boston Common but rather a place she'd never seen before: a ruggedly impressive mountain range topped by menacing storm clouds tinged red by the setting sun, suggesting a serious but not imminent threat.

The room, simply yet pleasantly furnished, seemed to have been long abandoned by its former occupant. A thin sheen of dust covered the windowsill, the dressing table, the mirror hung above it, and the surface of the small, elegant oak writing desk.

Letha rose and walked to the desk, stooping to retrieve a fountain pen that had fallen to the floor. I can still write the letter to Venus, Letha decided, now while the storm is in abeyance. I'll put it in the evening mail; the westbound train leaves at seven.

She peered into the darkened recesses of the desktop, searching for stationery, but discovered instead a picture frame tucked into one corner and turned upside-down. She picked it up and was startled to see a portrait of a distinguished blue-eyed gentleman, the same man who'd been at the train station, the one she'd mistakenly assumed to be her husband Vernon. The man in the photograph was posed with care, leaning on an oddly-angled walking stick, his hair and moustache perfectly groomed, his trim body luxuriously outfitted in a tweed three-piece suit, his tall shirt collar anchored by a perfectly fashioned necktie.

As Letha held the photograph in front of her, she thought she saw a subtle smile escape the man's mouth. In stark contradiction, his solemn blue eyes focused just beyond her, burdened by private knowledge of what they'd seen, with implications so unsettling he could not decide how to reveal his findings, or to whom. Then the blue eyes shifted and gazed straight into hers, as if she were transparent and he could peer directly into her racing heart.

"Believe me," Letha thought she heard him say as she hurriedly replaced the portrait in its hiding place. She couldn't tell whether his muffled words were a well-voiced instruction, or an anguished plea from a sorrowful man who'd left his family for the noblest of reasons.

The blue-eyed man had used Vernon's voice, but a version that was thin and echoing, suggesting that her husband was far removed from this time and this place.

We are both dead and gone. Letha understood in that instant that her time on Earth was finished and, moreover, that she need look no further on this planet for her errant husband. Searching the remainder of the universe – that would take some time.

She wiped her hands together vigorously to get rid of the dust they'd picked up while exploring the abandoned room. She took a resolute step forward and then another, carrying her out the door and into a hallway. With the next step, however, she plunged into the sudden darkness of an open trapdoor and vanished.

-11-

My suitcase is packed and sitting by the front door. Charles nearly trips over it as he rushes in, grinning with unrestrained confidence. I'm sitting at the kitchen table, sipping one final cup of tea.

"I thought you were mad at me," I say.

He ignores my comment, opens the clasp on a big manila envelope and spreads its contents out on the table in front of me.

"Take a look at this."

He points to a glossy photo printed so recently I can still smell the chemicals. It's a picture of a fuzzy circle marked with soft highlights and shadows.

"Mars," he announces. He points to a blurred white spot just below the equator. "And that's a dust storm."

"It's a white smudge."

But he's insistent, showing me another photograph. On this one, the smudge is absent.

"Any visible change is meaningful. Short term variation is almost always weather, but this one's more important than most. Remember I told you there would be a surprise for the scientists at JPL?"

I'm feeling edgy again.

"They'll be surprised all right," I tell him, "at being handed such terrible prints. Work this bad could cost me my job-" I stop short; I forgot I'd been fired.

And Charles has forgotten I'm supposed to be leaving now. "You think you can do better?" he dares me.

"You got a darkroom?"

"This is the headquarters of the International Planetary Patrol," he reminds me. "Of course we do."

I follow him across the courtyard and into the Planetary Research Center. I enter a tiny but reasonably well-equipped darkroom, its shadowed contents minimally visible under the soft orange glow, the enormous enlarger mounted front and center as critical to seeing in this room, as is the telescope under the dome.

I load one of the 70mm filmstrips into the negative carrier and project it onto the easel below, cranking the enlarger way up high to get the largest image possible. I turn the enlarger light on and adjust the focus knob until the projected image is clarified.

There on the surface of Mars is the tiny fluff, the thing Charles has designated as a dust storm. This photo, I note, was taken by the same telescope Dr. P had used to view and identify his canals, the same telescope Great Aunt Lulu had used to study the blemish – just like the one in front of me – for what it actually was. But what was it? She'd never said. Only that there was something there, some meaning in the disturbance. A Martian story shrouded from view. An enduring mystery.

I look closer, zoom in more and crank the focus knob for all it's worth. When the startling details within the blemish begin to reveal themselves, I hold my breath, shut off the light, set the timer and expose the moment on the photographic paper in front of me.

Curious what you can see in the dark, I muse as I take the exposed image through the developer, the wash, the fixer – tapping my foot and clicking my tongue, anxious to get to the end of the process. When the resulting print emerges, dripping, from its tedious journey, I hang it up to dry and try again.

I spend the next few hours loading different negatives into the enlarger, dodging and burning, trying different filters to boost the contrast and bring out the detail. When the resulting print is less than perfect, I go at it again, using my considerable darkroom skills rather than scientific algorithms to tune and finesse the visuals. Each area of the planet's surface must be encouraged to reveal its secrets; each highlight must be crisply delineated from its shadowy surroundings. There must be the suggestion of dimension – mountains and valleys, deep canyons with dense cloud patches floating above them. Moreover, there must be drama – a Martian story unfolding in intervals crafted over time. Each exposure I fashion in the dark illuminates more. With each enlargement I print, a new truth emerges from the rugged surface of the brooding planet.

At JPL I'd performed my darkroom tasks dutifully without feeling any of the excitement I feel right now. Then, I was obeying the rules, making Mars look exactly how the scientists wanted it to look. Now, I'm in gleeful violation of the rules, even etching my own hand-drawn dust particles into the negatives. *I know I'm not supposed to add information, Dr. Dick, but look how well it works!*

The darkroom is only large enough for one person. Charles has been waiting as impatiently as an expectant father in the hallway outside, jumping up now when I exit with a slightly damp print carefully pinched between finger-and-thumb of each hand. One print contains the white area; the other, taken 24 hours later, does not.

"You nailed it," he gushes over the two photos. "This is exactly what I need."

Of course I'd nailed it. I can do even better when I get back to JPL, to my own darkroom. Shit, I'd forgotten again about getting fired.

"This is really bad weather," Charles explains, pointing to the well-defined white spot just below the equator. "It's headed in this direction." He points toward the other side of the planet. "And it's moving fast. This may be the prelude to a massive dust storm that will erupt any day now. No one has predicted this."

"That's the secret?"

"If the storm is as big as I think it will be, there may be nothing for the Mariner to see. Nothing but a huge cloud of dust."

He indicates its enormity by extending both arms. And just that quickly, he's back in his hero-astronomer role, deeming the small disturbance a harbinger of disaster: "The television experiment you were working on at JPL may be doomed—" He paces as he delivers his well-rehearsed lines, "—unless I can get these to someone who might be able to intervene."

He stops to look into my eyes with all the gravitas he can muster. "Will you help me do that? Surely you must know someone…"

But I'm not listening to him, sidetracked by my own epiphany, a truth delivered to me over generations but making itself known in one enlightening darkroom session: *There is something more to be seen. Details that may not be visible must be clarified nonetheless. The story of the disturbance itself must be told.*

I'd proven this to myself and now I need to prove it to Dr. Dick and the Dicklings. want my job back and finally know how to get it. For the first time ever, JPL needs me.

Charles is still busy admiring the prints I'd made. "We could use someone like you in the darkroom here," he tells me. "Want me to see about getting you hired?"

It's almost as if he's gotten down on one knee and proposed to me. Laughable, really, but sweet.

"Thanks, but I've got to get going," I tell him, already heading for the door. I'm not sure whether I'm running away from something or toward something else, not sure whether this is goodbye or hello. Either way, I reason, I have to keep moving. The present is nothing more than an uncomfortable moment, and it's already over.

Venus on Mars

- 1 -

After sitting for days, my car wouldn't start, so I had it towed to the Esso Station in downtown Flagstaff. Turned out all I needed was a new battery. I had just enough cash to pay for the battery, a bottle of orange soda and a package of peanuts. So I've got my wheels back and I'm heading west on I-40.

I'm pleased to have the Mojave Desert all to myself. Its barren aesthetic appeals to me: areas of low-growing scrub arranged neatly, with almost equal distance between each; boulders strewn everywhere haphazardly, then piled high in amazing mounds erupting from the desert floor; the occasional brilliant white sand of a dry lake bed. No water but this place seems to work without any.

The stunted trees alongside the road make me uneasy, though. I'm used to towering palms. Here most trees have grown no taller than me, and they're unusually bent and deformed, as if they've suffered more than anything else here. I feel a little sorry for them, stuck where they are, while I whiz by in my little car, nearly outpaced at one point by a long-legged jackrabbit sprinting alongside the road. I wonder if he's running toward something, or away from it, or if he's just running because that's what jackrabbits do. can relate to that.

I passed through Needles around 11 a.m., making good time. I can drive all day and be home by tonight. With the air conditioner on high and the windows rolled up, I'm comfortably and neatly isolated from the desert surrounding me. I no longer need to experience this trip, I tell myself, I just need to finish it.

The big manila envelope in the passenger seat me voices encouragement. Tomorrow I'll waltz into the Image Processing Lab with the envelope containing the extra set of prints I'd made for myself and announce, "I'm back!" just like Great Aunt Lulu. Offering not a word about where I've been or my adventures along the way.

Once I deliver my remarkable prints to Dr. Dick and explain their significance he'll forgive all my transgressions and hire me back in a heartbeat. We'll use the photos to show the clueless scientists how easily a large-scale dust storm could compromise Mariner's planned activities – and give them vital lead-time to consider possible revisions. *Venus does Mars, and saves the Mariner mission!* I'll be written up in the newsletter, and not because of my miniskirt or boobs. The Dicklings will respect me at last. I'll not only be one of the boys, I'll have become the very best one of them. It'll be like I've grown a huge dick and know exactly how to wield it.

A sudden and unsettling bump: I've hit a major pothole in the road. I didn't see it coming.

The whole car rattles and shimmies side to side, trying to recover. I grip the wheel, downshift and let off on the gas. Finally the steering corrects itself and I'm still on my way to Pasadena. I take a deep breath and let it out slowly.

But what if Dr. Dick is not so happy to see me? I hadn't told anyone about the discrimination complaint I'd filed against JPL. What if Dr. Dick found out about it and that's why he fired me? What if he's already replaced me? What if she's prettier, flirtier, with shorter skirts and taller hair? What if they're boogeying right this minute across the shiny tiled floor of the IBM room?

As if bowing to some cosmic cue, the entire landscape dims as a cloud parks itself in front of the sun. I realize I've been far too busy fantasizing about my glorious future at JPL to recognize my precarious present: The unusual beauty of the desert landscape hiding its own version of evil, revealing its subversive self after only hours of driving through its unvarying and innocuous features. While Texas was merely boring, this place is starting to feel downright sinister. The road has become uncommonly narrow, with minimal shoulders and yawning ditches beyond them waiting to swallow my little car whole. No mile markers here. No road signs. No phone booths or emergency call boxes. Just the road through the desert and my car and me.

Past, present and future have merged into one unending moment. I'm perpetually centered on a vast dirt-hued plateau framed by sheer-sided mountains. The wheels on my car are spinning and my foot is heavy on the gas pedal, but I'm not going anywhere. The more I drive, the less distance I seem to cover; the mountains remain stubbornly distant.

I'm stuck here, in this instant, in this location.

It's an illusion, I remind myself. Distances can be deceiving in places like this.

Although the vast uncivilized space between the road I'm on and the mountain range I can never reach appears barren, I know there's life there – but a malignant kind, hiding and waiting to pounce the moment I show any sign of weakness. If I have a flat tire, if I run off the road, if my engine overheats, I'll have to get out of the car and then I'll be screwed.

Okay, now I'm just messing with myself, scaring myself for no good reason.

Quit that, Venus, I tell myself. But the uneasiness builds rapidly toward what surely will erupt into panic if I don't get out of here soon. And still I can sense no forward progress.

I notice a worrisome sentinel off in the distance, a rushing swirl of wind and dust rising confidently from the desert floor. It hovers until it spins itself out, then slowly it spreads and dissipates. Nearby another forms to take its place.

The growing dread I feel is palpable. I look straight ahead and concentrate on driving, trying to ignore these itinerant dust devils. My stomach is queasy and my heart is racing, but stopping until I can calm down is out of the question. I have to get out of this place I'm doing nearly eighty now, as fast as my little car will go. If only I had bought that souped-up Mustang instead, I'd be home by now.

Then the ultimate desert drama unfolds: An immense dirt-red wall that shouldn t be there rises in the distance. It looks soft, like dirty cotton candy, yet solid like a misplaced mountain range. All the dust devils have converged, consolidating into a crowded phalanx marching toward me. I'm driving straight toward it because there is only one road through the desert and I'm on it – and because I'm in California at last, only a few hours from home.

Instinctively I turn on my radio to see if I can get some news, forgetting I don't have one any more. Since I set out through the desert several hours ago, I've seen hardly another soul. Maybe they got a warning and went some other way. Damn my dead radio.

When I first encounter the dust it's thin and white, reflecting the sun above and almost pretty. But as I drive further into it the vast cloud thickens, commandeering the view through my windshield and obscuring the road ahead. The sky disappears, and the air around me turns dark and dense.

The wind picks up; it's audible – a howling horror-movie sound far more sinister than the impish air currents swirling around Mars Hill.

If I've learned one thing from the Book of Great Aunt Lulu, it is to face an oncoming storm head-on, to open my eyes and see in the disturbance whatever it may reveal. I'm determined to keep driving – even though bits of sand caught up in the wind begin pelting my windshield like bullets, and I can no longer see the road ahead.

My little bug of a car can't maintain its forward momentum. The winds push it sharply to one side. I try to hang on to the steering wheel...

But I've run off the road. And then off the narrow shoulder.

I'm tumbling and bouncing across the dust-shrouded desert floor.

Daylight has turned pitch-black from the pulsating storm surrounding me. The winds do not subside. I'm suffocating inside my twisting, turning car – but I dare not open a window even a tiny crack. I'm powerless against this force. Unprepared to deal with the massive storm I should have known was inevitable.

Hadn't everyone warned me about this?

Why didn't I pay attention?

- 2 -

The unsettled sunset Letha had seen from the tall windows in the comfortable bedroom was by now a rosy memory. In its place darkness had spread in all directions, and there were no stars visible.

She found herself stepping cautiously along a stone-cold, pitch-black passage. Not because her vision had failed again, but because the brass sconces mounted at regular intervals along the walls offered no illumination, as if there had been a power failure.

The storm, she remembered, *it must have hit after all. That's why the lights are out.*

She heard muffled footsteps passing above her, a heavy door opening and quickly closing: a sudden departure.

"Wait!" she shouted, but no one heard her.

At the end of the passageway, she reached a set of rough wooden stairs and hurried to climb them. At the top she encountered a trap door. She pushed hard but could not open it. The trap door must be locked from above.

"Please, I have to get out of here!" She pummeled the door with both hands and shouted until she was hoarse, but no one answered.

Struggling to breathe in the stifling air, Letha sensed the panic building inside her. She listened but heard no wind howling, only the leaden silence of complete abandonment.

She must be deep underground, she concluded – trapped where she'd so recently been placed, dead and buried, in Holt Cemetery in New Orleans, one of the few graveyards in the low-lying, water-lined city where you could be laid to rest *under* the ground, not above it.

All those other places she'd been – the quaint train station, the vast red-hued desert, the pleasant room with the writing desk and the mountain view – were in her imagination, or a dream. This part – the silent, suffocating darkness – was real.

There was no one to help her. Vernon had left this Earth long ago, her brother Ollie was back home nursing a second shot of whiskey by now. And Venus – well, she had her own problems to deal with. Really big ones. It seemed her reckless daughter had climbed out of the frying pan and plunged headlong into the fire.

Letha crept back into her satin-lined box, the only comfort left in her afterlife, closed her tired eyes, and wept into her pillow.

- 3 -

The storm had hit, just as Charles had predicted, with a maniacal vengeance, stirring up dust on the Martian surface, forming a dense disturbance that rose several hundred feet in the air, swirling in all directions, spreading until the massive cloud enveloped the entire planet. Even Charles had not predicted the full extent of the storm's magnitude.

An astronomer at a South African observatory had first spotted the disturbance: a brilliant white streak erupting suddenly, in a single rotation, just below the equator. Since then, all observers working with the International Planetary Patrol had tracked the storm as it surged and spread. The massive white cloud turned dirty yellow as billions of dust particles were sucked up and suspended in the Martian atmosphere until no surface features were visible. Within two weeks, the planet seen through telescopes worldwide no longer appeared red but rather a soft dull yellow. And remained stubbornly so, as the Mariner spacecraft arrived right on schedule and eased itself into near-perfect orbit above the shrouded surface.

According to the mission plan, the scientists working in the Spacecraft Operations Center at JPL had activated Mariner's cameras during its final approach, only to be shocked that the initial images transmitted back to Earth revealed no craters or crevices, no surface detail at all, save for four soft mounds. Were the onboard cameras malfunctioning? Had the computer given the cameras flawed instructions? Because the equipment on the orbiting spacecraft was not performing as planned, the mystified scientists turned to ground-based telescopes for answers. When they called the astronomers at Lowell Observatory, they were not only told about the planet-wide dust storm, but also that an observer working on Mars Hill had predicted this event.

"Put him on the phone, then."

Charles was pleased with himself, his unique knowledge suddenly in demand, and was eager to make himself available. Soon he was busy not only advising the mission specialists at JPL, but also coordinating International Planetary Patrol photos of the Martian storm being rush-shipped to Flagstaff from around the world, as well as observations by hordes of amateur astronomers who by now worshipped him. Each day he received more fan mail, grown now into a sizeable stack on his grand new desk in the Planetary Research Center. He spent several hours each day trying to keep up with his correspondence. He'd had a new photograph of himself taken at the historic telescope, wearing his red beret and the vintage three-piece suit. The astronomers he worked with privately ridiculed the way he was stage-managing his newfound notoriety, walking around Mars Hill "all puffed up," they said of their earth-bound superstar.

This morning Charles is penning answers to questions written out in longhand and mailed to him from the editor of an amateur stargazers' newsletter, *The Strolling Astronomer.* They'd also requested two photos – one of the Martian disturbance and another of Charles himself which he happily signs.

The Strolling Astronomer: *How did you know the dust storm was going to happen?*

Charles: I've long studied the Martian dust storms. There's a seasonal cycle to them, a period during the Martian spring when they are most likely to occur, when cool polar winds sweep down onto warmer slopes, basins or plains to create an atmospheric disturbance of sizeable proportion.

Once formed, a sufficiently large dust storm may easily become "self-perpetuating." The dense clouds absorb sunlight, cooling the planet's surface. This atmospheric temperature change may increase local winds, thereby stirring up more dust. Any local clearing warms the surface, generating new winds and re-stirring surface dust.

The Strolling Astronomer: *How long will the storm last?*

Charles: If history is any indicator, the storm may play itself out within a few weeks, or it may lessen and then grow strong again, extending into several more months. The clearing will be gradual when it comes.

The Strolling Astronomer: *Any way to equate this storm to similar weather events on Earth?*

Charles pauses to think before writing an answer to this question.

Charles: Imagine yourself trapped in a wall of dust thirty miles high, caught up in winds of over three hundred miles per hour. The four points of reference seen by Mariner upon its arrival are the four tallest mountains on the planet, each one many times higher than Mount Everest on Earth. Everything else on the Martian surface is entirely buried beneath the storm.

Similar storms occur in the Sahara, the Gobi and the deserts in the Southwest of this county, but none approaching this scale. Because Mars is smaller than Earth and has a thinner atmosphere, Martian storms can travel faster and farther, the planetary winds propelling the dust forward at speeds that may approach that of a jet airplane.

"You wouldn't want to be there now," Charles proclaims out loud.

KING OF MARS HILL

wake up, unable to breathe, upside down in my car. The dirt has forced itself through one broken window, across the dashboard, and into my throat and nostrils.

I gasp and kick the opposite door hard with both feet because I can see daylight beyond it. The door opens, and I shimmy outside onto the ground. I roll over, stretch out my arms and legs, and lie face up, staring into a putrid orange-yellow haze. The air around me is thick with dust, but the dust is no longer swirling.

It's eerily quiet now, except for each labored breath I find myself pleased to take.

I can't remember how I got here. But when I sit up and take one look at my upturned and half-buried car, I know I'll need some other way to get out of here and back to Pasadena.

I pull my t-shirt up over my mouth and nose, and the breathing gets a little easier. I stand up cautiously and take a few steps to make sure I can walk. My head hurts. I must have bumped it when my car rolled over. Otherwise, I don't think I'm injured. That's the only good news.

The desert has delivered on its evil promise. I'm in big trouble. I retrieve my bottle of orange soda and package of peanuts from the wrecked car, my only provisions until I get out of here.

All directions look the same through the thick air: rust colored dirt strewn with rocks and low-growing scrub brush. With the sun masked by thick dirty clouds I have no way to determine east, west, north or south. Moreover, what little I can make out looks nothing like what I remembered from before the storm. The wind must have re-arranged everything.

I can't stay where I am, so I choose a direction at random and start walking. No matter how vast this desert is, I reason, there have to be boundaries on all sides because no desert goes on forever. It only seems that way.

L etha stirs in the darkness of her satin-lined box. She was sure she'd
been left alone, abandoned and beyond retrieval, but now she hears
shuffling nearby, like a group rearranging itself in cramped quarters.

She offers a confident greeting, "Hello," then anxiously awaits a reply.

An unseen man clears his throat, then steps forward to take her arm
and help her stand.

"Step carefully, ma'am," the invisible companion advises her.

I've been unearthed, Letha thinks as the doors are pushed open and
she emerges from the underground train station into painfully bright
sunlight.

She shades her eyes and steps without hesitation to the street-side
door underneath the giant eyeglasses.

She is not disappointed: *Open*, the sign says.

Vernon's journey had been instantaneous. He'd found himself back
underneath the giant eyeglasses and this time he knew just what to do. He
pulled the keychain from his pocket, found the key that fit, unlocked the
door and pushed it inward, listening for the comforting jingle of the bells
mounted above the door.

It was as if he'd never left: All the eyeglasses still rested in the big display
case front and center; the shiny mirrors here and there for customers to
check their appearance and vision; the darker room in back with the tall
padded chair; the big paper with progressively smaller letters hung on the
far wall. And he'd found his ophthalmoscope right where he'd left it, on
the table where he also kept eye drops, salves, ointments, balancing stones,
and eye pumps – all treatments and devices he now knew to be worthless.

He sat down at the table, pulled a notebook and fountain pen before
him, and wrote the only true thing he knew: *Vernon Dawson, Vision
Specialist.* He added the one-word location where his customers could find

him: *Cosmos.*

When Vernon hears the bells above the street-side door tinkling again, he walks into the outer room to see a rotund, middle-aged woman who looks vaguely familiar.

"I'm here to get my eyes tested," she tells him. She hurries surefooted ahead of him into the examination room in back as if she's been here before.

Vernon follows her into the darkness, confident he now possesses the knowledge she'll need to see clearly.

"This time," she instructs him as she climbs into the big chair, "You must tell me what you see."

"No more secrets," he promises her.

A short while later, Letha exits the optical shop into a brilliantly sunlit afternoon. She realizes this is not Kenmore Square, but an idealized, paint-by-number version of her former life, each shade of each color distinct and extravagant in its saturation: smiling pedestrians outfitted in peacock-hued suits and dresses; resplendent automobiles with polished bodies trimmed in shiny chrome; glorious pastels in the bouquets for sale from the colorfully attired streetside flower vendor.

Letha observes her own reflection in a glass store window as she passes by: her quaint straw hat trimmed with billowing yellow ribbons; her dress a profusion of soft blues, cheerful golds and rosy reds; her shiny patent leather pumps gleaming in the sunlight.

At last she understands why she hadn't been able to tell her daughter the truth: She hadn't seen it for herself until now. Like Boston's complicated underground rail system or a prism struck by sunlight, the route they'd taken had, from the very beginning, split and separated into multiple colorful bands: green, orange, red, blue. There had been choices all along the way – choices not made.

Early on, Letha had chosen an itinerary she believed would insure for Venus the things she'd not had for herself: a secure home with books to read and a fancy new dress from time to time; a husband who would be there always; and a way to look at the future clearly. She'd worked hard to manage the journey for her daughter, but now she pauses to wonder whether the goals she'd set were in fact the proper ones. Or whether other choices, other routes drawn in other colors, might have proven more beneficial.

Letha looks into the sky at the fiery mass of the sun that holds the solar system in place. She judges how much time is left, how much longer her struggling systems will sustain her, and determines precisely how to spend the precious bit of eternity she has left.

She'll have to hurry now. She grabs a sheet of paper from the air swirling around her, positions the fountain pen she'd found on the floor near the desk in the cozy room, and begins scribbling her impromptu thoughts, turning the paper sideways when she runs out of room in order to continuing writing:

Dear Venus,

Finally I have found the time to write. You have been on my mind constantly; you know how worried I can get when you're so far away.

I'm sorry I did not tell you everything when you were young and full of questions. I had to keep us both going, and the truth would have broken us. I only told you the stories I could bear to tell, the ones with happy endings, even though you begged for more.

There were no pictures of your father because I never actually saw him, my eyesight being what it was. But he was real and I have finally found him after a lifetime of searching. He is exactly as I'd imagined him — handsome and clear-eyed, deep-voiced and kind. I found him standing underneath the giant eyeglasses, preparing to open up his optical shop. Not the

giant eyeglasses in Kenmore Square; no, these
eyeglasses are much larger, and the lenses more
powerful. I'm wearing them now, and I can see
forever, beyond the giant storm that will pass
and leave you intact. And then you will have a
decision to make, about what happens next.

This is the hardest part to write, Venus, the
critical truth I never told you: I don't know
what you are looking for, but I want you to
know that you will find it if you look hard
enough and long enough, just as I have. You are
a clever and industrious young lady, but these
qualities are not enough. You must also read
the book. All of it. Even the missing pages,
which you must reconstruct according to your
needs.

The writing will not be quick or easy, but it
is a worthwhile pursuit. I have done it at
last; writing my own pages has allowed me to
find your father. And I have discovered that
he too read the book, and constructed his own
pages which took him to a far-away place, a
place so distant that he could not find his way
back home. He has apologized for leaving and,
of course, I have forgiven him.

Long ago your Great Aunt Lulu filled the missing
pages with her own truths, but she was afraid
and so she removed them and hid them away.
She has set in motion this tradition that we
must follow, so please be patient. The words
for your pages will come to you when they are

ready, and not before.

I can no longer see you because the storm,
always on the move, has placed itself squarely
between us. The dust caught up in the unstable
air hides many details, but there is knowledge
contained within it, truths suspended,
constantly shifting and moving, not yet ready
to settle down and make their meaning known.

You are like that, Venus. You are like the
dust, part of the storm as it passes, part of
what it leaves behind.

When the dust settles, you will find out who you
have become.

Before she can finish the letter, Letha is interrupted by a sudden gust
that snatches the paper from her hands. She watches it twist in the wind
as it sails away, and fervently hopes her words will find their way to their
intended destination, into her daughter's hands. She hopes that Venus will
not need a carefully penned signature to understand who wrote the letter
and will read the cramped and chaotic sentences without questioning how
they could have been written by the mother she'd just buried. She hopes
that Venus will not question how the letter has been delivered through
time, across space, and despite the enormous windstorm raging across the
Solar System. A spectacular event that shows no signs of abating.

- 6 -

The dreadful autumn of your passing has given way to a melancholy new year. The relentless snow flies past my window, keeping me homebound for most of January. One raging snowstorm after another has painted all of the sky a lusterless gray, and there is no good seeing – or being seen – until the weather clears.

But I have made a fortunate discovery while delving into the dark recesses of my hallway closet and opening a long-sealed case I have found there: Even if I cannot see you, I can still talk to you. The ability to do so has been hiding inside my typewriter. I had nearly forgotten about its remarkable abilities!

I am still your secretary because I never resigned. I can always type a letter for you. There's always a place in the universe where you will be able to receive it.

I click open the wooden case and set the exquisite machine on the windowsill in front of me. My busy fingers type your address: *the Cosmos.* Then I push a key with a scientific symbol on it and feel a slight pulse, as if years of words unspoken between us have been stored inside the metal fittings and are just now being released. The message floats suspended in the air around me, waiting for a respectable breeze to carry it toward you. I open the window to a brief burst of cold air, and my words commence their long journey through the turbulent skies.

When the universe is this unsettled, I think heartfelt messages may travel more easily across its wide expanses, while a calm, clear atmosphere may restrict progress of the same. Senders and recipients who never thought they'd correspond again may come in contact, trading long-repressed affections and admonitions whispered in heavenly alcoves, where tender, truthful words authored by long-ago confidants hover and pause before continuing their extraordinary journeys.

Thoughtfully, Letha pulls another piece of paper out of the tumultuous wind swirling around her, holding it firmly in one hand, her fountain pen in the other, determined to have her say. She's nearly out of time and almost out of energy.

She takes a deeply labored breath, exhaling as she slings her final thoughts onto the paper. Thinking and writing have fused into one frantic act. She's whirling with the wind, like a dervish, pulling just enough of its energy inside herself to complete her task. She knows her efforts are the cosmic equivalent of placing a message in a bottle and tossing it into the sea, but it's her only chance to get these words to Venus – words Venus will need to compose the missing pages of her own life.

My Dear Venus,

Here is another thing I never told you. I went back to cleaning houses and caring for the indigent when my vision was so poor I couldn't see the keys on a typewriter or cash register. I cleaned her house on Newbury Street for several months before they put her in a home.

She was old and already dotty; she sat up in her bed and told me stories while I swept, mopped and dusted all around her. Endless stories about Mars and the Martians, her own people, she called them.

She described the love of her life, a brilliant astronomer who had fallen into disrespect; he'd died and moved to Mars where he was appreciated and even revered, she said.

A boy child she'd carried but lost... She didn't know where he'd gone. What she'd seen but couldn't say, when she looked though the telescope.

"I kept secrets," she'd stage-whisper. "In those days proper ladies were expected to behave with discretion. I learned to choose my words very carefully."

That's when I found the book, under her mattress, one day when I was turning it.

Now here is the irony of my find. Inside the book I knew there were words written specifically for me, but I could not see well enough to read them. I never had the book and good vision both at the same time.

Time on Earth is like that: One day follows another, and you can't revisit any of them until you're dead and buried. But that's when it all comes apart, and you can put it back together any way you want.

Your father can come home again. He didn't break the telescope. Aunt Lulu lives with us and she's not demented. I find the book under her mattress and I can see all the words inside.

Goodbye truly is the beginning of everything that happens after that.

Believe me.

                              Your mother,

                              Letha Broussard Dawson

Letha releases the final missive into the air and watches it fly away.

There is nothing left to say. She has exhausted herself with her difficult revelations, and even more so with her clever inventions.

She closes her eyes, opens her arms, and lets go of the fountain pen.

She steps forward to catch a gust of wind that will propel her to a final resting place, somewhere in the infinite universe.

t turns out Dr. Dick and everybody else in Image Processing was wrong – the indisputable proof surrounds me. You have to add more information to what's there; it's the only way to make sense of it.

As I make my labored way across the ugly desert I'm constantly conjuring up pictures of my eventual destination: a breeze-cooled oasis where I'll sit under a palm tree and order another Piña Colada.

I'm not there – I'm still stranded in this God-forsaken place – yet the oasis is here, right in front of me. It's like the desert and oasis are two different pages in a picture book I'm mentally composing, and I can flip back and forth between them in my mind.

This is what my mom has been trying to explain in the letters she keeps sending me through the wind: her final thoughts about the oddly arranged book, how it must be read, taken apart, augmented and then reconstructed.

But the truth she is finally sharing with me has come too late: I left the book behind, in the back seat of my car that's now buried in the dust. Whatever was there on the pages, whatever was missing... None of it matters now.

I find my way back onto an actual road, which seems promising. Roads always go somewhere, don't they? Let's hope it's somewhere I actually want to go, although I really can't afford to be choosy right now, can I?

One dogged step leads to another, and another.

I'm trudging though the hostile desert. I'm relaxing and sipping that chilled coconut Piña Colada.

Charles has been in constant contact with JPL since the planet-wide Martian dust storm first materialized. The tiny Mariner spacecraft taking faraway orders from scientists is now dependent on one observer's limited view through an antique, 24-inch telescope once used to chart fanciful Martian canals.

The irony of his recently elevated situation is not lost on Charles, especially whenever he thinks of Venus, the glum but intriguing girl who got away. Surely she must have talked her way back in at JPL and is back at work. Surely she's heard of his success. She's most likely twiddling her thumbs these days, since there are no Mariner images to process. If only she'd stayed in Flagstaff, there'd be so much they could do together, just like the two who'd worked here so long ago, the founder and his secretary, inseparable soul mates, the original Martians of Mars Hill.

Charles has even created a compelling script for their astronomical drama, inspired by her outrageous behavior under the dome the day before she left and the outfit she'd worn: On special occasions, he would dress up in the founder's vintage three-piece suit and convince her to put on the white ensemble. They'd welcome visitors to their Observatory on Mars Hill, the maverick astronomer and his unconventional assistant, a beautiful and brilliant couple – only she'd have to promise to keep her big mouth shut.

In one of his telephone conversations with the JPL science team, Charles asks about Venus Dawson, whether she's back at work there, thinking he will at least offer a quick but sincere "hello" and invite her back for a visit sometime.

"Just a moment, sir."

He's transferred immediately to Arthur Dickson, Ph.D., Director of the Image Processing Lab.

"Where is she?" Dickson demands. Venus had been right about him;

the man has no manners at all.

"She left Flagstaff a while back," Charles replies. "In a huff. That's why I hadn't tried to get in touch sooner."

"Sounds like Venus — hot and bothered."

"Yep." Both men laugh and agree.

"She'll show herself when she's damn good and ready and not a moment sooner," Dickson predicts.

"Well, when she does, give her my regards."

As both men hang up their phones, one in Pasadena and the other in Flagstaff, each has the same sobering thought. Venus left one location and still has not arrived at the other. She's got to be stuck somewhere in-between.

Within minutes, the highway patrol has been notified and the rangers who routinely patrol the Mojave Desert in off-road vehicles have been mobilized. Venus Dawson's solemn official JPL photo has been copied from her personnel file and couriered to every law enforcement agency between Flagstaff and Pasadena.

"She's got to be somewhere," Dickson fumes on the phone with the Barstow police captain.

"We're trying our best, sir," the captain assures him.

"Try harder," Dickson growls back.

"The dust storm may have shifted a great deal of desert sand," Charles, on the phone in Flagstaff, explains to the Needles deputy sheriff. "You should look again. You may have missed something the first time."

"Let me ask you this, sir," the deputy replies. "Are you absolutely sure she wants to be found? We have people who go out into the desert all the time — sometimes to ponder life, sometimes to end it. They don't want to be found. You know what I'm saying?"

"I know what *I'm* saying," Charles replies. "You have to keep looking."

-9-

've been walking for hours without making progress. The same desert landscape surrounds me and the same thick air chokes and envelops me. I've coughed my throat raw. My irritated eyes sting and burn. My lips are so dry they're about to split open. I'm tired of holding my mouth clamped shut to keep the dust out.

I sit down on a rock, duck my head to keep the dust out of my face, drink the soda eat the peanuts, then bury my trash in a shallow hole I dig with my fingers because I may die soon and don't want to be remembered as a litterbug.

I no longer expect to find my way out. I no longer expect to survive.

I don't want to die alone. I didn't want to live alone, either. It's just that somebody I could get along with never showed up.

And why is that, Venus? What's wrong with you? I feel a rant coming on but can't afford the energy to let loose my anger. So I work to tamp it down.

The dust-laden air gets darker, gradually permeated by what must be nightfall. get up and continue walking because there's nothing else to do.

Gradually, as my vision adjusts to the darkness, I discover I'm not alone after all. Through the haze I see a tall, well-dressed man standing up ahead, smoking a cigar. An elegantly dressed woman, nearly as tall, approaches him, lifting her long skirt to reveal crimson stockings. He smiles at her daring. They link arms and stroll away. She's whispering secrets into his ear. He leans toward her to catch every word.

A young slender version of my mom stands fidgeting and whistling off-key under a gigantic pair of eyeglasses, waiting for the optical shop to open. When it does, she rushes inside.

Harry sits on a boulder smoking a joint, his motorcycle parked nearby. Or is it Jorge from Amarillo?

"Want some?" he asks and I sit down beside him, take a big hit and hold it. When I finally exhale, I release not only smoke but all the dust I've inhaled along the way. A huge amount. My own private dust storm, the one I've been holding in far too long.

Everyone disappears, obliterated by the dust.

The sun has set and it's cold, too cold for my bare arms. I rub them briskly, trying to warm them. My feet are numb; I can't stand up.

This is the end. I'm reliving the past because I'm dying. Isn't this what people do? But it's not only my life that's flashing before my eyes, but everyone else's, too. Shouldn't Dr. Dick be here, yelling at me? Shouldn't Charles show up soon, with coffee and doughnuts?

-10-

As long as the dust storm rages, the surface of Mars cannot be seen or photographed. With no dissipation in sight, the Mariner mission director, desperate to salvage the "television experiment" part of this mission, makes the only reasonable decision: He orders the Mariner cameras shut down to preserve the limited power onboard the spacecraft. While Mariner naps, the science team must fidget and wait until the Martian air clears and their cameras can photograph the surface they'd sent it there to see.

With no images from space to be processed, all support personnel are encouraged to schedule vacations now, in advance of the work that surely lies ahead. No one can say how far ahead.

On his first weekend off in nearly a year, Arthur Dickson is relieved to dress casually in a white t-shirt, plaid Bermuda shorts and tennis shoes with no socks. Only the JPL logo on his baseball cap hints at his identity. He treks across the JPL campus to claim the van he's reserved from the motor pool. He stocks it with food, water, an entire carton of chewing gum, and a first aid kit he's borrowed from work. He pops several sticks of gum into his mouth before beginning the drive east toward Barstow and the desert lying beyond. Whether Venus is in trouble or just hiding out, he's determined to find her. Whether he'll yell at her or kiss her hard on the mouth, he hasn't yet decided.

On the other side of the desert, Charles sets out, heading west in the big white Observatory van. He's earned a day off, he reasons to himself. The least he can do is drive through the Mojave on the road she would have taken if she were returning to Pasadena. Armed with a thermos of coffee and a half-dozen glazed doughnuts, and wearing his white cowboy hat, he's prepared to be the hero.

It's a windy day, kicking up dust devils, innocuous little whirlwinds that rise with surprising ferocity from the desert floor. But they soon die down and disappear, and clear blue skies prevail.

The desert has brought them together.

Arthur Dickson spots the Observatory van and waves it down. Greetings are exchanged and the two men decide to travel together, unlikely road buddies united in their quest to find out what has happened to the one acquaintance they have in common.

"She never really liked me," Dickson tells his passenger Charles, who silently studies his map, glancing up occasionally to survey the road ahead.

"For Chrissakes, I tried to get along, but she wasn't about to give me a break."

"Not exactly personable, as I recall," Charles finally offers.

"I mean, what the hell did she want from me? I was her boss, not her boyfriend."

"Pull over up ahead," Charles interrupts, pointing to a mound of sand off to the right.

The two men exit the van; a short trek across the desert floor reveals the abandoned little car, half-buried in the sand. They sift through its interior for clues, but the only item they recover is a bright red billfold. There's no identification card inside, but the Polaroid photo that falls from it – of Venus and Dickson posing together – confirms the worst.

"It's not like I was supposed to marry her, you know," Dickson laments.

Charles attempts to comfort his distraught companion. "I don't really think she was looking for a husband."

– 11 –

've conjured up two new pages for my mental picture book.

I'm still lost in the desert, but I've been rescued. I flip back and forth between the page showing my unconscious form lying prone on the dirty desert floor and the page showing the spic-and-span hospital where I'm being treated for heat exhaustion, dehydration and a mild concussion. In one picture I'm hopelessly doomed; in the other I'm relaxed and fully medicated. In the desert I'm dying alone; in the hospital room three suitors show up in turn by my bedside.

"I've been looking for you everywhere," the young man in a Kmart suit announces as he hurries into my hospital room.

"How'd you find me?" I'm groggy, but I recognize him. He's the man from the Equal Employment Opportunity Commission who'd written my workplace discrimination "statement" so many months ago. He apologizes for the delay – backlog of cases to blame, a lot of discrimination being reported these days.

"I've got everything ready for you to sign." He pulls a stack of paper-clipped pages from an envelope in his briefcase. He seems in a hurry as he hands them to me, along with a ballpoint pen he's already clicked open.

I begin flipping through the pages, thinking I'll just add my name and this part of my past will be all over. But when I get to the last page, just before the line he's prepared for my signature, I read a hand-written addendum: *I agree to go braless for all future appearances.*

I look at him, incredulous, and he smiles back – leers, actually.

My anger takes over. I grab the pen and draw a sharp line through this sentence, then throw the papers back at him. The paper clip comes loose and the pages go flying everywhere.

"Get out!" I yell at him.

"I just got here," says Dr. Dick, who's come to my bedside. He's grown sideburns! His face is full of concern, but he quickly masks it with derision.

"You're a fool," he rants in my face. "You could have died out there."

"Thanks for caring," I growl back at him.

"And you look terrible," he adds.

"But I'm not wearing a bra," I announce, instantly breaking through his foul mood.

We both laugh hard. It hurts to laugh, I realize.

"You have a cracked rib," he tells me.

"I have more than that." With some effort I sit up and grab the envelope from the table beside my bed. "Look at this..."

But now I've got the two envelopes confused. One has the exquisite photos of Mars that will get me my job back; the other has my discrimination complaint that will banish me forever from JPL. I'm not sure which one I'm about to show him.

But before I can hand him either one, he's gone – and without offering me my job back.

"Do you know where you are?"

"Flagstaff General?"

"Nope."

"JPL?"

"Not even close."

"The Baronial Mansion?"

"Don't you start with that again..."

Now it's Charles by my bedside, wide-eyed with enthusiasm, recounting everything I've missed.

"I called it," he tells me. "The dust storm, spot-on accurate. Thought you'd like to know."

"I'm sort of famous now," he adds. "I've just been interviewed by *Popular Astronomy*. I can send you an autographed copy when it's published."

But I'm not listening to him because someone else is trying to get my attention: faint broken signals from far away. As I strain to hear the high-pitched clicks, clacks, whines and squeals, I can tell this is not an orderly message, but more like a distant and intermittent half-melody searching through relentless static for lyrics that eventually will organize its sounds into meaningful and melodic thought.

"Shhh," I hiss loudly. Everyone in the room, even the hospital itself, vanishes. I'm alone in the desert again, surely near death, unless I can sift through the space chatter and hone in on the one signal that will save me.

-12-

The lion-like March winds have delivered your reply!

The keys on my typewriter emit tiny pulses when I touch them, your words strung across the heavens now touching down on Earth, coalescing on my windowsill as a sweet and sacred evensong.

I listen, straining to hear your faint yet coherent message sent from so far away, an answer to my long-ago question: *What did you see that took you away from us?*

"I saw myself, not on Mars Hill, but on Mars. Not as a reflection of myself on Earth, but as one settled down among the Martians.

"There *is* a way to get from there to here. I saw the route extending through the telescope; I closed my eyes on Earth and opened them on Mars."

My breath catches in my throat as your message continues:

"We shall be wed when you join me here," you promise me. "In the spring, the canals will be flowing with fresh clear water from the melting snowcaps. Jonquils will be blooming; I shall pick some for your bridal bouquet.

"We shall climb to the top of the highest peak to survey everywhere we have been and all things we have done.

"No one will see us there, unless we decide to be seen. I shall be able to stay by your side forever."

Your words bring me more pleasure than can be imagined!

I must prepare for this joyous occasion, our eventual reunion on the red planet when I shall see you again face to face, the moment when we shall wed, a time when no force on Earth, nor in the cosmos, shall be able to separate us again, where we shall live as man and wife for all eternity.

Now what did I do with my wedding dress?

My mom once showed me what she called her "wedding ensemble", an absurd little outfit unearthed from a long cardboard box, cradled in layers of yellowed tissue paper. She gently lifted from the box a tiny chocolate brown two-piece suit with real mink trim on the collar. No lace, no ruffles, no veil, no train, and none of it white. Wrapped separately in tissue paper were diminutive brown leather pumps I couldn't get my size-seven feet into, and a narrow brown Robin-Hood-style hat adorned with goofy orange and yellow feathers.

"I weighed a hundred and two back then," she laughed, holding the jacket up against her ample chest while I tried on the silly hat.

"That doesn't look like a wedding dress to me," I said, doubting her every word.

"It was a sunrise service," she replied. As if that explained everything.

Didn't my parents do anything like normal people?

"Six a.m. we said 'I do' and by six-thirty we were off on our honeymoon. We took the train out to the Cape and stayed there overnight. I didn't even have to change clothes."

"I've kept it all these years," she said wistfully as she gently lowered the outfit back into the box, covered it with tissue paper and carefully replaced the lid, "thinking you could wear it some day for your own wedding."

There's another reason I should never, ever get married: I'd look ridiculous in that outfit. Dr. Dick would make all matter of fun over it. Not that he'd be there when I got married. If I got married. And not to him.

But here I am, stepping carefully across the dust-blown desert, dressed in Great Aunt Lulu's elegant white dress, following a faint but steady signal leading me toward a lush oasis not yet visible where the wedding guests are waiting. I have no idea who the groom might be; I only know I'm expected to marry.

But the white dress does not fit. I have to suck in my breath to keep the delicate buttons fastened at the tiny waist, and the skirt is much too long. I'm still wearing my flip-flops. One of them gets all caught up in the hem, and I pitch forward. I realize I'm falling. This time there is no ground to catch me: I continue falling endlessly through time and space.

In the distance a rugged red planet grows larger.

"Open your eyes," a hushed voice insists.

I'm thickheaded but awake. I hear uncomfortable shuffling nearby. There's the smell of cheap toilet water, stale cigarette smoke.

"What do you see?" someone asks.

Cautiously I open my eyes to take it all in, but the details are blurred and indistinct.

"I can't see anything," I have to admit.

"Keep looking," someone else insists, and I work to steady my vision, to see into and beyond the dust-flocked surface of history and imagination.

I see the truth of a faraway world that is barren, but not without life.

I see swift changes that may indeed take place there: entire civilizations that can come and go, canals that can be built and then fall into ruins, summer gardens that may be tilled and planted before withering and dying, buried beneath deep winter snows, and yet none of this is visible because we are observing the past and evidence of these events has not yet arrived on Earth.

What we Earthlings see will never catch up with clever time or the Martians who hide in its wake. They're there now, watching our progress. Seeing and being seen are compatible events; it's just that the insurmountable time delay throws the whole universe out of sync, forever veiling the truths told on one planet from those observing from another.

"Step carefully," Lulu stage-whispers from atop the highest Martian peak, her cautionary words from long ago just now arriving in my ears.

But it's too late.

I've collapsed on the red soil, too exhausted to walk further. I know what I'll see if I close my eyes: the rest of my life flash-forwarding in a nonsensical dream.

I struggle with my last bit of energy to stay awake.

I'm lying on my back, staring into a featureless sky, when the blind Navajo woman shows up, leading her cow with a rope.

"Is that cow named Venus?" I ask her.

But she's too busy to answer. "Get up," she orders me, and I'm instantly on my feet. She points to a patch of white up ahead, a piece of paper on the desert floor.

As soon as I pick it up, she points to another.

"You can't keep them," she tells me, once I've amassed a decent handful of pages.

"Why not?" I challenge her. "I found them."

"You know why," she tells me. She's speaking her own words, but using my mother's voice.

"You can't use another one's pages," she continues. "You have to make your own."

The Navajo woman and her cow disappear into the haze while I stand waiting for a sturdy breeze to kick in. When it does, I fling all the pages into the air. Some sail far away, while others whirl madly around my head. The blind woman was not Navajo, but my recently departed mom. I must be near New Orleans; we've just buried her. I've paid the preacher and the mortuary. I'm heading toward the cemetery curb where I remember parking my car, when a deep voice calls out:

"Wait!"

Uncle Ollie approaches, treading carefully, using his diamond-encrusted cane to steady himself. But this time there's nothing to wait for; he's empty-handed.

The book he's supposed to give me no longer exists; it's come unbound and its pages have all flown away. Even the words themselves have jumped off the pages, tiny airborne signals darting ahead and then hurrying back again to find companions, their verbal essences combining to form new entities from whom they too will soon separate, destined to repeat the never-ending cycle of mystery and meaning.

This is why I'm here.

Instead of telling my story to the dust-laden air, I'm receiving it as a dance of words and pages, eyes and brain, all suspended in the heavy air surrounding me.

I'm drawn into the dance with them, twirling around like a dust-devil dervish, when I hear the coyote howl nearby. A mournful and distorted sound. Its pitch bent by the passing windstorm into a sliding scale of anger and regret.

-13-

V. M. Slipher had made the regrettable decision. The Baronial Mansion must be torn down. Built over time as it had been, with rooms added on as deemed necessary but with no overall structural plan, the aging building had weakened. Ceilings sagged. Chimneys leaned. Walls had ventured measurably out of plumb.

He made one final visit, taking careful steps across the rotted wood floor of the veranda, noting that the shiny pair of blackbirds nesting all lovey-dovey in the eaves would soon have to find another perch to call home.

He walked through the dining room, the library and the kitchen, then to the other end of the house, opening each door, briefly scanning each bedroom. The furnishings had already been removed and sorted through. Any items of historical significance had been stored in boxes in the basement of the administration building that now bore his name

Pausing just outside the darkroom he'd used so often before a new one had been built, he leaned over, pulled open the trap door he'd once fallen through, and lowered himself into the passageway running beneath the main floor – the passageway that the former director had insisted on adding to the Mansion. Slipher never had figured out what purpose it served. He knew Lowell visited her bedroom; everybody knew. A waste of time and materials, and so oddly built, running diagonally underneath the rest of the house, the underground passageway was a likely contributor to the building's structural failure.

Making his way through the darkness by touching a cool wall with outstretched fingers, he moved forward slowly, listening for footsteps passing overhead, voices reverberating from the rooms above him, the music box being cranked into operation. He began tapping his fingers on the wall now to a merry waltz. He listened to the dancing feet counting beats in threes on the wooden floor above him, soft laughter and a sudden high-pitched whine, coming not from the rooms above, but from a dark alcove behind the stairs.

He looked into a tiny pair of glowing eyes: A diminutive gray fox raced past him, escaping into the light through a fist-sized hole that had not been there when the structure was in use.

The small shaft of daylight coming through the opening provided just enough illumination for Slipher to see the dirty sheets of paper tucked behind the stairs, rolled and tied with a soiled blue ribbon, something the movers had missed. He retrieved them and carried them outside to study in the daylight.

Page after page of familiar perfect circles, each one filled with the most incredible detail, with color and dimension. Each circle was initialed with the letters "WLL". Below each one the "seeing scale" had been marked as "0," the worst viewing conditions possible. No one had ever observed when the seeing was this bad, he remembered. But someone had: Miss Lulu. And here was the evidence.

Unlike the previous director, Slipher was more pragmatist than visionary. *Perhaps the past has been kept alive too long,* he thought, releasing the untenable drawings by an untrained eye and hand into the stiff breeze issuing from one side of the mesa. It struck him that this was the prelude. All the stories that have been told here will be released when the Mansion comes down, the sifting debris of memories that need no longer be preserved in one time, in one place.

You'll not send me away! the pages shout as they pivot and dart into the unsettled air.

But the wind is relentless, and has carried them far into the heavens long before Slipher turns to walk away from the now thoroughly abandoned and lifeless Mansion.

Liberation at last, my pages announce!

When reading a book, I can only be on one page at a time. The pages are bound, locked in place as shackled prisoners, not allowed to come and go as they wish. When I turn to the next page, I am no longer on the previous page, but have arrived at an entirely new location marked with new words and new thoughts. I can always look back or peek ahead in the story, but no matter what, I'm only on one page at a time.

What if the pages were released from their binding and allowed to float freely? What if they could move in any direction? I could still choose one page or another, but the pages themselves could make their own choices, approaching or retreating in order and time, one page snuggling next to another, or racing far away from its kin. The loosened pages from one book might choose to march alongside the pages of an entirely different volume, fiction and reality combined, or fanciful poetry settling down next door to serious prose.

Reading and understanding might then offer the same impromptu pleasure as dancing across a wooden floor, out the door and underneath the stars; changing partners as easily as we change direction, leaning and twirling with the music toward a destination not yet in place; believing fervently as we gather the pages once more that our story will be assembled in time for our arrival, that all the stars and planets will be perfectly aligned, that our future is fixed and certain – until the next moment, when an insolent breeze arrives to rearrange everything.

Good Seeing

– 1 –

The mission director has declared it: *Good seeing at last!*

The science team awakens the computer onboard the orbiting Mariner and reactivates its two cameras. The eyes and ears of the slumbering spacecraft pulse back to life and begin their long-postponed work in earnest.

A long-distance dialogue ensues between the Earth-bound scientists and the faraway Mariner:

What do you see?

So much. I see so much. You'll not believe all I can see.

Tell us everything, then.

The data gathered in surging bits of blacks, whites and shades of gray released from Mariner's onboard radio antenna begins its long trek back to Earth, where an enormous white dish rising from the desert floor adjusts itself like a giant catcher's mitt prepared to receive the signals tossed from 40 million miles away.

Relief and justified pride are evident in each carefully fashioned transmission. The interminable journey has not been in vain.

LIFE ON MARS

-2-

open my eyes and spy it in the distance: an oasis uglier than any I've ever imagined, so ugly it must be real.

No palm trees, no lush lagoons dotted with slow-moving, curved-necked swans. Instead, squat, brown, nondescript buildings nestled beneath an enormous white dish curved and tilted like a giant ear eavesdropping on the heavens. A tiny figure outfitted in navy blue has scaled the sturdy tower supporting the dish and is preparing to nudge it into position – the Harry of this alien place, the dish porter!

"Hello," I call out, my voice weak, scratchy, and barely audible.

But someone hears me.

It's Linda the waitress sprinting from the building, kicking up miniature dust storms in her path. *Didn't I warn you*, I think she's going to fuss at me. But instead she pulls me to my feet.

"Com'on, hon," she encourages me. Linda's gone now; in her place is a pert fake-blonde woman wearing a blue jumpsuit. "Let's get you inside."

She's supporting each step we take toward the building she'd run from. "We've been looking for you everywhere," she tells me.

We reach the formidable steel door and she pushes it open with a firm forward kick. She's in a hurry.

"Welcome to Mars," she says and grins.

In a dimly lit room inside I see blue-suited Martian men and women huddled in pairs around workbenches, examining television screens, oscilloscopes and other displays I can't identify. No one looks up as we approach; they're focused on the tasks before them.

Complex Supervisor, says a small sign on top of a workstation elevated above the others. I think it's intentionally humorous until I realize these creatures are not native English speakers and must have problems dealing with the idioms of my language. Their leader looks remarkably human.

"Excuse me," I say to the man stationed there. "I need to get a message to Earth. Can you help me?"

He smiles as he picks up the telephone. "Miss Dawson. I'll let them know you're here, the old-fashioned way."

It takes the smell of Campbe l's Chicken Noodle Soup to finally convince me I'm still on Earth. The blonde woman, whose badge reads "Marie," opens a can she keeps in her locker and heats it on a hotplate before presenting it to me in a steaming mug.

"We get stranded here from time to time," she explains. "It's best to be prepared."

"Stranded where?"

"You're in the Goldstone Mars tracking station complex in the Mojave Desert," she says before taking her place at one of the workstations. There's intense excitement in her voice. "We're just getting the first signals from the Mariner television cameras."

"Can I see?"

But she tells me there's nothing to see – the radio signals are still just pieces of information. They won't become pictures until they arrive in Pasadena, where the Dicklings will process and assemble all the picture elements – or "pixels," as Dr. Dick called them.

I'm sitting quietly in a darkened room filled with streams of space chatter arriving in varying pitches and volumes. The messages from space are bouncing everywhere.

This is the place, I think, where all the signals that have traveled by radio waves and sheer persistence through all of space converge, seeking someone who will gather and arrange them in some order that makes sense. The information sent from the Mars Mariner must be a tiny part of a much greater conversation, one small machine babbling in a language nearly lost among all the others.

The signals must be what I heard in the desert. What I followed to find my way here. The same way my mom found my dad, the way Lulu talked to Dr. P using her inventive typewriter, the way my mom sent me post-mortem letters. If space goes on forever, and time extends both forward and backward from the present moment, then all the messages sent never end their journeys – they just bounce from one space and time to another.

I've entered command-central, a busy post office in the desert that handles correspondence for the entire universe, a complex telephone switchboard with the ability to connect anyone with anyone else, anywhere, any time, dead or alive.

I wander awestruck into another room, and once again they're all too busy to notice. This area is lined with row after row of vertical racks. Mounted in them are electronic devices I don't understand, each one laboriously performing a task I cannot fathom. Some screens display changing waveforms. On others banks of miniature lights flash off and back on. On another, big double reels of tape spin as information is received and recorded.

I see an old Underwood typewriter sitting on a desk nearby. When I approach, I notice that its keyboard displays not only the alphabet but also odd scientific symbols, like the keys on the one Great Aunt Lulu must have used.

I pull up a chair, sit down and lightly touch one of the dusty keys. As soon as I do, I feel a mild shock, some kind of electrical current pulsing through my body. I push another and another, sending messages I don't understand to destinations I can't comprehend. Already my signals are on their way to the very edges of the expanding universe. *Is anybody out there?*

"You should take a typing course," my mom used to tell me, but I'd resisted, thinking that if I knew how to type I might get stuck in some job where that's all I did. I'd learned to type on my own, my primitive hunt and peck finally evolving into decent typing skill and admirable speed. My mom would be so proud. I could get a job now, working for some man I could fall in love with and marry. But I'd worked for Dr. Dick and we hadn't fallen in love. Someone else would be helping him process the Mariner data. There are so many Ednas in the world waiting to take my place, and only one Venus trying to figure out where she belongs.

It didn't matter any more, all the work going on at JPL without me: the close-up photos from the orbiting spacecraft capturing the rugged terrain of the entire Martian surface, the algorithms and careful image processing to make it all presentable, the endless JPL press conferences where proud Mariner mission specialists would project huge slides on a screen and point to them with a long stick, saying, *Here, look, this is Mars.*

Because the Mars they show us is already becoming something else. No matter how diligent their efforts, how determined their quest or how sophisticated their machines, the highly trained rocket scientists and clever NASA engineers will never be able to see Mars as it really is. Their careers are much too brief.

"Ma'am?" a young man in the blue jumpsuit so ubiquitous here approaches shyly, as if he's hesitant to interrupt my concentration.

"I'm not doing anything." I jerk my fingers away from the keyboard.

"The first courier's leaving for Pasadena," he tells me. "We thought you might want to catch a ride home."

I accept the offer, knowing even as I climb on board the white van with the blue and red NASA logo that I don't live in Pasadena anymore, but it'll work fine as a launch pad for wherever I end up next. Soon I'm traveling on a bumpy two-lane road alongside real signals from Mars, delicate radio waves embedded in heavy, durable reels of magnetic tape.

The desert surrounding us on all sides has turned benign. The sun polishes its rock formations. A lone cactus blooms though its season is long past.

Pasadena is 85 miles away, a trustworthy road sign assures us.

"Pretty far out, all this Mars stuff, huh?" The driver attempts small talk, but I have no honest answer to his question.

When the signals we carry with us arrive, they'll be loaded into Dr. Dick's speedy new IBM computer and transformed within hours into visual form, showing up as images on the television screen mounted at the far end of the room. All the Dicklings and possibly a few new Ednas will gather in awe around the unprecedented display.

"It's our turn now," Dr. Dick will tell them. And the Image Processing Team will jump into action, writing and rewriting algorithms, judging each new image once the algorithm is applied, as to whether it can be improved even more. Clarity, contrast, geometric adjustment, definition, but no new information. These are the rules.

I no longer belong among the scientists. Their code of conduct is far too restrictive for my artistic urges that arrive in fits and starts – even though I have no notion what to do when one erupts. Color, drama, compelling narratives are the elements I want to add to the raw data. Dr. P added the Martians to a planet where they could not possibly exist, but he did not consider them his own creations – he actually thought he saw evidence of their existence on the red planet's surface, one man's optical illusion fashioned into an entire alien culture.

If you look at the same thing over too long a time, you'll run out of actualities. There will be no new data to observe, but the lust to see and know more will not stop. That's when invention begins. It's inevitable. With the entire universe as a sketchpad, the observer can continue looking, then recording the results that make themselves known not only through the lens of the telescope or camera, but as magnificent apparitions appearing within one's mind.

The imagination cannot easily be silenced.

The advantage of looking at change is that it's always changing, the information continually refreshed, always offering more than can be spied in any one image, one instant, one frozen moment in time. You can keep looking over time and never run cut of information. There's always more poised to reveal itself, more of the unruly universe to ponder.

The guard waves us past the familiar security checkpoint and we drive right up to the Space Operation Control Center where impatient scientists rush out – not to welcome us, but to celebrate the arrival of the data recorded on the big magnetic tapes they can't wait to get their hands on.

I get out of the van and stroll across the well-tended campus. Nobody stops me, even though I'm not wearing a badge. I head down the steps and past the cafeteria, the visitor's center and the auditorium that's now packed full of antsy reporters with strict deadlines. They're setting up their gear in anticipation of the news conference that can't begin soon enough for them. Image Processing is upstairs in the next building – Building 168. I think I'll just stop by to say...

Hello.

Here, There, Everywhere

Each morning just before sunrise, with the gray sky turning rosy in anticipation, I walk outside to observe the impressive network of canals: deep, still water contained within perfectly manicured banks, quaintly curving footbridges crossing them, and towering palm trees gracing the oases of their intersections. Living at Venice Beach has its advantages. I can be close to normal in a place where most folks are too busy expressing their own weirdness to notice any of mine.

I bought a camera and set up my own darkroom in the hall closet. But recently I abandoned it in favor of a sketchbook I bought at Hiromi's in Santa Monica, where I have a part-time job. I haven't decided yet how to fill its pages, but sometimes I stay up all night just thinking about it.

That's when I hear the Martians strolling past, sometimes singly, often in couples, occasionally whole crowds of them. Their chatter fills the dark corners of the walkways and seeps into the shadows under landscaped shrubbery and beneath sturdy rowboats anchored securely to deep-set moorings. I know that if I lift the curtain and peek out my front window I'll not see them; they do not want to be seen.

So instead, I sit quietly in the dark, listening to the stories they tell: stories of survival.

This is the truth I have learned from Lulu's journal: *We are all citizens of the universe, and we carry the universe with us wherever we go.*

So, I am a Martian. All of us are Martians, Neptunians, Mercurians, Saturnians...

We are built from comets and stardust. We cannot escape our cosmic identity or distance ourselves from our planetary kin.

At last I have located myself within the cosmos. I am Venus – not Venus the goddess of love, not Venus the cow, but Venus the shimmering, shrouded orb. I am full of light and mystery, and will reveal myself in my own time and on my own terms. Just as Lulu revealed herself in bits and pieces on the untidy pages of her journal.

Surely she must have revealed even more in the pages she removed – pages that may have told the truth about my lineage, pages that are circulating even to this day somewhere in the universe, like all the missing pages of our lives, those pages not yet written.

I have learned another thing from the oddly-styled book, and that is to have my best outfit ready, my fancy hat and crimson stockings on hand for when the proper time comes. Not the time to marry, but rather the time to step outside and join the eternal promenade of the universe, to tell my own story.

I'm inventing it now.

EDITOR'S AFTERWORD

In the years that have passed since that summer when I lost my mother, found my "Great Aunt Grandmother Lulu" – and "found myself," as we young folks used to say – clever Earthlings have launched powerful space telescopes to peer into distant sectors of the universe. We have sent plucky rovers to explore the rugged surface of Mars where water, we have learned, flowed abundantly in the past and most likely still lingers underneath the desert sand and rocks.

We seem primed to visit the red planet ourselves in the not-too-distant future.

Absolute evidence that life exists on Mars still eludes us, however. Like the unusual contest sponsored by a wealthy Frenchwoman back in 1899 – offering a prize of 100,000 gold francs to the first person to make contact with extraterrestrial life, but excluding the Martians because everyone assumed mankind was on the brink of establishing such contact – we are still on the brink; we are still that far away.

Which means that life on Earth stays pretty much the same. The women's movement has come and gone – twice – first during Lulu's lifetime with the bloomer-baring suffragettes and later with the bra-burning feminists of my own generation. Despite our efforts, my gender has yet to achieve full parity with the male of our species, even though today there are many more women in science, engineering, and technology: Women sitting in the dark peering through the world's largest telescopes. Women living and working on the International Space Station. Women visionaries who dare describe the universe on their own terms.

It seems fitting to spend time editing, augmenting and revising Lulu's story, along with my mother's story and my own, as part of a much larger tale that brings to the surface the little known contributions women have made to astronomy, to rocket science, to scientific, philosophical and practical vision – even though our activities may seem peripheral.

But please mark us as present, because we *were* there. We may be missing from the scientific textbooks and professional journals, but if you go to the primary sources – the diaries, conversations, letters and drawings these women have created – you may discover the actual progenitors of today's far-flung and ever-expanding space age.

Near the beginning of time on Earth, the Navajo woman was busy ordering the universe, naming and describing each part of it, when the trickster coyote stole her bowlful of stars and flung them into the sky, interrupting her story and creating a cosmic imbalance that still exists.

There can be no return to order until all stories are told, until each star has been located and described, until the grand meta-tale that contains all of our individual stories is complete.

This is the story I've created – my own missing pages – right here in the book you're reading. It is my modest contribution to restoring order in the universe.

So, you know what to do now: *Create your own pages*.

The universe awaits.

AUTHOR'S AFTERWORD

Wrexie Louise "Lulu" Leonard was an amateur astronomer who worked as a secretary at Lowell Observatory in Flagstaff, Arizona, from 1895 to 1916. The character "Lulu" is portrayed according to evidence in the historical record, although the journal forming the core of this narrative is fiction.

Astronomers Percival Lowell, A. E. Douglass, V. M. Slipher and Charles "Chick" Capen were real persons whose well-documented lives have been used to construct the characters of Dr. P, Mr. A. E., Mr. V. M. and Charles.

Dome porter Harry Hussey and Venus the cow were also real.

All other characters are inventions

ARCHIVAL PHOTOGRAPHS

Wrexie Louise Leonard

Percival Lowell

Charles "Chick" Capen

V.M. Slipher

Harry Hussey

A.E. Douglass

Venus the cow

ACKNOWLEDGMENTS

Wrexie Louise Leonard has been with me so long now that it's hard to imagine a time when I did not know who she was.

I came upon a photo of her in Victorian garb, looking through the 24-inch telescope at Lowell Observatory, while browsing the Observatory's online archives soon after reading Sally Stephens' "History of Women in Astronomy," in which she emphatically states, "women were not allowed to look through the big telescopes until the 1960s."

Wrexie was indeed "a lady way ahead of her time," her great-niece Helen Klauk wrote to me just months before she died; as a teenager Helen had met Wrexie and remembered her as sophisticated, cultured and exotic.

So here are three people to thank already: Helen Klauk, Sally Stephens (who by now has abandoned astronomy in favor of another noble cause, dog advocacy), and especially Antoinette Beiser, Lowell's intrepid librarian and archivist (now development officer), who was incredibly helpful and supportive when I visited, and has been ever since; Antoinette verified the Sally Stephens statement about women's lack of access to major telescopes with none other than astronomer Vera Rubin of "dark matter" fame.

Thanks also to Lowell Observatory for awarding me a valuable writer's residency and letting me stay in the historic Slipher apartment, a place that so perfectly fit the time and place I'd gone there to research. Lowell outreach director Kevin Schindler was generous with his time and his incredible knowledge about the facility's rich history.

Additional thanks to Jan Michael Hollis, Mary Lou Evans, and Helen Klauk's son Bill Klauk, who helped me round out the Wrexie and Percy part of the story.

At the Jet Propulsion Lab, archivists Julie Cooper and Charlene Nichols made historic materials available to me and endured my sometimes unorthodox research methods – a very special thanks to both. Bill Green, retired director of Image Processing Lab, who developed many procedures described in this book, met me at JPL, walked me around and answered my technical questions about image processing. We went through an earthquake together, always a bonding experience, and we have continued to stay in touch. Thanks, Bill.

Bill put me in touch with another retired director of Image Processing, Tom Rindfleisch, who met with me and offered his take on image processing methods and workplace ambience during his tenure at JPL. Thanks, Tom.

While comparing the information Tom provided me with the information from Bill, I realized I'd set my story on the very cusp of workplace equality there, a fact developed into a major theme in my story. (I must state for the record that my character "Dr. Dick" is based on neither Bill nor Tom, both delightful men.)

I'd also like to thank retired JPL employee Thedra MacMillan, who told me about the "space-themed" beauty contests once held there. My favorite – for its name alone – was "Miss Guided Missile."

Follow-up research on Charles Capen's "dust storm" work at Lowell Observatory led me to Roper Mountain Science Center in Greenville, SC, where Capen's papers are archived. Staff astronomer Doug Gegen was a gracious and helpful host and stayed late to let me look though the "sister" telescope to Lowell Observatory's Clarke telescope, a 23-inch refractor formerly installed at the Naval Observatory and at Princeton University, before it was moved to South Carolina.

Thank you to Jenny Benjamin at the Museum of Vision in San Francisco, whose exhibit on "quackery" informed me on many questionable treatments for vision problems in the late nineteenth and early twentieth century that helped me develop the character Vernon Dawson and his work as a dispensing optician who yearned to be much more.

In Boston, Lynn Matis at the MBTA transportation library not only made historic railroad materials available to me, but also put me in touch with Leo Sullivan, a wealth of information on early trains, train stations and train travelers. Also in Boston, Kimberly Reynolds and Aaron Schimdt at Boston Public Library guided me toward historic documents and photos in their collection.

Nearby, at Harvard's Houghton Library, I was able to examine a rare handwritten journal by Percival Lowell, illustrated with his original photos as he traveled through Europe in the summer of 1904. Lynda Leahy at Radcliffe's Schlesinger Library made available the archived materials of Boston's historic YWCA, where I learned of the incredible support this organization offered to young single women. Thanks to all my Boston area contacts.

At Goldstone Deep Space Network in the Mojave Desert, Karla Warner was my super tour guide, escorting me to the historic radio dishes, while retired DSN employee Marie Massey sat and told me stories about how it used to be.

San Francisco State University awarded me a faculty sabbatical, providing me time not only to write, but also to wander the streets of Boston and remote sites in the Mojave Desert, allowing me to create authentic locations in my book. Thank you, SFSU.

My volunteer readers, in addition to Antoinette Beiser and Bill Green, also included friends Harriet Ellenberger and Al Sincerco, who read and commented on the finished manuscript. Dr. William Sheehan, who has written and published widely on Mars and Venus, also read my manuscript and offered several critical insights that have helped in the final stages of writing and editing. Thank you to all.

Thanks to editor Carolyn Fireside for her invaluable suggestions and for working with me over time to perfect my story and characters.

A very special thanks to Dale Bailes, valued friend, fellow writer and editor extraordinaire, who assisted greatly with refining and finessing the final manuscript.

Ongoing thanks to my husband Phill Sawyer, who, as always, provided support and encouragement throughout this sometimes tedious writing and editing process.

And finally, if the cosmologists are correct and there are extra dimensions and multiple universes out there, it is hypothetically possible that Wrexie is still around, perhaps living on some alternate Mars-like planet. If so, I'd like to thank her across time and across space for her early astronomical efforts that have helped insure women access to the heavens ever since.

ABOUT THE AUTHOR

Jan Millsapps, Ph.D., is a pioneering digital filmmaker, an early web innovator, and a versatile and accomplished writer. She has produced films, videos, digital and interactive cinema on subjects ranging from domestic violence to global terrorism, and has published in traditional print and online venues.

Her media work has been shown at the Smithsonian Institution, the Kennedy Center, the International Center of Photography in New York, the National Educational Film and Video Festival, the Mill Valley Film Festival, San Francisco City Hall, the National Latino Health Conference in Washington, D.C., Bay Area Kaiser Permanente medical centers, and USC's "Interactive Frictions" conference on new media theory and practice.

Her scholarly, political and personal essays have appeared in the journal *Film Literature Quarterly*, in the book *International Film, Television and Radio Journals*, in the *San Francisco Chronicle*, on the *New York Times* wire service, and in the inaugural issue of *Sinister Wisdom*. Her early web work was cited in a 1995 book, *The 500 Best Film & Video Sites*, and in the *Journal of the Writer's Guild of America*. In 2007 she published her first novel, *Screwed Pooch*, about the Soviet space dog Laika. She has been a featured blogger on the Apple Learning Interchange and a contributing editor for the online, rich media journal, *Academic Intersections*.

As professor of cinema at San Francisco State University, she created and taught the first "Cinema as an Online Medium" class and founded a unique Interdisciplinary Digital Arts program; currently she teaches courses in digital cinema, interactive cinema, web cinema and short format screenwriting. She was profiled as an outstanding California educator in the 1998 television series *Quest for Excellence*, and in 2004 she was named an Apple Distinguished Educator.

She earned her B.A. with honors in Creative Arts at the University of

North Carolina at Charlotte; her M.A. in English at Winthrop University; and her Ph.D. in Rhetoric and Composition at the University of South Carolina. She also holds an academic certificate in cosmology.

She lives in San Francisco with her husband, music and media producer Phill Sawyer.

JAN MILLSAPPS

The Venus on Mars Collection

includes an full-color illustrated paper edition, black-and-white paper edition, ebook, and study guide, *Mars: Your Guide to the Red Planet.* Also included is a transmedia documentary film, *Madame Mars: Women and the Quest for Worlds Beyond,* to be released in 2015.

Sound for *Venus on Mars* is available on CDBaby.com, and at hundreds of download sites. Search for "**Suite Venus**" by Phill Sawyer.

About the Musician

Phill Sawyer is a music and media composer and producer with half a century's experience, beginning in the Hollywood recording studios of the sixties, where he worked on classic sessions with Frank Sinatra, Bing Crosby, Johnny Mathis, the Beach Boys, the Mamas and the Papas, and many others. His essay on working with Sinatra appears in the Sinatra family's 2007 release of "Sinatra: Vegas."

Sawyer's career shifted to the San Francisco music scene of the late sixties/early seventies, where he engineered recordings with rock notables Jerry Garcia, Grace Slick, Paul Kantner, David Crosby, Graham Nash, both the Jefferson Airplane and Jefferson Starship, and with jazz virtuoso Denny Zeitlin. His work in the San Francisco recording studios is documented in the book "If These Halls Could Talk."

His composing credits include "Titanic" on the Kantner-Slick "Sunfighter" album, "XM" and "Home" on the first Jefferson Starship album, "Blows Against the Empire," an original score for the musical "Cactus," which he co-produced, and sound design for the shadow theatre production "In Zanadu," which he also performed.

His movie credits include Phil Kaufman's "Invasion of the Body Snatchers" and "The Wanderers," Jon Jost's "All the Vermeers in New York" and "Sure Fire," and Emiko Omori's "Hot Summer Wind."

He has collaborated with Jan Millsapps as sound designer on multimedia works "Episodes," co-produced with La Casa de las Madres, "Coverage," featured installation at the 2002 Mill Valley Film Festival, and "Building Without Boundaries," a live performance celebrating the opening of the new Fine Arts Building at SFSU.

For nearly a decade he taught sound design and production for film in the San Francisco State Cinema Department, and more recently worked with the University of California's Continuing Education for the Bar during their transition from analog video and audio production to digital and online media.